The Cormorant Club

Anji Nolan

Avon, Massachusetts

This edition published by
Crimson Romance
an imprint of F+W Media, Inc.
10151 Carver Road, Suite 200
Blue Ash, Ohio 45242

www.crimsonromance.com

ISBN 10: 1-4405-5232-0
ISBN 13: 978-1-4405-5232-8
eISBN 10: 1-4405-5231-2
eISBN 13: 978-1-4405-5231-1

Dedication

FOR DAD, WHO GAVE ME WINGS,

FOR MUM, WHO LET ME FLY,

AND FOR BOOJ,

WHO WAS ALWAYS THERE TO PICK UP THE PIECES

XOXOXO

Acknowledgments

Thank you to all Vietnam veterans. Your service and sacrifice will never be forgotten. And a special thanks to my brothers of the 3/17th Air Cavalry HQ Troop, Communications, Signals and Avionics. I will be eternally grateful for your love and support. To Editor Barb, Susan Permenter, Kay Norris, and Sue Carroll for your invaluable input. And R.T. Anders, keep opening those *One-sided Doors.*

Chapter One

Putting as much weight as he dared on his right leg, torn and deeply embedded with gravel, Scott swiped at blood seeping from the gash over his eye. His head pounded as he squinted under the blazing sun, but he could make out a pool of motionless chocolate, about fifteen feet from where he landed. Pain shot through his body as he limped to his companion, and dropping onto the scarred tar of the roadway, he stroked her still-warm flank. There was no reaction from the most important female in his life.

"Thank God you're okay," came a voice from behind him. "That woman aimed straight at you."

"Can you help me get my dog to the vet?" He shifted to get up, but a hand pressed firmly on his shoulder.

"Be still," said the Voice, shucking off her over-shirt. "That gash looks deep; you're probably going to need sutures." She poured water on the pristine cotton, and pressed it to his brow. "Just sit, an ambulance is on the way."

"What about Laverne? I can't leave her here."

"We'll see to her later; for now, you need the attention."

He vaguely recognized the comforting voice, and as he struggled to place it, another female, harsh in the background, wailed an excuse for an apology. Caring nothing for what sounded like empty sincerity, he blocked her out and tried to rise again. Soothing Voice wouldn't let him.

"Be still," she insisted, using her Evian to flush blood from his eyes. "I need to check for damage. Here, take the compress and press it firmly on your eyebrow." Scott took hold of the bloody wad that was her shirt as she ran her hands over his arms and legs. "You'll be black and blue tomorrow, but your nose is the only thing broken. You're not half as disfigured as you could've been, considering you just butted heads with a Cadillac."

Scott wasn't sure whether it was the sunlight, the blow on his head, or advancing years, but his eyes weren't adjusting to her proximity. "Thank you, I appreciate your kindness."

"I'm sorry I can't help your dog, but I can run you through a couple more checks. Do you know what day it is?"

"Friday."

"Where are you?"

"Arizona."

"How many fingers am I holding up?"

"Three . . . er . . . four, can't be sure, no glasses."

"Who's the president?"

"Alfred E. Newman."

She smiled. "Well your sense of humor is intact. Do you know your name?"

"Morgan . . . Scott Morgan; are you a nurse?"

Upon hearing his name, she sat back. "Excuse me a minute," she pulled back the leg of his shorts and saw the scar. "I can't believe this; Scott it's me, Holly . . . Holly Winthrop."

"Holly? What the . . . can you see my glasses anywhere?"

"Sunglasses, way over there, but they're pretty trashed."

"Need 'em anyway, they have prescription lenses; can't see squat without 'em."

"Don't move; I'll get them."

Scott followed her blur retrieving his glasses, and after she carefully slipped the eyewear back on his nose, a familiar angel of mercy came into focus. "You look exactly the same as you did in Vietnam."

"Nonsense." She self-consciously ran a hand down her cheek, "You're obviously delusional."

"Am not. Seriously, you haven't changed one bit."

"Neither have you; you're still full of it, and I remember you were seriously worried about. . ." she pointed to his groin, "two inches north and you'd—"

"Be singing with the Vienna Boys Choir."

"Good memory."

"Not a wound you'd easily forget."

"You had a little crush on me back then, as I recall."

"Major passion, more like." He took her hand. "So my unbridled lust meant nothing to you?"

She smiled. "Here's the ambulance. Now shut up and let the medics do their job."

Scott saluted. "Yes ma'am."

Chapter Two

Scott had quickly determined it wouldn't be years before he saw Holly again, and the day after their trip to the emergency room, he called the number she gave him. "Hi, er, Holly, it's me, Scott. I'm sorry, in advance, if I sound like a babbling imbecile, I'm hopeless on these machines. I wanted to thank you again for rescuing me; I can't tell you how thankful I am you were there. Oh, I said that already. Damn, I hate talking to dead air, words get all, well, you know. Look, if you're not doing anything tomorrow, if you want to that is, can I buy you lunch, here in Prescott at the Eagle Lake Cafe." Scott couldn't help recalling how infatuated he'd been with Nurse Holly back in Vietnam, until he discovered she was married to a Colonel Tremont "Tug" Winthrop. And his brief contact with that notoriously predatory military intelligence officer popped into his mind as he blustered on. "Er, sorry, forgot the most obvious, the invitation includes your husband; can you call me back when you hear this?"

*

On cloudless azure-blue days, Prescott's mountain air is intoxicatingly thin, and while it was taking Scott a while to get used to it, the occasional headache and nosebleed didn't stop him from loving it. He never tired of exploring the Prescott National Forest and was always surprised to come across an iridescent jewel of a lake, surrounded by tall pines set in the rolling hills of Arizona's high desert. Locally known for its bald eagles and cormorants, Eagle Lake was his favorite, and as he watched the majestic birds soar and the coal black divers swoop, barely a shadow reflected on the placid water.

It was a perfect day for lunch and bird watching, and Scott was loitering in the café's garden when a silver BMW roadster maneuvered into a parking spot. He knew immediately it was Holly, and his heart fluttered as he stepped forward and opened her car door.

She emerged in a pale apricot dropped-waist flapper dress amid a wafting of delicate perfume. "Look at this," she said, glancing at the expensive concoction of gold and diamonds about her wrist. "One-thirty exactly. I almost got lost, you know, shot right past, and went down to the boat ramp in the cove. God knows I wasn't getting out there—it's all sand and men in waders."

"Did you ask for directions?"

"No, just turned around, and saw the café sign as I was heading back to Route Sixty-Nine."

Scott pecked her on the cheek, again marveling at how young she looked. "Well, you made it. I know it's off the beaten track, but I had every confidence you'd find it."

"I'm pretty good with 'off the beaten track.' Besides, I have an ulterior motive for being here."

"You do?"

"Of course. Hippocratic Oath and all that, wanted to see how my patient was doing."

"Just that?"

"For now."

He smiled. "You should have said you're not familiar with the area. I could've picked you up and saved you the hassle."

Seeing two Dodge Rams and a beat-up Ford in the lot, Holly wrinkled her nose. "No offense, Scott, but I'm not sure Gucci would go with a truck."

"Don't drive a truck."

"So where's your car?"

He inclined his head and pointed to the lot next door. "This place will be thick with Hummers and SUVs in half an hour, and

I've been dinged twice, so I keep my distance."

She stepped up onto the curb and adjusted her sunglasses. "Oh my," she giggled infectiously, "what is that little creature?"

"Morgan Plus 8, classic British racing green with saddle leather interior and hood straps."

She grabbed his hand and took a couple of steps toward the shiny import. "How divine! Let's zip off somewhere right now. I'm overcome by a positively Isadora moment."

"Hold up there; God forbid I should strangle you on our first date."

"Okay, but I want a rain-check."

He pulled her closer. "That mean you'll be seeing me again?"

"Sounds like that, doesn't it?"

"So you're not Mrs. Colonel Tug any more?"

Her voice faltered. "Not exactly."

"Sounds ominous. Anything complicated I should worry about?" Her smile conveyed everything he needed to know, and caused the sort of excited tingle he'd not felt in some time. Cupping her elbow, he steered her toward the café. "Come on, then; let's eat."

As they stepped into the dim confines of the café's outer gallery, Holly scooched closer to Scott. "Yikes," she said, eyeing a motley assortment of animal heads adorning the walls. "Are we expected to eat with those looking at us?"

He smiled. "Don't be put off by the carnage out here. It's different inside; not a dead animal in sight."

"Good, had a horrible déjà vu thing about a nightmare weekend in Tug's hunting lodge."

"Trust me, just keep going."

A delicate wafting of rosemary and garlic enveloped them as they arrived at the hostess station, but Holly was diverted by the dining room's unobstructed wall of glass. "Gosh, you were right—look at that view."

Several couples were already seated, and a strikingly attractive waitress, dressed in the guise of a German peasant girl, recognized

Scott. "Nice to see you again, sir. Would you like the terrace or a window table?"

"Window, thank you."

The waitress straightened the lace on her intricate costume and led them to a table.

"Thank God for the European café," whispered Holly as the waitress left menus and departed. "I was beginning to think myself alarmingly over-dressed."

"You look stunning."

"Why, thank you. I like your look, too. That blood-soaked thing you've had going in the past clashed with everything in my closet."

"Well I'm all better now, thanks—again—to you."

"Scott . . ."

"Yes, dear?"

She smiled at the endearment; it felt good to be a 'dear' again. "Are we sitting on glass?"

"Fabulous, isn't it? You get the same view of the fish as the eagles and cormorants."

"Are we safe?"

"Don't worry; if we go through, I'll save you."

"Thought saving was my job."

"Was. Not any more. What are you going to eat?"

As they reviewed the menu, the waitress set down an ice bucket filled with a bottle of Veuve Clicquot. Her accent confirmed she was of German descent, and Ilse, as her name badge attested, filled their champagne flutes and took their order.

"This is spooky," said Holly, beaming approval.

Scott lifted his glass and chinked it to hers. "Welcome back into my life. What's spooky?"

"You seem to know I have a penchant for European sports cars, and you bring me to a German restaurant. Did I tell you at some time my mother's family was from Germany?"

"No."

"Your choice to eat here was pure coincidence."

"Not entirely."

"What then?"

"Years ago, after Vietnam, I was prompted to do some research on your husband."

"Why on earth would you do that?"

"That's not important any more. The war was a long time ago and things change, but I remembered your husband's bio said he was married to an army brat he met in Germany. I guessed that was you, and figured you might enjoy a return to your roots."

"Do you make a habit of filling your head with useless information so you can pull it out at a moment's notice to surprise the heck out of a lady?"

"Yep, sort of goes with who I am."

"And who are you, Scott Morgan?"

"Then or now?"

"Let's start with now, and if I like what I hear, you can work back."

"Now: I'm retired, single, and thanks to some fortuitous investments, very comfortably off."

"Excellent ending; you may work back."

He grinned. "Pretty single-minded, aren't you?"

"A lady has to look out for herself." As she took a sip of wine, her hazel eyes sparkled over the rim of her glass. "This champagne is yummy," she continued. "Don't tell me a booze preference was in my husband's bio, too."

"No, just a guess. Besides, this is a celebration. It's the second time you've saved my life."

"Hardly. I simply provided moral support."

"And a deliciously healing touch."

"Thank you again, kind sir."

"Something's been bothering me, though. When you picked me off the blacktop, you said, 'that woman aimed straight at you.' Why did you think that?"

"Maybe it was an illusion caused by the sun, but the Cadillac seemed to appear out of nowhere, and came down Keats Street very fast, heading straight for you."

"Did you see the whole thing?"

"Yes, I was at the corner waiting to make the turn. You took a few steps across the road, and paused like you saw the car coming; you turned to pick up your dog, and bang, the car was on you. No brakes, no swerving, just you in the air, then bam, down on the hood, and crashing to the ground. There were other people around; surely, they saw what I did. Didn't the police talk to them?"

"According to all accounts, they saw nothing. You are the lone witness."

"That's odd, how could they not see what happened? No offense, but you're a big guy, towing a large dog. Did the police at least charge the woman with speeding or reckless driving?"

"Nope, it was something like 'failure to control a motor vehicle,' a slap-on-the-wrist type of deal."

"So she gets away with running you down, and killing your dog. That's not right. You should speak to a lawyer and sue her."

"I tried. Lawyers are only interested in lost limbs or major carnage, and dogs—don't even go there, Arizona just classes them as property. I've little choice but to put the whole thing behind me and move on."

"Pretty generous of you; I'd have wanted some major recompense."

"Oh, it'll come; I just hope I'm around to see it. Anyway, let's not dwell on it. There has to have been a lot more interesting water under the bridge since you last saved my bacon. What's been going on with you?"

"Not much; I ostensibly played the dutiful wife tagging behind Tug for more years than I care to remember. Then he killed himself."

Scott almost choked on a mouthful of wine. "Excuse me?"

"Killed himself, or at least that's the official story."

"Whoa, whoa, back up. That's a bit much for an old guy's ticker; you better start at the beginning."

"Sorry, but you did ask, I'll try to give you some warning about any future bombshells."

Scott mouthed a "thank you."

"Well, you already know I'm an army brat. My dad was a brigadier general, married to a German national and had a permanent attachment to the embassy. My mom often entertained visiting officers when they came to Berlin, and Tug and I met at one of her parties when I was fifteen. Apparently, he saw something he liked in me, and though he primarily kept in touch with my father, there was always a little something for me in his communications. He sort of inspired me to join the army, so when I was old enough I became a nurse and volunteered for Vietnam. With me going my own way, Tug and I lost contact for a while; then we stumbled across each other when I was passing through Saigon. Within a week, we were married. All very impulsive, very unlike him, and—eventually—very painful for me."

"You mean violent-type painful?"

"Nothing so dramatic; that would require a loss of control I don't think was part of his nature. Tug certainly wasn't known for his spontaneity."

"But you just said you two got married on an impulse."

"That was the exception that proved the rule; I learned later our joining wasn't the least bit coincidental. Apparently, a senior officer's record looks better if he at least appears to operate within the normal rules of society. Not only did he need to marry a woman he could implicitly trust, who was suitable to show off at highbrow embassy and military functions, but she had to accept the nature of his business. Knowing my military upbringing, he felt confident in my discretion, and orchestrated the whole thing."

"Damn, that's cold-blooded."

"That was Tug." She sipped her champagne. "Don't get me wrong, within the confines of his rigid paranoia, he treated me very well; there was just so much about him I didn't know. Anyway, let's not rehash that old news now—here's our lunch. "

*

The pair kept the conversation light while they ate, and it wasn't until they shared coffee in the viewing lounge that Holly continued.

"Scott, thank you; it was wonderful tasting authentic *wiener schnitzel* again."

"My pleasure. It's the least I could do."

"And news of Tug's death didn't spoil it for you?"

"No, I was simply surprised to hear something so uncharacteristically desperate came over a man who was so—"

"Sure of himself?"

"I was going for stoic; what on earth could've penetrated his sort of emotional armor that he felt it necessary to kill himself?"

"My feeling exactly, which is why I don't believe he did."

"Sounds like you have unresolved issues; I'd like to hear 'em if they're not too painful."

"They aren't now. You know, we're practically strangers, but I feel like I can talk to you about anything."

"You can. Besides, we've twice come together in a moment of crisis, so there's a bond."

"Um . . ."

"You okay?" he asked, following her stare.

"Yes, sorry, something caught my eye. You said your brain is full of useless information."

"It's a curse."

"Do you know what that wall plaque is?"

"Rotary Club."

"Not that one," she pointed, "the bird-looking thing."

"It's a cormorant; there are hundreds of them outside."

"Right, but I've seen that same outstretched wing presentation before."

"I'm sure it's pretty common. They all do it to dry their wings."

"Nah, something's funky with the head; I saw that same odd shape on letterhead that fell from our safe after Tug died."

"Maybe he was a member."

"Excuse me a minute. I need to ask the waitress something."

Holly disappeared into the animal gallery and returned with a puzzled look on her face. "You're right; it's a bird-watching group called the Cormorant Club. They meet here every month, and, according to Ilse, the group is very secretive."

"That goes along with being a bird watcher. Sounds like Tug was right up their alley. What the heck, everybody should have a hobby. Maybe his was watching birds."

"The only bird Tug had any interest in was the lightly browned variety, covered in gravy, with a dollop of mashed potatoes."

Scott laughed out loud; he felt much the same way. "So he was a closet bird watcher. We all have a secret or two."

"That would be one secret I wouldn't mind knowing about him; they riddled his life, and I know they're what killed him. For example, I recall an incident the week before he died. He'd had way too much brandy and as he loosened up—something rare for him—he started mumbling numbers and cursing about people abusing his animals. His vagueness wasn't new to me, but even I had a hard time coming to grips with that."

"You had animals?"

"Not so much as a gerbil. He always said they're too much work. There were so many what-the-hell-is-going-on moments between us, and I never knew exactly who he was, why he treated me so deferentially, or why I cared so much for him. And since he died, I've tried to put what I did and didn't know about him into some sort of perspective. There's no doubt we had a strange relationship—"

"Strange in what way?"

"The contradictions of the man."

"He certainly had a few of those."

"It sounds like you knew him."

"In passing only."

"Well, there you go; you hardly knew him and could see what he was like. Suicide wasn't in his nature. Why couldn't his colleagues and friends see it? All I want is for someone to tell me the truth. I want to know what caused him to kill himself, or who killed him."

The shadow of skepticism crossed Scott's face.

"I've done it now, haven't I? Are you sure you want to know a gal who sees conspiracy at every turn, but might simply be going nuts?"

"I think you're okay. At least two doctors have to declare you nuts; self-recommendation doesn't count. Look, if you still want to talk, we can go back to my place."

She smiled. "Pretty smooth segue for an old guy."

"I try."

Chapter Three

When they arrived at the exclusive enclave of Poets Corner, sitting in the folds of northern Arizona's high desert mountains, the gates were closed. Scott activated his remote, waving Holly through, and as she razzed over the gate's grid, he noticed the ripple of sheers in the house occupied by the community's unofficial gatekeeper, an ex-cop. Routinely irked by the community's rules, fired by champagne and more mischief than was good for any sixty-two-year-old, Scott piggybacked across the grid and waved at the elderly busybody.

His Morgan and Holly's BMW fit comfortably on Scott's drive, and handing her from the vehicle, he led her into his neo-Victorian cottage. "Welcome to my humble abode."

"Not so humble. How big is this place?"

"The original deed says thirty-seven hundred and fifty square feet, but that's not counting the sun room my brother-in-law added."

"This is his house, then?"

"Was; he and my sister died six months ago. Their wills directed I should have the place. But I've been having a hell of a time since, trying to sort out a weird reverse mortgage clause, which made the place forfeit after they died."

"Once you sort that out, are you selling it or staying in Arizona?"

"Originally thought I might, but having been here a while, I realize I like more water and land around me. These houses are so close together, I can feel the pain in my neighbor's bunions."

"I know what you mean. I'm looking after a friend's house in Paradise Valley, north of Phoenix. It's on two acres, but developments with houses barely bigger than shoeboxes are springing up all around. Arizona seems to be building like there's no tomorrow, and you're right—God only knows where the water is coming from."

"Thankfully, we can drink wine. Want a glass?"

"After champagne? Are you trying to get me drunk?"

"Will it further my cause?"

"It might."

"Then I'll pour you a large one." He emerged from the kitchen with wine, peanuts, crackers and cheese, and set them on a table beside her chair.

"You're quite the host; do you entertain a lot of ladies?"

"Oh, yeah, I have 'em trooping in and out twenty-four-seven."

"Umm," she said, settling back in her chair. "Nice wine. You have good taste, and this is a lovely room; makes me sad for what I lost. Are you really interested in hearing the rest of my tale of woe?"

"If you don't mind sharing that part of yourself."

"Okay, but don't say I didn't warn you."

His hand gesture indicated he understood.

"At the time Tug died, he was a major general with all the privileges that go along with the rank, and his record, at least as far as I knew, was impeccable. Tug was working in Washington at the time, and one afternoon, I left our home in Alexandria and joined my friend Poppy for lunch at The Ritz Carlton. She was attending some sort of travel agent gathering, so she couldn't stay at the house with us." Holly took a sip of wine. "Maybe if she had, things would have been different."

"Anyway, I arrived home about three-thirty, and the place didn't feel right. Mrs. Cross, our housekeeper, didn't open the door, and when I went inside it felt like Tug was home, though he never got off the hill much before seven. For some time, I puttered around waiting for Mrs. Cross to return, and then I remembered Tug had dropped a bottle of burgundy in his study, which not only stained the rug but splashed onto the drapes. Guessing Mrs. Cross had taken them to the dry cleaners, I went into the study to check." Her eyes glazed as she took a breath. "Tug was slumped in his chair wearing full dress blues, giving me more than a burgundy stain to worry about."

"I assume he was dead."

She nodded. "The uniform didn't register as odd at the time; I'm not even sure his being dead registered. I was numb, and simply called the MPs, told them who I was, and said Tug wasn't moving." She took another sip of wine. "Within minutes, the army arrived. A snot-nosed lieutenant made a perfunctory examination, and declared Tug put a gun to his head and pulled the trigger. I was blind-sided. That wasn't the man I knew, he always said suicide was the coward's way out. Believe me, Tug was a lot of things, but a coward was most definitely not one of them."

"Was there a note?"

"Not anywhere I could see, though I never really looked, and before I could ask any questions, I was hustled away to a hotel. Can't remember which one, but I spent two days there before the army allowed me back to the house to get my personal effects. Some goon from the military was behind me every second, reviewing and cataloging everything I removed, and at no time would anybody tell me anything. I never saw Tug again until he was cremated in a chintzy ceremony at a local crematorium; it was the only thing I could afford."

She swiped angrily at a tear. "He should have been buried with full military honors, Scott, with colleagues and friends around him. Instead, he got nothing. He did so much for this country, and in a split second it was all forgotten."

Scott reached over and placed a hand on her knee. "You don't have to continue if it's too painful."

"I'm all right, really; I have to talk to somebody who'll believe me. I've been holding this in for so many years: once I get by this bit, I'll be good.

"The day after the funeral, Mrs. Cross called me at the hotel and said men with military identification were ransacking the house. I called Tug's office and asked the officer in charge for an explanation, and was treated like a pariah. That same afternoon someone came to the hotel, escorted me back to the house, and demanded I open the safe because the contents were being confiscated. I'd never opened the thing before and didn't have a clue what the combination was, but I knew it was in Tug's computer. One bastard stood over me as I accessed the files, and then he took over and did whatever computer geeks do to someone's hard drive. Another large blond specimen with wicked bad breath watched me open the safe, then bagged everything before I had any chance to protest. The only thing I saw was a couple of sheets of paper that fell to the ground, and Halitosis Harry practically flattened me in his haste to get at them. I wrote off the whole incident as another secret in the catalog that was Tug. Do you mind if I pace a bit? It calms the demons."

"Go right ahead."

"As you've probably guessed, in the military and civil authorities' infinite wisdoms, Tug's death was declared a suicide. Everything he'd worked his entire life putting together was so much smoke. They confiscated papers, bank books, cash, everything. The only thing they would tell me was that Tug had business dealings with 'anomalies needing investigation,' and the discovery of his ties to those entities were what caused him to kill himself. Load of B.S. is what I call it, and if I live to be a hundred, nobody will ever convince me he committed suicide; it wasn't his style. He wasn't *Good Housekeeping*'s idea of the perfect husband, but he was my best friend, and I know he'd never have done anything to jeopardize my financial security."

"Don't you have any money of your own?"

"You mean that I earned, from a job?"

Scott nodded.

"No. After Vietnam I never worked. Tug wanted me around

whenever he was home. He gave me an allowance, of course, bought me everything money could buy, but we never imagined I'd need an independent source of income."

"How about a life insurance policy?"

"He didn't believe in them, said it was tempting fate. But because he was in a dangerous business, he set aside money to protect me should anything happen to him in the field. We had money in the safe, lots of it; I simply never used it. Most of my purchases were on credit cards—why would I need cash?"

"So how are you managing financially?"

"When the government froze our assets, they threw me a crumb here and there, but the house, the car, and many of the possessions I thought were ours turned out to be privileges of his rank and disappeared the minute he died."

"Surely even the government can't cut you off and throw you out on the street."

"Don't be naïve, Scott, they can do what the hell they want—especially when they think one of their own has betrayed them. What little money I could scrape together paid for the funeral. After that was gone, I relied on sympathetic and generous friends."

"Count me in."

"That's very nice of you, but before you commit, maybe I should tell you the rest."

"There's a rest?"

"Warned you." She retook her seat. "As you probably remember, having absorbed his military record into that prodigious brain of yours, Tug was a lot older than me—twenty years in fact—but he had the voracious mind of a teenager. I said before he wasn't openly Mr. Personality, but there was something almost Svengalian about him; he held me like a magnet. I couldn't best him at anything, and I spent our entire married life on a quest to find something I could do better than him. It was an ongoing, mind-blowingly exciting game, and fostered a unique relationship between us;

more like God and disciple than husband and wife."

Scott's raised eyebrow accompanied "the look."

"Correct, Mr. Head-Full-of-Useless-Information, we had neither a conventional mental or physical relationship, and I do know how weird the God thing sounds."

Embarrassed at the transparency of his unspoken admonition, Scott braced his hands in front of her in a gesture of submission. "I'm not saying anything, really, nothing. I have no right to throw stones."

His charming contrition made her smile. "You don't have to. You're a man; I can feel the cogs turning. Anyway, let's get by that. I did years ago. Tug was very open with me, and said when he was away, I could see whomever I liked as long as I was discreet. I was. Then when he returned from whatever junket he was on, we resumed our role as a devoted couple until he was called away again."

"Called away?"

"Didn't I say? He was a spy."

"You knew that?"

"Didn't you?"

"Actually, I did. Our paths crossed at an intelligence testing session after basic training. Then after I was injured, and found out you and he were married, I was prompted to find out more about him. You were such a sweet, straightforward person. I couldn't quite get my head around you marrying such a creepy character. I was young and curious and wanted to find out what attracted a women like you . . . but that's my story. Let's finish yours."

"You weren't the only one who was curious. In the beginning, I really didn't know he was with military intelligence; like everyone else, I thought he was a liaison officer. Then after Vietnam when we actually had the odd occasion at home together, there were phone calls in the middle of the night, cryptic messages I couldn't begin to understand, and obvious hang-ups when I answered the phone. We weren't sleeping together, so for the longest time I thought he had another woman."

"Did that bother you?"

"Not really. I told you our marriage was unconventional, and I was certainly no angel on his frequent trips away. We simply agreed that when he wasn't on a mission, we would go about our lives as if the way we did things was perfectly normal. And, in my selfish acceptance of everything a high-ranking officer's wife has access to, I drifted along with little thought for anybody but myself. It was years before it dawned on me there was no other woman, never had been; his obsession was worse. His all-consuming love was military intelligence, and she was having him play truly nasty game with some extremely dangerous competitors."

"But you knew what he did."

"Does anyone married into that sort of arrangement ever truly know what their loved one is doing? I don't think so. For our entire married life, I'd glossed over who and what he was, because our lifestyle suited me. And I probably would have gone along wallowing in ignorance had he not returned from one escapade in a wheelchair. Thankfully, it was temporary while his gunshot wounds healed, but I was never given an explanation of how he got them."

"He probably wasn't allowed to tell anyone what he was up to."

"I realize that, but in the past, he'd dropped enough hints to let me know where he was, and then it became pretty obvious what he was doing. He trusted me, and God knows I wasn't about to say anything that might jeopardize his position."

"So did the wounds prevent him from going on more missions?"

"No, although it was more than a year before he was called back into the field. Ordinarily, I would've played the dutiful wife and continued to say nothing. Unfortunately for him, and the people having to listen to my tirades, I was a manic menopausal woman who suddenly became sick and tired of being in the dark. Driven by something outside my control, I wanted straight answers, and when I didn't get them, I started poking around. I uncovered computer information relating to bank accounts and safety deposit boxes in several countries, and found a bunch of files I couldn't make any sense of."

"Did you ask Tug about them?"

"Sure. He said the bank accounts were our retirement nest egg, and he dismissed the files as unimportant communications with his subordinates. Then calmly as you please, no discussion, no 'is-this-something-I-should-really-do,' no 'what-do-you-think-honey,' he declared he was retiring from the army. He wanted us to enjoy life, veg out and see the world together before he got too old. I was excited about the prospect, and the government owed him that. But he never got to do it."

"So he wasn't depressed, he'd just had enough?"

"Right, he was upbeat and committed to us, for once. I liked the new guy."

"Then came the suicide."

"The official line was that he killed himself because of his involvement in government corruption, overseas money laundering, and an affair with a young male soldier, who threatened to expose him. The homosexual thing would have meant a dishonorable discharge, but it was the other charges that resulted in my being left with nothing."

Scott knelt before her chair and laid his hand on hers. "It doesn't matter what you lost—put it behind you. I've found you again and we can move forward from here."

"It's not that easy. I'm not like you, Scott, I can't let it go. At least not until I know the truth and somebody pays."

"Sometimes the truth can be worse than not knowing."

"And that's reason to remain in the dark? I remember a heated phone conversation Tug had with someone the day before he died. For the first time in a married life full of mysterious calls at all hours, I actually broke my own law and picked up an extension. I clearly heard a man saying, 'Whether you agree or not, you are part of this, and you will keep your mouth shut.' Then the line went dead."

"Did you recognize the voice?"

"No, but Tug was a major general; not many people had the balls, let alone the authority, to tell him what to do. I was really worried and went into his study. He was visibly shaken, looking like a whipped old man facing something he couldn't handle. That wasn't him—he could handle anything from anybody. The next day, I arrived home and found his body."

"Was there nobody you trusted to talk about all this?"

"My savior was my dear friend Poppy. She was a rock, and without her, I don't know what I would've done."

"Did she know someone who could get you answers?"

"Unfortunately, no. Her husband had been a big somebody in Canadian government, but like me, she was cut out of their social circle after his death. She was just so grounded, knew all the right things to say to make me feel better, and when she realized I was flat busted, she invited me into her home. Later, she paid me to housesit, shared everything in her life, and I couldn't have wished for a truer, more generous friend. Damn it, I hadn't realized how comfortable my lot had become until I saw that Cormorant plaque."

"It's a bird-watching club; why does it bother you?"

"I'm not sure, but it drags up all sorts of questions again. I haven't moved on, I haven't forgiven and forgotten; all my hidden resentment and pain is still inside waiting to come out. But it's not about losing a husband any more—it's about justice and truth and somebody giving me back what I'm due."

"You think a bird club might help you get that?"

"I don't know. I simply thought the plaque might belong to a military social club, where I'd find somebody who knew Tug. They could have insight into a side of him I didn't know, maybe even lead me to understand why he'd kill himself. Then I'd have an opening to speak to the military again. Military intelligence might be full of smoke and mirrors, but what I do know is the papers that fell from Tug's safe had the exact same Cormorant logo above a list of animals, and that must mean something."

The mention of a list set off alarms in Scott's memory. "What animals were they?"

"Animals . . . er. . . alphabetical order, aardvark, bison, donkey, elephant, like that."

"Do you remember 'C'?"

"Now that, I do remember, because I don't think it was an animal, at least not one I've ever heard of."

"Was it cassowary?"

A frightened look clouded Holly's eyes. "How could you possibly know that?"

"It's a bird, and the list you saw is part of a code."

"A code?"

"Again, that's my story. Finish yours, and I'll put in my two cents worth."

"I don't think so; you've got me worried now. Please don't tell me you're ex-military intelligence. I've had a belly full of their nonsense."

"Am not, and never was, I promise; I abhor all that 'Big Brother' stuff. For thirty years, I was a hardworking airline stiff whose sole claim to fame was expertise with cargo and dangerous goods."

"Dangerous goods, like in explosives, weapons, stuff like that?"

"Well, yes, but I also know the toxic interactions of overheated shellfish and coffee beans, and the hallucinogenic properties of decomposing melon and tobacco juice. I'm one of the good guys, Holly. Look, I can see how passionate you are about getting to the bottom of this mystery, and I'd really like to help find out why somebody wanted you—and everybody else—to believe your husband committed suicide." He lifted her hand and brushed his lips across her fingers. "Speak to me; I'm on your side."

"Okay, but no more freaking me out."

Scott gave her the Scouts Honor sign.

"As I said, I live in my friend Poppy's house. She has pots of money and travels a lot, so I don't see her much."

"The Beemer?"

"Hers; told me I should take it out for an airing now and again. That's what I was doing the day you were hit. I was delivering some tickets for her right here in Poets Corner. I was on my way back to Phoenix when I came across you in the road."

"Lucky for me, or I could be dead now. That ditz who hit me didn't seem to know whether she was on her ass or her elbow."

Holly giggled at the description of the elderly woman driving the offending Cadillac. "As I remember, you have a very hard head. Although, after your skirmish in Soui Dau, I also recall advising you not to go barreling into solid objects."

"Seems to be an occupational hazard. But get this; a couple of days after the big confrontation, illustrating the mentality of the aforementioned ditz, I found a message on my front door with a bill attached for car repairs. Apparently, the colossal weight of my person dropping from a considerable height caused several hundred dollars worth of damage."

"Dear God, what nerve. Is she that broke?"

"Look around; nobody in Poets Corner is short of anything, least of all cash. But apart from the formal accounts, which are gone, didn't you and Tug have mad money put aside?"

"Told you, it was in the safe, but I couldn't get at it. The clean-up team made sure of that."

"You said the government gave you money."

"Sure, while the investigation was ongoing. But once it was over, my 'allowance' wasn't enough to rent a Washington storage locker, let alone support a woman who hadn't had a job in thirty years and was used to a, shall we say, up-market lifestyle."

"Investigation or no, no one has a right to reduce you to living in someone else's house."

"They said Tug accumulated his wealth illegally."

"Were you told exactly what that meant?"

"The military won't discuss it with me. It's a 'classified/need-to-know' status."

"I'd have thought you, of all people, needed to know."

"Apparently not."

"How was the suicide verdict confirmed so quickly?"

"A letter was hand-delivered to his aide."

"That's why you didn't find anything. How convenient. Do you know what it said?"

"The gist was, Tug had taken a great deal of money from certain foreign governments to facilitate the removal of their bad elements and had laundered his ill-gotten gains through legitimate businesses. Supposedly, he'd used U.S. government personnel and equipment to accomplish the tasks and indicated he could no longer live with the lies and guilt."

"Bull crap. He worked for military intelligence. He had no conscience to produce guilt, and lies were a major part of his life."

"You're preaching to the choir. The letter also indicated he was being blackmailed by his homosexual lover."

"Well, that certainly doesn't wash with me. If he can go about randomly disposing of a nasty international element, wouldn't bumping off a disgruntled lover be a piece of cake?"

"At last!" Holly threw up her hands, "Someone else sees it my way. I told the jumped-up pipsqueak of an investigator precisely that, and he told me I was overwrought and should think about seeing a grief counselor, the little twerp. Anyway, there was a huge investigation—"

"Why wasn't it on the news? Seems a high-ranking military official, assassin to the world, with a homosexual lover would be right up the tabloids' alley."

"Again, that crossed my mind a million times. Nevertheless, under the guise of national security, the entire proceeding was kept top-secret and heard behind closed doors. I was allowed to attend once; the day the prosecution produced the maintenance pool corporal who said he was my husband's lover."

"And was he?"

"Don't even think it, Scott. I admit to being so blown away by the insinuation that I wasn't absorbing many of the details, but of one thing I am absolutely sure: my husband was not gay. I said our physical arrangement was unconventional. I didn't say it was non-existent. Besides, I feel sure had my husband been gay, he would have had a lot more discretion than to tackle someone under his command."

"Did you tell the authorities that?"

"Of course. What I also shared was that the sex allegations were bogus because an injury during one of Tug's sorties in Vietnam had rendered him impotent. Stuff just didn't work properly."

"Why didn't you get a medical assessment?"

"They beat me to it, the lying sons of bitches; by the end of the day, they made him sound like a flaming queen. And once that was bandied about, nothing I could say would erase the damage." Tears formed in Holly's eyes. "I'm gut-busting angry, and as I've come this far, I'm going to finish my story."

"Then you'll need to stay with me tonight. It's getting too late to return to Phoenix, and you're not only upset, but you've drunk quite a bit—"

"Damn, you're good—get me drunk, then take advantage."

"I didn't mean . . . I have two bedrooms, there won't be any—"

"Calm down, Lochinvar, I'm teasing. Thank you for your generous offer, but I have to get back. I don't have so much as a toothbrush."

"I do."

"Oh, you're really good."

Scott smiled and refilled their glasses.

Chapter Four

Scott woke to the heady aroma of Blue Mountain coffee and Holly humming *By the Time I Get to Phoenix*. The serene rightness of her being in his home evoked a dream of a life with her, and throwing on robe and slippers, he flip-flopped into the kitchen.

"Why'd you let me sleep? It's my job to make coffee and pander to guests."

She turned, fresh from the shower, face devoid of makeup, hair in a towel. She didn't look a day over thirty. "You'll get your chance. I can't cook worth beans."

"Darn it, neither can I. Would you settle for whole wheat toast spread with a very nice English marmalade, courtesy of Fortnum and Mason?"

"I haven't had real marmalade since Tug and I were stationed at Mildenhall."

Scott flipped the toaster. "Did you sleep well?"

"Divine. That wasn't your bed, was it?"

"Would it make a difference?"

"Sure. I have a rule never to climb into a man's bed on the first date."

He loved her humor and wondered whether the innuendo meant she'd actually thought about them sharing a bed. He knew he had—a million times over four decades. As they sipped coffee and munched on toast, a comfortable contentment settled about them.

"So," she said, breaking the silence, "I bared my soul last night, and you promised to tell me your story. Want to go for it now?"

"I'll need to go way back; it could take a while."

"I've got the time if you've got the inclination."

"You're very disarming, you know that?"

"It has been hinted a time or two."

He smiled, wondering how he had survived so long alone. "Let's take our coffee into the den. These chairs give me a backache."

It was Holly's turn to smile. Like herself, Scott was in great shape for his years and alluding to aches and pains was the first time she'd even considered their ages. Pulling a tray from the counter, she loaded it and ushered him forward. They'd spent the previous evening in the formal sitting room, so in the light of a bright mountain morning, she got her first glimpse of the rear of the house.

*

When they entered the den, it was clear Scott was a world traveler with a penchant for aviation. Several model airplanes hung from invisible ceiling lines, and an antique wooden propeller surrounded by historical photos and all things relating to aeronautics plastered the walls. The masculine room also contained a wall of books and videos, Mission style furniture, and four huge club chairs. Holly sat back into the soft buttery leather and let its bulk envelop her. "I love this room," she said, "it reminds me of a pilot's ready-room in an old war movie."

"That was my intention."

"So you're the airplane nut."

"Guilty as charged. Chuck and my sister had only been here a month when they died, and except for your bedroom and the sunroom, the place was empty. I moved some of my stuff from Boston, originally planning to stay here during the winter, but frankly, I miss New England. There's something about the coastline, Salem during Halloween, Christmas at Faneuil Hall . . . " His eyes misted. "But enough of what I miss; grab your coffee, I'll show you around."

Opening glazed pocket doors at the den's far end, they entered the sunroom. Banks of tropical plants kissed windows and ceiling and spilled into the circulating water of an indoor pond. Reaching behind the waterfall to a small refrigerator, Scott pulled out a container and threw food into the water where several large koi meandered about.

"Did you just throw in frozen peas?" asked Holly.

"They love them. Put your mug down and hold out your hand." He dropped in some peas. "Now, lay your hand in the water so the peas stay in your palm."

As Holly did so, the fish came and took them. "This is surreal. It feels like little fishy kisses."

"Doesn't it? I spend hours watching these beautiful creatures, and after I feed them, they thank me with kisses."

She shot him a look.

"That's my story and I'm sticking to it."

She smiled. "Not afraid to be a big softie, are you?"

"Nope, and proud of it. Come, sit, watch them a while. It'll make you a koi lover, too."

Wicker furniture adorned with bright floral cushions sat atop slate floors, and Holly curled up in a rocker below a large wicker fan circulating the air. "It's so cool in here," she said. "It must be heaven in high summer."

"It is; throw in a Singapore Sling and cucumber sandwiches, and it's like being at Raffles."

"Have you been there, to the real Raffles?"

"With my sister. It's probably changed since we went, but back then it was very British Colonial. She said once she got her own house, she'd create a Raffles room."

"Well, she certainly did that. It's lovely in here. You said she died recently; were you close?"

"We were. She was ten years younger than me; so after our folks died, I was it for her, support-wise, for a while. Then Chuck came along, and though they couldn't afford a house back east with a sunroom, as soon as they moved here, it was the first room they put together."

"It has a wonderful Zen-like vibe."

"That's what Amanda said. She wasn't at all well in the months before she died, and spent most of her time in here, reading and watching the fish."

"I know why," said Holly, "I could easily get used to rocking back and forth just listening to the sounds of running water." A cricket chirped. "He sounds quite at home, too. Why would you want to sell this house?"

"The house is nice, but the community makes me feel like a square peg in a round hole."

"Maybe the residents simply need time to get to know you better."

"I don't think it's that. Chuck and Amanda raved about this place from day one, but for me, there's always been an undercurrent of something uncomfortable."

"Undercurrent sounds ominous, and what sort of uncomfortable?"

"I can't put my finger on it. I've had the same feeling several times in my life, and strangely enough, it usually occurred when I was near your husband."

"I thought you only knew him in passing. When were you near my husband?"

"My best friend, Tim Bowman, and I were shunted to one of his testing sessions after basic training in '66."

"You must have been impressive young men; he didn't let just anyone try out."

"We were simply enlistees ripe for recruitment into military intelligence, something neither of us had any interest in. Not that that made any difference to the colonel. Wherever we were in 'Nam, Tim and I were approached to join intelligence, thus confirming my belief that Big Brother was, is, and always will be watching us."

"Yikes, that's some pretty heavy paranoia for breakfast. Don't like the military much, do you?"

"Depends on what a government uses it for. Don't get me started on all that 'service to country, necessary to safeguard our way of life' hocus-pocus. I'm an honest, up-front, meat and potatoes sort of guy, and I don't like not knowing why I'm doing something. Vietnam was one of those what-the-hell-are-we-doing deals, and like thousands of others at that time, I just wanted to complete the dance card assigned by Uncle Sam and get the hell out. Joining military intelligence and playing at James Bond was not my idea of fun."

"But you must have had an ability the military felt they could use to defeat the enemy."

"I did—codes and ciphers—but I found the whole notion of being a spy distasteful and rather ridiculous."

"I'm impressed; you refused Tug's job offer. Your will must be stronger than mine. His voice and manner were extraordinarily persuasive, and pretty much had me from the get-go."

"That's how I feel about you." He took her hand and brushed his thumb across her skin.

She pulled her hand away. "Stay focused, mister. Are you suggesting there may be a connection between military intelligence, the papers that dropped from my safe, and this Cormorant Club?"

"I'm not sure, but coincidences give me a headache, and there are enough here to give me a migraine. That testing was clearly your husband's way of identifying people with unusual communications abilities and recruiting them into covert operatives."

"But you declined the job."

"Right. Tim and I wanted to stick together. We knew each other before the army, we were drafted on the same day, and in the end, we were assigned to the same unit."

"Wasn't that a monumental coincidence, two guys, friends before, both being good at codes and ciphers?"

"Touché, but we were Eagle Scouts. That's where our interest in codes and puzzles came from."

"Somehow I knew you'd have an out, but how do you tie in the papers in our safe to a code?"

"Nobody in combat has much time for relaxation, and being in a foxhole does heighten your awareness of certain things. When we weren't getting blasted, Tim and I discovered that among other things lacking in a logistically impossible war halfway around the world was reliable communication. Being fair, we had basic communication, but we both felt the need for something unique, like that of the Navajo Code Talkers, because everybody was exposed to our patterns on a daily basis. It wouldn't take a genius to work out what we were about, so we decided to come up with a code even the brains at Langley couldn't crack."

"So when it was done, why didn't you just send it to them?"

"It was a game between us, something to prevent us from going crazy between having our teeth rattled by air support and our brains blown across the camp by the VC. Some drank, plenty had a high time with Mary Jane, Tim and I played with code. It satisfied our egos and gave us something to talk about other than death. I don't think either of us anticipated it would actually be put to use, although it does appear something similar was on the papers that fell from your safe."

"You put that thing together over forty years ago. Surely it's no use after all this time; don't they have computers that can crack anything now?"

"Sure, but it's the simplicity of this code that makes it unbreakable. Using a conventional pattern of transposed letters, it takes numbers established from an agent's location, then adds a random alphabetized animal primer to establish 'A.' The same message, to the same agent, would mean something entirely different if he—or she—moved three houses down the block."

"Yikes, too much information. You lost me on transposed. Do you think you could write the whole thing down? It might make it clearer for me."

"If I can remember it all, but what's the point?"

"Maybe possession of this code was the reason for Tug's death."

"That's possible, but I'm not sure how we'd go about establishing a connection, and even if we did, who'd listen? We'd be fighting military intelligence."

"I'd still like to try."

"I'm retired, and I've got nothing else to do. Something is odd, though. How did the code get into your safe? Only Tim and I knew it, and he can't tell anybody."

"Why not?"

"Because he's dead."

"When did that happen?"

"December '68. He came into your MASH unit the same time as me. Head injury, turned out to be brain damage; he died before you guys could get him moved."

"No, he didn't."

"Didn't what?"

"For a smart guy, you're being remarkably dense. He didn't die."

"I went to his funeral. They handed his wife a flag. I held his kid for two hours in the pouring rain."

"Well, I don't know anything about that, but he most certainly didn't die anywhere near my MASH unit. The day after you were shipped out, he was accompanied from the unit by a couple of guys who worked for my husband. I know for a fact he was still with Tug in military intelligence fifteen years after the fall of Saigon."

The color drained from Scott's face. "What the hell . . .?"

Chapter Five

When it sunk in that Tim Bowman was still alive, the brotherly concern Scott had suppressed since Vietnam exploded into a burning need to know. It was undeniable the military intelligence machine had fabricated his best friend's death, but it was the reason for the action that concerned Scott. He couldn't understand why Tim simply hadn't formed an alliance with Holly's husband, a man whose unsavory reputation in covert operations became legendary, and put up with the stern lecture about hypocrisy and betraying one's principles that would certainly have flowed from Scott's lips. Then, over time, all would have been forgotten.

Instead, Tim had chosen to abandon his family and betray their friendship. Now Scott needed to talk to him, and find out why he'd felt it necessary to hurt and deceive everybody for so many years. Moreover, putting aside selfish underhandedness, if Holly was right about the papers she saw, had Tim, in his revised government capacity, been using a code they devised for fun for an entirely different classification of games?

The more Scott dwelt on the code's reappearance around someone who'd died under suspicious circumstances, the greater his curiosity. Holly had said the men emptying her safe had identification, but she admitted being unqualified to distinguish real from fake. However, she was certain of two things: their attitudes didn't feel right, and they went to extraordinary lengths to prevent her seeing anything they removed. Scott was a firm believer in gut feelings, for they had served him well. Now, it was his analytical side that spurred him to prove or disprove any connections between his code and the bird club meetings in a Prescott café.

Scott spent a sleepless night trying to connect the seemingly unrelated occurrences that had dogged him and those close to him over the previous few months. And the more questions he added to his list, the surer he became that they were not random happenings. Why would anybody want Holly to think Tug Winthrop committed suicide, and how did his code get into their safe? What had prompted his family's attitude change about Poets Corner, and why would they will him their house, knowing it became forfeit under an HOA reverse mortgage clause? Did his potentially fatal encounter with the Cadillac have anything to do with him challenging the mortgage company, and why was Holly the only person present at the accident who saw what happened? Most importantly, exactly what had Tim Bowman been doing since the sixties, and what was he doing now?

*

It was around noon the next day when Scott decided to go along with Holly's idea of eliciting help from the waitress, Ilse. They drove back to the Eagle Lake Café. But even though the place was packed with diners as waitresses bustled about, Ilse was nowhere in sight. The duty hostess told Scott she was due on shift in fifteen minutes, so after purchasing glasses of wine and munchies from the *Appetithappen* Bar, he and Holly adjourned to the terrace to await her arrival. They'd been sitting less than five minutes when Ilse's athletic figure came into view. She strode straight toward them, heading for the back door of the café.

Scott smiled, and waved.

"Back so soon," Ilse answered, recognizing him. "I guess you really like our food."

"We do, but today we're here for another reason."

A worried look shadowed the young German's eyes.

"My friend and I," Scott gestured to Holly, "wondered whether you can help us out."

She smiled timidly. "I'll try. What do you need?"

"We have some business with that cormorant bird group that meets here each month. Would you know the name of the organizer?"

She forced a smile. "I'm sorry I don't, but they're meeting here at five. Maybe you should come back then."

At this point, the last thing Scott wanted was to contact anyone; he was simply fishing for information. However, he was curious about the worried look on the waitress's face. "That's too bad; we have to be in Phoenix at five. Might you have a list of members?"

"They do sign in before every meeting, but I could get into major trouble for showing you that."

Holly interjected in German. "We desperately need help, Ilse. Couldn't you do it just this one time?"

The strategy worked. Hearing her native tongue gave Ilse a sense of security, and she lowered her voice. "I should, because I hate dealing with them. Mrs. Voldheim, the café's owner, is paid extra to look after the group herself, but she's incredibly lazy and makes me do everything."

"Makes you?" Holly inquired. "How can she make you?"

"Um . . . this is . . . um . . . I am so—" A tear slid down Ilse's cheek.

Holly put a hand on the waitress's arm. "What on earth is the matter?"

"I've been really stupid and have to talk to somebody."

"You can talk to me. Let's go over there, where it's more private." Ilse and Holly moved to the far side of the deck, deep in the shadows.

"I met a guy who wanted us to be together, so I quit school and came to Prescott because he said he had a business."

"Well, that's nice."

"No, it isn't. I came here on a student visa, and one day while I was at the supermarket, he left me. He took everything, including my passport."

"Why didn't you go to the police?"

"I was ashamed and too frightened to talk to anybody. My boyfriend's 'business' was selling drugs. I should have left him as soon as I found out, but I didn't."

"Do you use drugs?"

"No, I would never do that; I might be stupid, but I'm not suicidal. I saw some of his customers; they were being eaten alive by meth, and I wanted no part of it. At first, being alone wasn't bad. I thought I could get a job and make my own way. But everybody wanted proof that I had a work visa, which I didn't. Then the rent came due. I told the landlord I had no money, nowhere else to go, and because I had no green card, I couldn't get a job. He told me about Mrs. Voldheim, and I came here begging for help. She said I could live rent-free in her guesthouse as long as I work in the café."

"That was good of her; she really stuck her neck out for you."

"I suppose, yes, and things did go well for a while. But when I asked her to consider paying me a little, because I couldn't live on tips, she became angry. She said if I didn't continue to do what she asks, she will turn me over to the INS, and I'd be deported back to Germany in disgrace. I couldn't go back like that; my father would kill me. He's not rich and worked hard to get money for my education. I blew his dreams apart the minute I dropped out of school. I am such a failure."

"You shouldn't think like that. All you have to do is get back on track. Look, my friend Scott over there is a wealthy man; maybe he knows someone who can help you."

"Why would he help? He doesn't even know me."

"Because he needs information. Perhaps you could trade?"

"What sort of information?"

"He needs to know about the Cormorant Club, but nobody must know he knows. Know what I mean?"

Ilse wiped away a tear from her cheek. "You sound like a

bad movie. Is he a policeman? Have those weird people done something wrong?"

"No. His brother, who died, was owed money by a member of the club, and he wants to know where that person lives so he can get it back."

"What does he need to know?"

"When does your shift finish today?"

"I'm here to set up the meeting room, then I go home and come back at five. It's really my day off; see how badly that witch treats me?"

Holly let that remark go. "For now, here's my cell number; when you finish setting up, call me, and we'll talk, okay?"

"I thought Scott said you had to be in Phoenix."

"You don't miss much, do you?"

"I was a chemistry major. I'm good with details."

"It was a little white lie on Scott's part. I'll be waiting for your call."

"Thank you for listening to me. I don't have any friends here, and I hope I've found some in you and Scott."

"You have. By the way, I'm Holly."

*

When Holly fetched Ilse from the café to Scott's house, he was surprised by the young woman's affectionate embrace. "Oh," he said, smiling broadly, putting her enthusiasm down to European idiosyncrasy. "Thank you for agreeing to help us."

"I'm happy to."

"At the café, you seemed nervous talking about the Cormorant Club. Why is that?"

"I don't like the way they operate. There's something uncompromising about them. Every knife and fork is precisely organized, nobody is allowed to enter the room after I set up, and no matter how many people attend, I'm not allowed to share the work with the other waitresses. Neither can I speak to any of the guests."

"If you can't speak," asked Holly, "how do you take their food order?"

"I get a sheet of paper indicating where to place the food, then I leave." She paused and laid her hand on Scott's knee. "I can't tell you how grateful I am that you're going to help me." His blank look indicated he hadn't been apprised of his role in the young woman's salvation, and she turned to Holly.

"There you go," chirped Holly. "That proves I can keep a secret. I didn't tell Scott about our conversation. I'm leaving that to you."

Ilse smiled thinly. "I appreciate your discretion, but I think you should have told him about our arrangement before I got here."

"Yes, I'm sorry. My bad," Holly blushed. "I'll bring him up to speed, but for now, finish telling us about the club."

"Mrs. Voldheim gets a call each month outlining the club's needs, table settings, meal requirements, wine, that sort of thing. But today's meeting is unusual because the last one was only two weeks ago."

"Two weeks," said Scott. "That would be around the tenth?"

"Yes, Friday the tenth exactly. I remember it because twenty-five members showed up, and I was run off my feet."

Scott fidgeted; he didn't like the coincidence. "Are these meetings some sort of benefit dinner?"

"You mean, like an award ceremony?"

Scott nodded.

"They might be. The club has its own silverware, and one of the knives has a crest on the handle. I put it in a specific place that is different each time. Maybe the one who gets it is a prize-winner."

Scott frowned. "Or a scapegoat."

Ilse raised an eyebrow. " Scapegoat—what's that?"

Scott hadn't wanted to say too much, particularly as Ilse seemed very intelligent and might follow up with questions he couldn't answer. "Someone who is made an object of blame."

"*Sündenbock*," Holly translated as best she could.

"Blame for what? Why would a bird club need a . . .scapegoat?"

Scott had guessed correctly; Ilse was very much on the ball. "Er . . . maybe when they were in the trees, they disturbed the nesting eagles. That's against the law, you know. Do you recall who received the special silverware at the last meeting?"

"I don't know names. She was just another guest."

That was enough information for Scott. "Tell us what happens when guests arrive."

"I serve drinks in the dining room. They can have whatever they want."

"Do they pay?"

"Not to me. I just keep serving until dinner."

"What sort of people are they?"

"They're all really old, like sixty, maybe more." Ilse interpreted the look between her hosts. "Sorry, I didn't mean to offend you. You know, not working people."

"Do they look wealthy?"

"If you mean do they have nice cars and fancy jewelry, yes."

Scott was getting into his stride. "And what sort of accents do they have?"

"I'm not the best person to ask about that. They sound like Americans."

"What do they talk about?"

"Mostly travel, and I hear them talking about repaying favors. But I have to be honest, sometimes Americans talk so fast it's just noise."

"Do they ever talk about birds?" Holly inquired.

"Now that you ask I don't think I've ever heard any mention of birds. Aren't they supposed to be a bird-watching club?"

Scott smiled. "Ilse, do you mind if I take some notes; this old man's memory isn't as sharp as it used to be, and I don't want to miss anything."

"That's fine. The more I help you, the more I hope you'll be able to help me."

When he again glanced at Holly, she smacked her palm to her head in a comical show of forgetfulness.

Scott shook his head and turned his attention back to Ilse. "Do the same people attend each meeting?"

"Pretty much. I photograph the whole group, then I take a single picture of the person with the magic knife."

"Can you get me any of those pictures, maybe point out the group leader?"

"No. Mrs. Voldheim dials and I simply aim a camera phone. The picture goes directly to whoever is on the line."

"You said you don't know anybody's name, but do you recall hearing any as you serve?"

"Not really. You know that sudden silence when you walk in a room because people are saying things they don't want you to hear? It's like that. But the guests sign a book at the hostess station."

"Could you take a look at it and memorize the names?"

"How many?"

"How many do you think you can remember?"

Ilse tapped her temple. "Photographic memory. Tonight there are twelve guests; as long as I can read the signatures, I can get the names."

"Excellent. So tonight you can call us with them?"

"I don't usually finish until after midnight."

Scott nodded. "I'll be awake." He handed over a slip of paper with his number. "Can you call without being detected?"

"I'll borrow a cell phone from one of the other girls."

"That's the ticket; we'll make a spy out of you yet."

"You know, now you have me thinking, I do recall something I heard."

"What's that?"

"The mail on your hall stand had a return sticker to S.J. Morgan. Is that you?"

"Yes, why?"

"At the last meeting, I heard one of the ladies say Morgan. Was that just a coincidence?"

A tic pulsed in the corner of Scott's eye.

Chapter Six

Holly returned Ilse to the café at four-thirty, and as she angled to the back door, she saw several luxury cars parked in the side lot. "Do those cars belong to staff?" she asked Ilse.

"Not on what we get paid." Ilse pointed to the line of cars. "See the bumper sticker on the gray Lexus? It's on all the cars over there. Looks like they're all bird watchers."

"Thanks, Ilse. You'll call Scott tonight?"

"I promise. *Auf wiedersehen,* Holly."

As the young woman disappeared into the café, Holly pulled a ballpoint pen and a notepad from her glove compartment and jotted down the parked car's license plate numbers.

*

Scott was waiting at the front door when she arrived back at his home. "Where've you been?" he asked with a worried frown. "I was about to send a search party."

"I drove straight there and back. Are you getting a little paranoid or what?"

"Maybe. Secret meetings on the day I was run down, cormorants coming out of the woodwork—God alone knows what's next."

She held up the notepad. "These, and as we have to wait to get names from Ilse, looks like I might be here another night."

Scott grinned and closed the door behind her.

*

They were enjoying a glass of wine when Scott picked up Holly's notepad. "Hon, this last number, 2321512. What sort of car was that?"

Holly closed her eyes to picture the scene. "Hmmm, I started at the left, so from the top it would be, Lexus, Mercedes, Beemer, Beemer, Mercedes, Jaguar . . .arghh . . . I can't picture the rest, but they were all expensive."

"Were they all Arizona plates? We normally have six numbers, and this is seven."

"That was another self-indulgent fat-cat's Mercedes, black on black with tinted windows."

"Whoa, where did that come from?"

"Sorry, had to be said. It was the last car in the row, parked at an angle, like drivers do when they're flaunting their new vehicle or are too bone-idle lazy to park properly."

"I can see that's a pet peeve of yours."

"I hate it. Be reasonable! There's a shortage of spots, and whoops! Some moron hogs two spaces. Makes you want to . . ." Holly could see her tiny tirade was amusing Scott and she blushed; she hadn't wanted him to see the volatile side of her quite so soon. "Sorry, went off on a tangent there."

"I liked it," he said as he covered her hand with his. "Shows you're comfortable enough to show me your feisty side. However, now you've got the parking issue off your chest, what are we going to do about the plate numbers? Even with names, we can't simply call up the DMV and ask somebody to match the owner information."

"That's not strictly true. I still have a few Washington friends who weren't totally traumatized by the circumstances of Tug's death. They might help."

"Good. While you're at it, do know anyone who can dig out Tim Bowman's new name?"

"New name?"

"Got to have one. He was recorded as dead."

"Right, forgot about that. I can ask." Holly looked at her watch.

"It's nearly eight-thirty in D.C. Maybe I should leave it until tomorrow. Damn, today's Friday. We'll have to wait until Monday."

"You'll be staying the weekend, then?"

"Is that a problem?"

"Not in the least."

She cuffed his shoulder. "So quit your grinning. You look like the cat that got the canary."

Her playfulness took him back, and the sight of her in his shirt and sweats, looking twenty years younger than her actual age, had his mind—and other uniquely sensitive areas—drifting to places too dangerous to contemplate. "Yes ma'am; I am quitting the grinning right now."

"Smart ass."

"I know, and you love it. It's early; want to take a walk? We could stop at the clubhouse and raid the video library."

"For what?"

"*Sound of Music, Christmas Carol*, stuff like that."

"What about the dishes?"

"Leave 'em. Let's be spontaneous, jump outside the box, and shrug off the encumbrances of mundanity."

"Good grief, is there any such word?"

"Not sure, but it sounded good."

She laughed. "I will accompany you, provided you absolutely promise not to subject me to either of those movies."

"Come on, Grinch, we need some exercise."

*

On a balmy evening with a light mountain breeze wafting up the valley, several walkers were about. However, apart from the occasional disdainful nod, nobody engaged them. Holly clung tighter to Scott's arm after each silent rebuff.

"Not very friendly are they?"

"And it's worse since my accident," he answered. "From day one, my brother-in-law raved about the friends he made here, and what great neighbors he had. Frankly, they've been glacial to me; another good reason to sell the place as soon as I get the paperwork sorted out."

"What's the problem with it?"

"Apparently, though Chuck and Amanda willed the house to me, the homeowners association has a kooky reverse mortgage deal wherein the house and any equity go back to the mortgage company upon their deaths."

"Is that legal?"

"Yes and no. Reverse mortgages have been around a while, and I'm sure they've helped a lot of seniors out of a financial hole. What I don't understand is how Chuck and my sister seemed to have totally misunderstood the details of their deal."

"Why do you think they misunderstood anything?"

"Because when I received their wills, they'd included a notarized addendum deeding the house to me. They must have known the lien holder takes everything after they die."

"Then sending you the addendum was odd."

"What's also odd—when I went through their personal papers, I found no evidence of a deed, mortgage payment schedule, or reverse anything papers. I also discovered the house is actually worth triple what they paid for it."

"That will be good once you sort things out and sell."

"According to my last heated conversation with the lien holder, the house and profits of more than two hundred thousand dollars are retained by the mortgage company to offset costs."

"You said your family was only here a month, so what costs could they have incurred?"

"My lawyer is wrestling with that as we speak. I tried to get information and was told in no uncertain terms that confidentiality laws prevent anyone from the mortgage company discussing specifics. They did, however, send me a copy of the deed, which mentions community dues, taxes, and medical costs."

"Dues and taxes I buy, but medical costs? That sounds bogus to me."

"I know; I just can't understand how anybody, especially Chuck, would fall for whatever scam was being perpetrated. He was a street-wise cop with the N.Y.P.D."

"What department?"

"Dangerous goods, bomb squad. Like me."

"Good grief, your family likes to live on the edge."

"That's what makes us so charismatic and devil-may-care."

"Fool." Holly squeezed closer. "You know what's really strange about this place?"

"Apart from the Stepford neighbors?"

"There are no cars parked on driveways."

"Rule 24, paragraph 14, subsection (c): only guests may park in a driveway, and then for no longer than eight hours."

"Well, that puts me well into a violation. What happens now?"

"I get a snotty letter, and if I rack up three, I'll be escorted off the premises."

"You're joking."

"Apparently the rule-makers are not. Sis told me a certain grieving widow got a pair of poodles to ease the pain of her dearly departed, and their constant yapping—and her unwillingness to do anything about it—drove enough people nuts, she was ordered out."

"And she went?"

"Yup. Here's the clubhouse—last chance at a movie."

"Do you think we'll find *The Devil in Miss Jones or Mike the Pike*?"

"Why, Mrs. Winthrop, I'm shocked. Never pegged you for a voyeur."

"You don't know the half of . . ." Her grip tightened, and a strange look shadowed her eyes. "Keep walking, act normal." She hustled Scott past the clubhouse doorway and stopped on the shadowed side of the building. "Squish in close."

He pinned her to the wall. "What's this all about?"

"In the lobby of the clubhouse, I saw someone I recognize. I think it's Marvin Shapler."

"Who?"

"A Washington attorney. Came in and out of our house in Alexandria several times, worked with Tug."

"So? He relocated to Arizona."

"What a coincidence."

"Touché, Mrs. W."

"Did you see the cars parked out front?"

"Yeah, five, I think, but you can be very distracting. What about them?"

"They all had the same bumper sticker."

"So what? Lots of people have stickers. Look at that fish thing, it's all over the place."

"I know, but we're trying to piece stuff together here, and Ilse told me all the bird clubbers have the same bumper sticker."

"Then we have twelve down at Eagle Lake and another five here?"

"Seems that way. So I ask myself, why isn't this lot at the meeting Ilse set up? Not only that, one of the cars at the clubhouse is the Cadillac that hit you. Call me crazy, but something screwy is going on here."

The walk back to Scott's house was considerably less leisurely than they'd planned, and the first thing Scott did was have Holly move the BMW into the garage. When she returned to the sitting room, he had a glass of wine waiting.

*

"You're right," he said, handing her a glass. "Things are getting weird. I've no idea what we're into, but I don't want you in danger."

"Why would I be in danger? You're the one they hit with a car."

"While you were moving the Beemer, I pulled out the code notes you asked me to put together and tested something." He showed Holly a chart. "If memory serves me right, the numbers of the seven-digit plate you saw translate to Zero."

"Zero? You've lost me."

"In Vietnam, my nickname was Zoom, and Tim Bowman's was Zero. That's one too many coincidences for me. My God, all these years I thought he was dead, and he pops up in a cockamamie bird club within a few miles of my house."

"Let's not get ahead of ourselves. How did we get sidetracked from finding out who killed my husband to reuniting with your friend?"

"What if it's all linked? Your husband dies suspiciously, Tim Bowman emerges from the grave, my sister and her husband die and leave me a house that's not theirs, and when I ask a few questions . . . kapow, I'm left for dead on the black top. And, circling it all, that damn cormorant."

Scott paused, digging deep into his memory. "Something . . . something about God, '*Thence up he flew, and on the tree of life, The middle tree and highest there that grew, Sat like a cormorant.*'"

Holly looked at him blankly.

Scott smiled. "It's a poem, *Paradise Lost* by Milton. Tim was a poetry fanatic, and it was one of his favorites. He's in this jumble somewhere, I can feel it, and he's doing what he always said he'd do: '*shove what you've got, right down their throat, 'til you make the weak and sickly choke.*'"

"Colorful character."

"He was . . . is . . .damn it, was. I have to talk to him, find out what's going on. I know he was a crazy rebel—we all were in the sixties—but we aren't in a war any more. Holly, this whole business is developing an ominous undertone."

"Which means?"

"We have to stay together."

Holly's eyes reflected a mischievous twinkle. "Is that a proposal?"

"Well, we've known each other for more than four decades, and every time we get together, I seem to be flat on my back, under your complete control."

"I'm delighted you think of me in those terms, but let's not move too fast. How about I zip down to Phoenix, collect a few things, come back for a few days, and see what develops?"

"Not necessary, I'll buy anything you need."

"I don't think so. Spending time together is one thing, but clothes . . .that's a bit much."

Scott put down his glass, lifted her hand, and kissed her fingertips. "Have you any idea how many times over the years I've wanted to be with you? Now I have the opportunity, and I want to take care of you."

"How could I know that? We were worlds apart, with no chance of meeting each other."

"Not quite. Your path and mine have crossed five times since Vietnam."

"Not possible. I'd have remembered."

"Remember, your husband and his associates tried to recruit me several times over the years. And though I didn't want any part of the government, I have lent my expertise when they needed to ship dangerous goods through non-military channels."

"That's not our paths crossing—that's you and Tug."

"As a thank-you for my help, the countries involved invited me to receptions: United Nations Malaysian Independence Celebration 1973, in 1977 the Consulate of Singapore, and in '82 the Burmese delegation. Then, after I was posted from New York to Boston, the State Street Bank Shareholders Meeting in '89, followed by the incredible bash for Ted Kennedy in the Faneuil Hall banquet suite."

"So why didn't you approach me or say something? Just watching is creepy."

"I was afraid."

"Of me?"

"Sort of, but mostly your husband. Every time I had dealings with him, his voice got to me. It was like he could get inside my head and scramble things. I wanted to refuse to help him, but he spoke and I went along. What was worse, I liked him. There was something almost hypnotic about him; he was in a dirty business doing crappy things, but in the time I was around him, I respected everything he stood for. You said he had a Svengali-like quality with you; it's a perfect description. I also felt those vibes, and had the hardest time distancing myself from him. If I had to talk to him with you as a distraction, my logic and good sense would have crumbled. So, it wasn't entirely you I was afraid of; it was the company you kept."

"Did you have feelings for him?"

"Jesus, where did that come from?"

"That didn't come out the way I wanted; I meant—"

"Am I gay? Go ahead, say it. It seems to be the new catch phrase."

"Scott, no, forgive me. It wasn't my intention to imply anything like that."

"You wouldn't be the first, especially since I decided to remain unmarried these last thirty years. It's pretty sad that after all the freedoms we shouted about in the sixties, our generation has fallen into the same patterns of uniformity and petty bourgeoisserie we fought against. Well, I, for one, don't feel I have to be what anyone else wants me to be. The rest of society can think what it damn well likes. My personal life is nobody else's business."

"You're right, I'm sorry. It's none of my business either."

"It is now. You opened the floodgates, and I want no secrets between us. I was married; for fifteen long, painful months to a girl who only wanted me for an American passport. We had a whirlwind affair while I was working in Israel, and we were married and back in New York before the ink was dry."

"So what happened?"

"I arrived home early from a trip and found her in my bed with another man. I later learned she'd not only redirected money from our bank accounts to support the creep she was screwing, but they'd been engaged in Israel and planned the whole thing to get into the United States. So there you go: a manipulated marriage, something else we have in common."

"Couldn't she be deported for doing that?"

"Nowadays, maybe. Back then, you marry an American, you're in."

"So all these years you never remarried. Didn't you ever want kids?"

"Did you?"

Holly shook her head. "You know Tug's circumstances. That wasn't about to happen."

"Of course; sorry." He took a sip of wine. "Anyway, that whole business soured my attitude, and although I've been moderately happy with live-in girlfriends, when marriage was suggested, I bailed. I never found anyone I loved enough to commit."

"But you remembered me, and the infinitesimal influence I had on your life."

"Maybe I was waiting to be with you." Change from Flush Left to Indent

"I knew you weren't entirely committed to Tug."

"How could you have known that, since I only told you yesterday?"

"Bob Lehman."

"How in God's name did you—how many more do you know about?"

"How many more are there?"

Scott's tone wasn't accusatory, but had a sarcastic edge Holly found distinctly uncomfortable. It was clear he knew things she would have preferred he not, and not wishing to repeat a life dominated by the mind games she'd played for years with Tug, she wanted out. Holly put down her wine glass and headed toward the bedroom.

"Where are you going?"

"None of your business!"

"I won't let you go, Holly."

"And precisely how do you intend to stop me?"

He went after her and grabbed the back of her T-shirt. "Please stop." He spun her around and locked his mouth on hers. When he released her, his eyes had misted. "Marry me now," he whispered. "This minute. We'll drive to Vegas."

It had been a while since Holly had been romantically involved, but no man had ever kissed her with such hunger. "Don't be crazy; we barely know each other."

"What's there to know? At our age, life's too short for analysis."

"That's odd coming from a ciphers nut. Besides, speak for yourself, old man; I intend to stay forty forever."

"Please, don't go."

She reached out and brushed a hand down his cheek. "I really should. Look, I'm sorry I over-reacted. It was just a shock to hear you knew something so personal about me."

"So I'll tell you something equally revealing about me. Go on, ask," Scott dared her.

"That's all right; it's best I go before something starts we can't finish."

"Can't finish? What do I have to do, tear off your clothes and prove something?"

His eyes said he was serious, and Holly was scared and exhilarated at the same time. "Don't think that's necessary, although I am wearing your clothes. Should you want them back, I can hardly refuse."

He took her hand and brought it to his heart. "Don't ever doubt my feelings, Holly; they've been around a very long time."

Before she could answer, the phone rang. It was barely ten. Needing to get her wits together, Holly squeezed from his arms and picked up the phone. "Morgan residence."

"Holly, it's Ilse."

"We weren't expecting you 'til midnight."

"I know, but this wasn't a normal dinner. One of the guests stayed long enough to eat, then said something about meeting at the corner."

"Are you sure?"

"Sure as I can be between hauling dirty dishes. Do you have a pencil? I'll tell you all the names I could read, but some of the handwriting was awful: Zoey Mitchell, Alice and Neil Bradshaw, Wally Carter, Duke Nyson, Eli Watson, Marvin Shapler, Ben Watkins, and Zack Patterson; that's all I could read. Hope it helps."

"It will, thank you so much. I'll be in touch."

As Holly handed Scott the list, she wasn't smiling. "Hate to say it, but I told you so. There he is, large as life, attorney Marvin Shapler. Do the other names mean anything to you?"

Scott reviewed the list and blanched. Moving into the kitchen, he opened a drawer and pulled out the Poets Corner Residents Directory. "There they are, front and center—the Bradshaws and Wally Carter." Flipping the pages, he found the other names. "Seems we might have something more to worry about than unsociable neighbors. I'm not letting you out of my sight, so first thing in the morning I'll follow you to Phoenix. You can pick up some clothes, leave the Beemer, and I'm not sure what we do after that. A call to your friends in Washington might help."

"If Marvin Shapler is involved, can we trust anybody in that circle?"

"Right now, my head is too full of 'what the hells' to think straight."

"Then why don't you gather some stuff and stay with me in Phoenix for a few days? We can't call Washington until Monday anyway."

"Okay, that sounds good. It would be best if we hit the road early tomorrow, so maybe we should turn in."

"We?"

He brushed his knuckles lovingly down her cheek. "I already made my move, so the next is up to you."

"Don't you know you're not supposed to rush a lady?"

"Holly, sweetie, I'm sixty-two. How much of a rush could I be in?" Kissing her affectionately, he headed to his bedroom.

*

Holly peeked in on him later, and found him asleep propped up on pillows, his reading light still on. His deep steady breathing comforted her; not so, a notepad covered in indecipherable scribbles at his side. Whatever he was working on was beyond her comprehension—complicated men with minds full of secrets seemed to be her lot. As she watched him sleep coverless, short pajama bottoms exposing irregularities in his tan, she was mystified how his disagreement with the road hadn't traumatized his muscles further. He now had modern 'war' wounds alongside the Vietnam scar on his cross-legged thigh, and Holly couldn't fathom how he'd escaped serious injury. She covered him with a sheet, kissed his forehead, and turned off the light.

*

Scott was aware of her the minute she stepped into his room. Now, with the memory of her kiss on his lips, he desperately wanted her. But he remained motionless. He'd waited too long to do anything that might drive her away. Breathing in her perfume, he struggled to maintain his composure. And while he half expected her to climb in beside him, when she did not, her presence was agony. He'd said the next move was hers, but when her lips brushed his forehead, he knew so chaste a gesture was not the one he'd been hoping for.

As the love of his life hovered above him, there was no mistaking the feelings enveloping him, and when she crept away, his disappointment was palpable. Listening intently, he picked up the sound of her in the next room, and when she climbed into bed and switched off the light, he put his fingers on the place she'd kissed and brought them down to imprint on his lips. He wasn't sure why she was holding back, or whether he could do anything to convince her how much he cared. What he did know; he'd never let her get away again.

Chapter Seven

When they arrived at Poppy's sprawling Tuscan style villa, with its stone accents and wrought-iron balconies, Scott was unprepared for its size. After parking in the multiple-car garage, he followed Holly through a side door into a large butler's pantry.

She dropped her bag and keys on an antique highboy, and kicked off her shoes. "I'll put coffee on. Why don't you take a look around?"

Passing through an archway, Scott entered a sizable living room where the vaulted and beamed ceiling balanced an impressive baroque fireplace. Underfoot, expensive Persian rugs covered honey-toned marble, and a mix of European and Asian furniture was dotted with multicultural objects d'art. Had it not been for a pair of leather club chairs in a sitting area by a window, there would have been nothing in the eclectic conglomeration to Scott's taste. Moving across the far end of the room, French doors opened to lush tropical gardens with a huge swimming pool and waterfall-splashed spa. Thinking how extraordinarily self-indulgent the house was for one person, he wound his way back through receiving and dining rooms, past the library and billiard room, to join Holly amid the granite and stainless steel of a gourmet kitchen. "This is some house," he said. "What is it, six, seven thousand square feet?"

"Eight. Wait until I show you upstairs."

"I'm not sure I'm ready for that. Is it as much of a mish-mash as down here?"

"You have to know Poppy; unrestrained is her motto. Personally, I think she has too much money for her own good; she sees something, buys it, and squeezes it in."

"You'd think she'd hire a decorator."

"She has, twice. Drove them nuts. Sit, I'll pour the coffee."

Pulling a wrought iron chair from beneath a substantial glass table in the breakfast nook, Scott sat and watched Holly bustle about. Being together felt good. "You say she lives here alone?"

"I'm here, too."

"Oh, right, I can see how that would fill up the place."

Holly giggled. "With all that business in Poets Corner, why don't you stay here? Poppy won't mind. It would do you good to swim and lie around, let those bruises and scrapes really heal. You'd get your tan back."

"How do you know I need to get my tan back?" Would she 'fess up to spying on him? He was ready to counter her bluster with a heavy dose of teasing.

"Saw you half naked in bed last night."

"Damn, now you've spoiled my fun. I felt sure you'd be too embarrassed to mention that."

"Embarrassed, are you kidding? I was a nurse. Besides, who do you think gave you a sponge bath when you were hauled into my MASH unit in Vietnam?"

Scott blushed. "You don't mean you washed everything . . ."

"Scotty, that wound of yours came within centimeters of your . . .what shall we say?"

"We won't say anything; just pour the coffee."

Smirking, delightfully confident, she wished she could go back to a time when they were both more innocent. "You really were a tiny bit in love with me back then, weren't you?"

"We all were. Nurses were like angels; it was almost worth getting wounded to have your hands on us."

"And all these years you've had a little torch flickering, waiting and wanting—"

"Do you intend to entirely embarrass the hell out of me, or—"

Bing-bong, bing-bong. The doorbell was as dramatic as the house.

Scott glanced at Holly quizzically as she got up to answer the door.

"No, you sit. I'll go," he said.

Confused by his firmness, she nevertheless smiled. It had been an age since she played the 'little woman'.

Striding to the front doors, the side window allowed Scott to see a tall, clean-cut man in his thirties carrying a suitcase. Behind him, a cab was leaving the drive. Flipping the dead bolt, Scott opened the door.

"Hi, I'm Jim Cromwell," said the man. "Poppy's nephew."

Despite being told to stay put, Holly joined them at the door.

Jim extended his hand. "You must be Holly; my aunt said you'd be here."

Embarrassed she'd forgotten this most important guest, Holly grabbed his arm and pulled him inside. "Oh my God, Jim, I'm so sorry. I was supposed to pick you up at the airport. I thought you were arriving on the 25th."

"This is the 25th."

"So much has been happening, I completely lost track. Jim, please forgive me; this is Scott Morgan."

"Your accent is Canadian," Scott said while holding his hand, "and my guess is Ottawa, though it sounds like you've been working in the States a while. You're losing some of the roll."

Jim smiled. "Amazing. Yes, on all counts."

As the men settled into the breakfast nook, Holly handed Jim a cup of coffee. "If it's okay with you, I earmarked one of the downstairs bedrooms overlooking the pool. The rooms are a bit smaller than upstairs, but you can fall right out of bed into the spa. Poppy said you'd be here a month, so if it's not enough space, there are plenty of other rooms."

"It sounds fine," he said as he took the cup from Holly. "Aunt Poppy probably told you I have a hard time staying in one place, so I plan to head out shortly, drop off something in Prescott, then explore Rim Country."

"You'll enjoy the cool air up there, and if you take Route 17 to 69, you'll pass right by Scott's house in Prescott Valley."

"Ah, a weekender. Do you also have a place in Phoenix?"

"Not on your life," said Scott. "Too darn hot. I'm from back East; need some mountains and water to survive."

"I'm with you there, although swimming year-round is pretty enticing."

"Once you've been here a while, you'll lose that notion," explained Holly. "Your blood thins, and winter is still too cold for swimming."

"Well gentlemen," said Holly, "much as I'd love to swap stories with you, someone needs to think about dinner this evening; I have to pop out and get some supplies."

"Thought you couldn't cook," said Scott.

"Can't, but I make a mean salad, and I'm sure one of you knows how to fire up the barbecue. Chicken and steak all right?" The guys nodded. "How about I show you to your room, Jim, and then you and Scott can chew the fat while I raid the supermarket."

"Lead on."

Holly left Jim unpacking, and headed to the mudroom with Scott on her tail. "Why are you hovering?" she said, scooping up her purse and car keys.

"I'm going with you."

"You don't need to do that. Stay with Jim, relax."

"Nah, I'll tell him you need a bag carrier. I'm sure he'll be happy swimming and lounging 'til we get back."

"You're being awfully paranoid."

He pecked her on the nose. "Part of my charm. I'll tell him we'll be back in an hour."

*

When they got back, Jim was swimming laps, and his emergence from the water, tanned and in excellent shape, ignited a fluttering in Holly. "Hey, young man, I hope you're putting on plenty of lotion. The Arizona sun is brutal."

"Yes, Aunt Holly," he said as he swept ebony hair from his face, and flashed her a devastating smile. "And I promise to renew it every two hours just like the bottle says."

She loved his hint of sarcasm and confident familiarity, but "Aunt Holly" certainly put things into perspective.

When Scott emerged with iced tea, lemon, and lime quarters, Holly was already settled on her lounger in a purple bathing suit with matching pareo. Scott poured drinks and settled beside her.

As Jim squeezed lime into his tea, he noticed Scott's traumatized skin. "Looks like you got the short end of the stick there, Scott."

"Car hit me. Nothing serious, did a bit of bouncing on the blacktop."

"Hope you sued somebody."

"Not that easy. Half a dozen people were strolling about, but all had temporary blindness when it came time to talk to the cops. Holly was the only one who came to my rescue." He reached across and squeezed her hand. "Just like she did forty-odd years ago."

"There has to be a story in that."

Scott relayed the story of how he and Holly met, and what transpired after his accident, but mentioned nothing specific about the Cormorant Club. Jim, however, was concerned the authorities hadn't done as much as they could to ensure the driver who hit Scott was punished, and suggested several avenues he might pursue to get results.

"Sounds like you know a bit about police procedure," said Scott, impressed.

"Goes with the job. Thought my aunt would have mentioned to Holly that I'm a sergeant with the Royal Canadian Mounted Police."

"How exciting!" Holly said as she beamed. "The only things she said were that I'd really like you, and that nobody would dare break into the house with you around. We're going to eat, and then, if you don't mind sharing a little more of your expertise, I have a project for you."

Jim looked at Scott. "Is she always this intriguing?"

"Trust me, she's just getting started."

*

Dinner was a leisurely alfresco affair and Scott couldn't help being impressed with Jim's exploits. Listening to an account of drug smuggling, a high-speed car chase, and an explosive standoff, he had no doubt Jim's determination to see a project to its end would make him the ideal man to help solve the mystery of the cormorants.

While Scott cleared the table and loaded the dishwasher, Holly had Jim to herself. "So Jim," she began, "if you can take a month off to explore Arizona, you can't be married, and obviously you don't have anything pressing at work."

Jim smiled. "Right on both counts. I never found a woman who distracted me long enough to make me settle down, and I've accrued so much vacation, I was ordered to disappear for a while." He took a sip of his tea. "Well, the part about the woman isn't strictly true, I did find someone, but as usual, the job came first, and she found someone else."

"That's sad."

"Not really, because she, her new husband, and his whole family took me under their wings, and have become dear friends. In fact, they conscripted me to deliver a package to their brother in Prescott; he owns a wine bar on Whiskey Row."

"The Grapes of Wrath?"

"Do you know it?"

"I'll say. They have a fantastic selection of wines, serve the only decent baked Brie and pâté in Arizona, and John Neverson, the owner, is a hoot. His wife, Cal, is more reserved, but when the two work together, it's worth the price of a bottle of wine to hear them go at it."

"Sounds like fun. I'd planned on going up next week."

"You should stay with us when you come up. I'll ask Scott."

Scott reappeared with wine and glasses. "Ask Scott what?"

"I thought as Jim is doing the grand tour north, he might stay with us for a few days in Prescott Valley. We could show him Poets Corner and our favorite café."

"Sounds good to me," said Scott, "but don't you think he should know what he's really letting himself in for?"

Holly pouted. "I was coming to that."

Jim enjoyed the way they sparred. "You two always like this?"

Scott brushed Holly's hand. "I love her to pieces, but she takes a dog's age to get to the point."

"And, he's always in such a hurry," continued Holly. "So, Jim, Scott told you a car hit him as witnesses' pled ignorance. What he didn't say was that the community where he lives has more than its share of odd happenings. To get the whole picture, you have to know something about Scott and his army buddy, my husband's death, and the information Ilse, a new friend of ours, gave us about a bird-watching group called the Cormorant Club."

*

By the time Holly and Scott had told the story, it was ten o'clock, and the trio had finished a second bottle of wine.

"So what do you think, Jim," asked Holly. "Can you help us?"

"You know," he said, sitting back in his chair, "if you'd told that story to anyone but me, your listener would think you were pitching a movie script. However, being a policeman, I've seen my share of weirdness, and I know life is often more unbelievable than anything Spielberg or Stone puts out. I have no authority to do anything here; I'd simply be an informed citizen who loves a good mystery. Having said that, I don't see any harm in tapping a few friends to help get you going in the right direction. The first thing I suggest we do—"

"We?" said Holly, "so you want to get involved?"

"Absolutely. This is exactly the sort of adventure I need. Two days on vacation and I'll be bored sick; this could keep me going for the whole month."

"Excellent," added Scott. "Where do we start?"

"First, I'll get some personal information on the owners of the cars whose plate numbers you spotted at Eagle Lake. I'll cross-reference those with your residents list, then take a quick look at everybody else on the list. It will be easy to run that Shapler character through the wringer; lawyers always leave huge paper trails. I'll try to dig up something on the new identity of Tim Bowman, but don't hold your breath. Worming anything from the military is difficult, but I know just the gal for the job."

"What can we do?" asked Holly.

"Not a lot right now. The beginning of any investigation is nothing more than information gathering, and because all this will be unofficial, it might take a couple of weeks to get anything tangible. Are you two staying here?"

"For a couple of days," said Scott, "then we were planning to return to Poets Corner. We thought going about our business would let whoever is trying to get us think we're clueless."

Jim loved the way civilians over-dramatized the criminal process. "You're right; often the best camouflage is normalcy."

"I was going to call a few friends in Washington to see if they can help," added Holly.

Jim frowned. "I wouldn't do that; let's keep things between us for now. Best you keep a low profile with no digging around, although I don't think an Internet search would be out of the question. Scott, do you have a computer at your house?" He nodded. "Pull any information you can find on your house's mortgage company, and research reverse mortgages and buy-back clauses on LegalBeagle.com. I'm assuming you got the insurance details of the person who ran you down?" Scott nodded again. "See if you can find anything on who is paying your medical bills, pain and suffering, like that."

"Medical bills, pain and suffering?"

"You haven't discussed that with the driver's insurance company?"

"I assumed, since I wasn't badly injured, my own insurance

would pick up the tab."

"Why? Unless you deliberately jumped on her car from the curb, the driver is at fault, and her insurance must pay. Get onto her rep; it's a routine procedure. You simply fill out the forms, and return 'em with your hospital bills. But be prepared to make some noise. You're the innocent and injured party, so why should your insurance company—ergo you, via increased premiums in the future—pay anything?"

"You're right. I never thought about it like that. I'll get right on it."

"Now about this Ilse—is she likely to alert anybody in the Cormorant Club that you've been asking questions?"

"Don't think so," Scott added. "She went to a lot of personal risk to get us information, and I think any loyalty she owed the café owner is already repaid with interest."

"What if the owner suspects something and fires her? From what you said, she'll have nowhere to go."

"That's something we were concerned about. We were thinking; since Holly will now be staying with me at Poets Corner, can we ask your aunt if she'd allow Ilse to house-sit here? She really needs to get out of her current situation, and we'll vouch for her."

"What sort of a person is she?"

Holly interjected. "You'd love her; tall attractive, blond—" Jim gave her the don't-start-matchmaking look that Holly deliberately ignored. "Educated, chemistry major, wasting her life as a waitress."

"I don't know. This house is a pretty big responsibility for a college kid, and despite the clutter, Aunt Poppy has some valuable stuff here."

"She stuck out her neck to help us," Scott added. "Whatever happens, we'll do the same. Getting away from Prescott would be an enormous boost to her confidence, and if she comes down here, I'd finance her getting back in school and sort out her passport before her visa runs out."

Scott was so earnest Jim couldn't see a way past him. "Okay, next time Aunt Poppy calls, tell her I'm for it. But Holly, I beg you: no matchmaking. My aunt also has a tendency to view every single female I come across as a potential wife, so promise me, no fix-ups, not even a suggestion, or the deal's off."

Holly threw up her hands in mock despair. "All right, all right. It's always the woman's fault. What's a gal got to do to get some respect around here?"

Jim smiled. "Leave us men to screw up on our own."

"Amen to that," added Scott.

"Well you two, I'm about done in. Jet-lag is finally winning, so if you'll excuse me, I'll see you in the morning."

Holly rose and kissed his cheek. "Thanks, Jim. We were going to try and do this alone, but with you on board, we'll make real progress."

*

When they were alone, Scott pulled Holly into his arms. "We will get to the bottom of this and somebody, somewhere, is going to give you back everything you're due."

Holly enjoyed the feeling of his body close to hers, but shrunk back. "Come on, it's late, I'll show you to your room."

"My room?"

"Your room."

His eyes registered disappointed acceptance. "Okay, lead on." As he settled into a guestroom, Holly's chaste kiss lingered, a stark brand of rejection on his cheek.

*

Holly could almost feel Scott below her, but the proximity of twelve feet was about as much intimacy as she could immediately handle. She'd been shaken from apathy seeing Marvin Shapler again, and imagining his association with an entity as close as the Cormorant Club returned vivid images of her dead husband to the forefront of her mind. And while nothing could erase the memory of that sight, it was the unctuous lawyer's sadistic smile and premature actions she remembered most.

She'd never forget his outrageous hypothesizing over Tug's shattered head, his endless pontificating about the pitfalls of an extravagant lifestyle, and his oh-so-quickly siding with the authorities on the suicide verdict. Then his deliberate silence as the authorities stripped her of possessions and dignity, leading her away to a hotel like an hysterical child over-reacting to something she didn't want to face. He was evil incarnate, and she hated him with every fiber of her being.

Tears were close as she thought how much she loathed Shapler, but she never imagined it would prevent her from giving Scott the attention he deserved. However, she did know that timing was everything in matters of the heart, and now was simply not Scott's time.

Swiping at her eyes, Holly donned a robe, and sat before her mirror bathed in the kindest pink light she'd ever encountered. And as she dabbed cooling emollient into tiny wrinkles, more imperfections from life's journey, Holly wondered whether the ravages of advancing years would ever let her be truly abandoned with Scott. He'd fallen in love with the pouting innocence of a rosy-skinned twenty-something, and had glimpsed her over the years, decked out in finery with professional makeup and a half-mile of ballroom between them. Now, at sixty, though she didn't look or feel her age, he must see every line and pigmentation as surely as she did.

It was true her eyes were piercing blue as ever, her hair shone with barely a gray in sight, and, touching manicured fingertips to still-full lips, she was, without doubt, more sensual. She smiled; it was all relative. She now knew things, had tasted life, and indulged in a variety of carnal experiences, and admit it aloud or run and hide, she ached to experience those things again. And as she shrugged off her robe, surveying her body in the cheval glass, her fingers flowed across goose-bumped skin. She wasn't cold, she merely imitated the frisson of his touch. As butterflies swarmed, she knew she wanted Scott desperately.

After slipping a silk nightgown over her head, Holly climbed into bed, pulled the sheets about her, and drifted into sleep. She'd lived two lifetimes before finding the one man who could give her everything she needed, and now something deep inside her kept him hovering, a fingertip away. But in that millisecond of unquestionable truth between conscious thought and the world of dreams, where everyone is young and beautiful again, though she convinced herself it was the image of Shapler keeping her from Scott, she lied; only her vanity was keeping them apart.

Chapter Eight

Scott and Holly returned to Poets Corner and, after a week of keeping a low profile, were eager to hear from Jim. A message brought them the news they wanted.

"I'll be in Prescott Valley around six. Would you like to accompany me to The Grapes of Wrath? I have some startling information to share. See you later."

Scott placed the last bag of groceries on the counter as Holly transferred a case of wine to the cooler. "Sweetie," she coyly asked, "do you have another set of sheets?"

"Laundry closet. Why?"

"Have to set up my room for Jim."

"And you're giving him your bed?"

"Where else would he sleep?"

"The den. There's a Murphy bed, pulls out of the wall."

"You want an honored guest to sleep on a wall bed?"

"No, but then you have to sleep with me."

"Is that a problem?"

He frowned. "Holly, you know how I feel about you; it could be awkward."

"How?"

"Don't play coy, you know what I mean."

"Heaven forbid there should be any awkwardness between us." Smiling wickedly, she entwined her fingers in his. "Walk this way, handsome."

"What about the groceries?"

"They'll keep. This won't."

*

Scott barely realized what was happening before irreverent piles of discarded clothes littered the floor, and Holly pushed him onto the bed. And as her hands began a tantalizing exploration of his body, she began to strip the years from him. He was a kid again, strong and full of youthful bravado; he the star quarterback and she the prom queen. He'd lusted after her, sweated agonizing nights with her near, yet so far. Now, she was atop him, beneath him, an impossibly sweet part of him, melding her body perfectly to the very core of his being. He was intoxicated by her dominance and wicked expertise, and when he responded with demands of his own, soaring highs and nerve-tingling lows undulating through their bodies, each surrendered to a love more than forty years in the making. And, in a perfect dance of desire, emotional maturity, and conjoined experience, they climaxed.

He clasped her hand as they lay back. "What just happened?"

She giggled. "I ravished you."

"Aren't I supposed to do that and rip off something in the process?"

"Darling, please, what century are you in?"

"Don't know what planet I'm on, let alone what century."

"You're very good, you know that?"

"Imagine what it will be like when I've had some practice."

"Oh, I think you've had some practice already."

"It's because I love you so much. You are just about the most perfect woman I've ever met."

"Shut up and get in the shower."

"Last time it was an ambulance, but this time no shutting up." He propped himself on an elbow. "I love you, always have, always will. I want to spend the rest of my life making love to you."

Her eyes were closed and he lay back to retake her hand. And as the exhaustion of indescribable ecstasy bound them, the world outside fell silent, and the cares of past traumas disappeared. But in the calm of those reflective moments, when every breath whispers soft in the mind, every heartbeat echoes loud in the chest, and each kiss carries the love of wasted years, Scott could not stay silent. "Holly, we belong together."

"I know."

"So will you marry me?"

Body spent, no more to prove, she knew he was the force she'd hungered for, the noble heart she'd sought, and when her lips brushed lightly atop the vein pulsing passionately within his neck, she said yes.

*

When Jim rang the doorbell, a radiant Holly greeted him. It didn't need a detective to interpret what Scott's arm possessively around her waist meant. And while he was pleased his new friends had found such happiness, he realized the news he brought might prove disturbing.

However, as Jim stepped into the hallway, he caught a faint wafting of a perfume he recognized, and it had nothing to do with Holly. He wasn't surprised to enter the living room and find an addition to their group.

A young woman sat in one of Scott's overstuffed armchairs. Her long ankle-crossed legs promised she would be tall, and her cropped blond hair surrounded a flawless face. Jim knew she could only be Ilse. He cast a questioning glance at Holly.

"I hope you don't mind," said Holly, feigning innocence. "We invited Ilse to join us. She's been so helpful getting information, and as I spoke to Poppy about that housing issue we discussed, she said if you meet and like Ilse, it's a go."

Despite his warning, Holly had gotten the better of him, and as Jim approached Ilse, she stood and extended a hand. Her stack-heeled pumps lifted her as tall as he, six feet two, and Jim found it curiously exhilarating to be on the same level as such an attractive woman's face. When she smiled, an easy, sensual action revealing perfect milk-white teeth, he took her hand. A tingle of electricity passed between them and her skin, brushed with a tinge of makeup, flushed, as if she understood his thought and was embarrassed by it. Her eyelashes, mascara-ed navy, closed self-consciously over the bluest eyes he'd ever seen. As Jim looked intently to see if vanity had prompted her to enhance them with lenses, she winked. Then, when her polite grip changed from a stranger's greeting to a seriously deliberate squeeze, the unexpected pressure caused something intangible to pass between them. She was playing, and Jim's heart skipped a beat.

"I'm delighted to meet you," she said, her German accent unexpectedly demure. "I hope I'm not intruding."

Amid a delicate haze of perfume and pheromones, the normally supremely confident aggressor was uncharacteristically rattled. "Cromwell . . . Jim . . . Jim Cromwell . . . likewise delighted . . . to meet you, that is . . . Ilse, hello."

His state wasn't lost on Holly. "Why Sergeant Cromwell, I do believe our guest has gotten you flustered."

The younger couple smiled and self-consciously dropped hands.

"Well, introductions being over," said Holly, "can I get anybody a drink?"

Nobody spoke.

"Seems I'm the only one with their wits about them, so here's the deal. Scott has a two-seater car. Jim, I presume you're driving the Beemer, also two seats. Unless anyone has any objections, I'll ride with Scott, and Jim, you're stuck with dowdy old Ilse." As the women exchanged a glance, Holly winked. "Okay, it's settled. Take your partner, and we shall depart."

Scott was having the hardest time not laughing as Holly worked on Jim's discomfort level. The more he tried to look calm and in control, the more she taunted him.

"Jim, don't forget to take a remote; if you can't get through the gate, you'll have to stay out all night. Final order; we discuss no business until at least a half bottle of something alcoholic has passed our lips."

"We shouldn't drink and drive," said Jim.

"So," said Holly, rubbing it in. "We'll all go our separate ways. Ilse, start walking; you have a long hike home."

A look of panic crossed Jim's face. "I guess one glass won't hurt. Besides, you got all dressed up, and Ilse came all the way from . . . where did she come from?"

"Heaven, Jim," said Scott, unable to resist getting in on the fun. "Heaven."

*

When they found parking spots in Prescott, the couples were separated by about a quarter mile. Nevertheless, Ilse knew exactly where the wine bar was, and linking Jim's arm, which he found entirely to his taste, she steered him to Whiskey Row. Scott and Holly were waiting in the wine-bar's doorway when Jim and Ilse arrived.

"I ventured inside," reported Scott, "the bar area is packed, and there are no empty tables in the body of the room."

"I think we arrived a bit late," said Holly, looking at her watch. "There is a rear patio, but chances are, it's mobbed, too. Do we stay, or grab some hors d'oeuvres, go home, and drink our own wine? What say you, Ilse?"

Running her hand provocatively down Jim's back, she settled about his waist and hooked her thumb into his belt. "I'm just glad to get an evening off in such pleasant company."

"It's your party, Jim," said Holly. "What's your vote?"

Pleasurable shock waves coursed up Jim's spine, and on several levels of his consciousness, he was content not to think about anything or anyone else within ten miles. "We've come this far, so I'll deliver the gift, and we'll check out that patio."

Fighting his way through the crowd, Jim waylaid a waitress

who said the owners were on a wine-buying trip. The patio was packed. "Forget the hors d'oeuvres," he reported to the group on the sidewalk. "Let's head home. I'd just as soon have cheese on toast and drink your wine."

Ilse smiled bravely, thinking this was as far as her evening would go, but Jim took her hand. "We'll meet you back at the house," he said. "Should we stop and pick up anything?"

Holly smiled at the intimacy in Jim's action. "We have plenty, so just drive carefully. We'll see you later." And the couples went their separate ways.

*

The Beemer was parked a few blocks away; not a long walk, but far enough for Jim to realize something totally unexpected and wildly exciting was happening between he and Ilse. Arriving at his parking spot, he didn't immediately let her into the car; instead, he leaned her against it.

"I'll be thirty-two next birthday, I have a dangerous job which takes me away a lot of the time, and so far my attention span with women has been questionable. Not entirely my fault, I might add, since my job invariably gets in the way. I'm a good guy, I don't smoke, swear, or drink to excess, and I've got all my own teeth." He manipulated his jaw. "Oh wait, no, lost one in Calgary. I work out, I've got no deadly diseases, and right now I am so attracted to you I can't think straight."

Ilse stared at him, her enigmatic expression giving nothing away.

"Er . . . I was born in Ottawa, come from a family of restaurateurs, and I loathe raisins."

She focused intently on him, her eyes picking up light from somewhere he couldn't detect, but still she said nothing.

"I love classic rock, hate poodles, can't stand bad manners, and I desperately need to kiss you."

She draped her arms about his shoulders, their comparable heights bringing her face tantalizingly close to his. "Then you better do it."

As he pressed his mouth to hers, Ilse's lips parted and her tongue touched his in a gesture of total acceptance and mutual desire. It was several minutes before they broke breathlessly apart.

"I should take you home before I do something I'll regret," whispered Jim.

"You would regret making love to me?"

Jim found her candor incredibly erotic, but without warning, she changed direction.

"Aren't Scott and Holly expecting us at the house?"

"I'd forgotten them. You're scrambling my brains. We have things to talk about."

"You can drop me off if you like."

"I don't like. Besides, what we have to talk about involves you."

"Me? Why would it involve me?"

"You're looking to escape the café, right?"

"How did you know about that?"

"I know quite a lot about you."

"That doesn't sound good." She smiled nervously, and moved aside for him to open the car door.

"I'm a policeman. Trust me, everything will be okay."

Her hand never left his thigh on the ride back to Poets Corner, and as Jim pulled to a halt on Scott's drive, he took her hand and brought it to his lips.

"I think we better go inside," she said.

"Why?"

"Because they're waiting. Look, they left the front door open."

Ordinarily, Jim might consider the open door a sign of something wrong; however, his police instincts registered no danger. His emotions were another matter. They told him he wasn't ready to share Ilse with anybody, and before she could open the car door, he leaned across and kissed her. She responded hungrily, and Jim knew however sensible he might want to be, he was in the grip of some delightful and long-overdue turmoil.

*

When the pair finally entered the sitting room, they found Scott and Holly already working on a glass of wine. "Hi, you guys," she said. "We were thirsty, so we started without you. Jim, glasses are out, wine and shrimp are in the fridge. Help yourself."

Jim brought in Ilse's wine and the shrimp, returned to the kitchen for his own glass, and rejoined the group as if nothing untoward was happening.

A blind man couldn't miss the unspoken emotion passing between them. While Scott was amazed Holly said nothing about the youngsters' flushed appearance or their delay coming into the house, he could feel the vibrations of her curiosity, radiating across the room. It was he who broke first.

"I guess the main order of business is to reposition Ilse. Have you given that any thought, Jim?"

Scott suppressed a grin, but the innuendo made Holly giggle.

"Thank you for the loaded question, Mr. Morgan," answered Jim, "I'm all for it, if she wants."

"Ilse," Holly began. "We promised to help you, and we have a plan. However, if you're not interested, we won't be offended. That said, my friend Poppy, who's never at home, needs a sitter for her house in Phoenix. We wondered whether you would you like to do that."

"I don't know; what's a sitter?"

"Like a caretaker, except this particular house has a housekeeper to clean and a gardener for the outside. It's a lovely place in a very nice area, has a pool and an exercise studio, and all you'd have to do is live there. If something goes wrong, get someone in to fix it.

You might have to change a light bulb or two, but apart from that, you simply live there."

"That's a wonderful offer, but I don't have any money. How would I pay rent? Without a green card, I couldn't get a real job in Phoenix."

"You don't pay to live there; the owner pays you."

Ilse raised an eyebrow.

"I know it sounds too good to be true, but it's a legitimate job that pays four hundred dollars a month. From that, you'd be responsible for your phone calls, food, toiletries, that sort of thing."

Tears welled in Ilse's eyes. "Who would have believed such a thing? Yes, I accept. What incredible friends you are; how can I ever thank you?"

"You already did," said Scott, "with the information you gave us."

"Oh, I almost forgot," Holly said. "There's one other thing; you won't be alone."

"Your friend has a pet, maybe. I love animals," Ilse responded.

"This is a different type of animal." Holly glanced at Jim. "For a while, at least, there will be someone else living there."

"I get on well with people, too; there shouldn't be a problem unless they don't like me."

Holly returned her gaze to Jim. "I can't imagine you'll have any worries there."

Trying to downplay his pleasure, Jim got up. "Guys, Ilse and I have something to discuss. Would you mind if we disappear?"

Holly assumed he wanted to take it from there. "Go right ahead."

"Let me give you something before we go." He went to the kitchen and returned with a pile of folders, which he split between Scott and Holly. "Read these while I take Ilse home. Make any notes you want and if you have questions, jot them down."

"Should we wait up?" asked Holly.

"By the time I get back it might be late. How about we go over things tomorrow?"

"Then take the spare key and remote from the hall stand."

"Thanks, Aunt Holly, and don't wait up—"

*

As soon as they were in the Beemer, Jim took Ilse's hand. "Hope you don't mind leaving so soon. I needed you to myself."

"Why?"

"I have to tell you something, make arrangements for your move, stuff like that."

"You could have done that inside." He didn't answer, but instead asked her to suggest a quiet place where they could talk.

They headed west from the valley toward Prescott, and turning into the Prescott National Forest, proceeded down an unlit road. Beneath the overhanging pines in such a densely forested area, he was reminded of Canada. Following Ilse's instructions, he meandered into the depths of the preserve and eventually reached the sheltered cove in which sat a log house.

Pulling to a stop, the unobstructed view over the lake offered a perfect platform for the rising moon, and with the evening clouds illuminated gold and orange in the night sky, light-beams bounced off the gently rippling water. It presented as romantic a sight as Jim could imagine. Walking around the car, he opened the car door.

"Would you like to see the house?" she asked.

Entering the cabin by a side door, they stepped into a single room with a wall of windows looking onto the lake. It was an unexpected bonus in the tiny space, and reminded Jim of the places he and his dad went fishing when he was a kid.

"What a phenomenal view."

"Isn't it? It makes the place seem bigger. Mrs. Voldheim rents this out, but I can stay here for free, as long as I work in the café."

"Sounds like a good deal."

The cabin was around twenty-five feet square; each corner being assigned a different purpose. The kitchen was an L-shaped counter top with a sink, drawers, and cupboards, on which a toaster, coffee machine, and microwave sat. A fridge occupied the other corner, and completing that end of the room, two stools beside a bistro table served as the dining area. Opposite that was a loveseat in front of a TV, but dominating the cabin's right side was a large bed with a side table, an ancient armoire, and a cushioned high-back chair looking out onto the lake.

Jim liked the place; it was rustic and unpretentious. "Do you have a bathroom?"

"Through there." Ilse pointed between the end of the bed and the armoire.

Jim entered a space the size of the rest of the cabin. "Wow, get a load of this." Containing the usual porcelain, it also housed a four-person Jacuzzi, boasting another great view of the lake, and an impressive steam shower. The log walls had been faced and tiled with mocha colored travertine marble, and all the fixtures were gold tone. "I think I could live in here."

Ilse came up behind him, her arms encircling his waist, and being as tall as he; her pelvis exactly aligned with his butt. "Mrs. Voldheim expected a huge profit when she expanded the house to accommodate a family, but the preserve people wouldn't give her planning permission to double the size of the living area."

The feelings being transmitted by Ilse were giving Jim dangerous ideas for two such new acquaintances, so he diverted his thoughts. "Wouldn't it have been smart to get permits before starting such extensive renovations?"

"For a normal person that would be logical, but you have to know her; she thinks she can bully her way into everything. She's not exactly what you'd call smart."

"Smart enough to own what looks like a very successful restaurant, and though small, this place is probably worth quite a bit."

"Wasn't always hers. She got everything from her husband; he had the brains, and the money. He died a while ago in a hit-and-run accident along the road out back. Mrs. Voldheim made a big fuss, hoping to get money from the city because they wouldn't put up streetlights."

"She has a point."

"Lights wouldn't have made a difference; people drive along this back road like lunatics. I felt so sorry for the poor man, run down, and left to die in the ditch. I found him when I came in for my shift; police said he'd been there for hours and bled to death."

"They know who did it?"

"The policeman said with a hit-and-run, they may never find the driver."

Jim's mind worked double-time. First Scott, now this revelation. It seemed cars and pedestrians didn't mix well in the Prescott area. "Did you know anything about him?"

"I know I liked him. We got on well, and spoke all the time about his plans for the restaurant, and his awful marriage. Such a sad man. He never actually said it, but I think he wanted to ditch his wife because she was so horrible to him. Left to her own devices, she couldn't organize a *reisauflauf*."

Jim looked confused.

"You call it, er . . . rice pudding."

"You don't care for her much, do you?"

"She's a hateful person who took advantage of a lonely man's vulnerability, and now she's doing the same to me."

"Hold on there; she gave you a place to live and a job, when you aren't supposed to have either."

"Why am I not supposed to have either? I work hard, I'm a good person."

Jim touched her arm. "But—"

"But what?"

"Don't you have some pretty serious skeletons in your closet?"

She blushed.

"Want to tell me about them?"

She pouted so adorably Jim wanted to kiss her. "Ilse," he said, brushing his fingers down her cheek. "We can't be friends if we lie to each other."

"What makes you think I want to be your friend?"

Jim kissed her deeply. And when she arched into him, and a satisfied moan escaped her throat, he desperately wanted to make love to her. "That's how I know."

"Jim, I'm sorry. When Scott asked me to go with you to The Grapes, I said I would before he told me you're a policeman. I couldn't back out then, and was afraid of what you might do if you found out about my ex-boyfriend, the drugs, and my student visa. I begged him not to say anything about me."

"I already knew."

"Then why haven't you told the police, called INS, taken me to jail?"

"I'm Canadian, and this is not my country. I occasionally follow criminals here and offer my expertise when I'm invited; that doesn't mean it's my business to expose people who don't have work visas. Besides, I know your ex-boyfriend stole your passport, but as Scott is willing to be your sponsor, and get you back in school, we'll probably be able to sort that out for you."

"We . . .meaning Scott, Holly, and you?"

"No, we, meaning us. Scott and Holly have enough to worry about."

"That crazy Cormorant Club person who owes Scott money?"

"We can talk about that another time. Tonight, you're mine and I don't want to think about anybody else. Tell me something I don't know about you."

"That could take some time."

"I've got plenty."

Squeezing from his embrace, she removed a bottle of wine from the fridge, and held it aloft. "Would you like a glass?"

"I don't drink and drive."

"I got that."

"So how will I get home?"

Her smile said he wouldn't have to.

Chapter Nine

It had been years since Scott or Holly had done anything resembling homework, but they diligently set about reviewing Jim's files. It was twenty minutes before Holly broke the silence.

"I never realized the general public had so much information floating about. I've got Poets Corner resident names, addresses and phone numbers, medical and financial data, and detailed occupational records and family histories. It seems rather intrusive to know this much about your neighbors."

"Don't look at it from a personal standpoint; we're investigating potential wrong-doing."

"I know, but shouldn't we have Jim hand all this stuff over to the local police?"

"To what end? We don't have anything concrete to tell them, we haven't established a crime has been committed and God knows to this point neither of us has had much luck getting the authorities in our corner. Besides, I'm sure Jim's on top of things and will contact whomever is necessary should we establish something tangible."

"Then I'll keep reading and hope something screams at me."

"Talking about screaming at you, remember those plate numbers you jotted at the Eagle Lake Café?"

"You recognize one?"

"No, but that funky seven-number plate belongs to a guy called Bryce Peterson, and five others belong to a company called Absit Invidia; mean anything to you?"

"Nothing. Why should it?"

"The Company was registered in the Bahamas in 1990, and its principal officers are Bryce Peterson, Persephone Collins, Douglas

Aitkin, Marvin Shapler—"

"Ah-ha, the rat resurfaces."

"Not finished . . . drum roll, please. . . the last person listed is Tremont Winthrop."

"You're kidding, right? Let me see that."

Scott handed over the file.

"I knew Tug invested internationally, but I was so preoccupied being a social butterfly, I took no notice. What the heck does all this mean?"

"Have you ever seen Absit Invidia on any of his paperwork?"

"Sorry, it doesn't mean a thing."

"Take a look at this list."

"'Activated Operatives-January 1969' and it lists fourteen names. Now that's impressive," Holly said as she smiled. "How on earth did Jim get a list relating to military intelligence?"

"Best not to ask, but look three quarters of the way down the list."

"Bryce Peterson; well, that's quite a coincidence."

"No such thing, Holly, and you know what's really bugging me?"

"The names are beginning to sound familiar?"

"Right."

"So, you want the familiar ringing." She picked up the thickest of her files. "This is the dossier relating to the Poets Corner Residents Directory. It shows that of the twenty-four houses in the community, twenty have at least one current occupant retired from government service."

"Well, that's certainly familiar," said Scott.

"There's more." Holly flipped to another section. "That comprises three from military intelligence, five regular army, one air force, four CIA, three FBI, and four police officers from major metropolitan divisions. Of the remaining five residences, four are occupied by spouses of a servicemen recently deceased or in hospice. And you, my dear, as a brother-in-law, are the only anomaly."

"Sort of explains the cold reception. Maybe if someone took time to get to know me, and found out I also served, they'd be nicer."

"You really think that?"

"No. Poets Corner has felt wrong to me from day one. What do you think the odds are that every house in a community is occupied by a retired government worker?"

"It's not so unusual; I've lived in military enclaves, at home and abroad. Servicemen like to hang together, swap war stories, and take advantage of the built-in support system if someone is on assignment."

"Maybe when they're serving, but there's nothing remotely resembling a military installation within a hundred miles of Poets Corner. It's too weird; I can't even see it as a case of old comrades sticking together. Look at these work histories. These guys and gals are from all over the country. I'll bet none of them even knew each other before hitting Poets Corner."

"Then you're right," Holly said, handing back the file. "The odds of every household coincidentally having such specific government occupations has to be astronomical."

"Astronomical indeed, and the people in Poets Corner don't just have the service connection. Jim and his people put together a medical survey. Every household contains at least one resident with an acute medical condition or a serious terminal illness. All have hypertension, diabetes, or osteoarthritis listed, and many are in the late stages of breast, prostate, lung, or other cancers, including Parkinson's and leukemia. Several are receiving expensive Alzheimer's care at private residential facilities."

"Aren't those things covered by Medicare?" said Holly.

"Sure, but there would still be considerable out-of-pocket hospital and practitioner expenses, as well as expensive medication co-pays."

"That's what secondary insurance is for."

"Yes," agreed Scott, "but there are still out-of-pocket expenses. Look here, and here, all residents are covered by an entity called Internos; a company which just happens to have the same board of directors as Absit Invidia. Jim's researchers have put together a minefield here. I'm an analytical sort, but this is more thorough than even I expected. I mean, look at this," he handed Holly a file containing a comprehensive analysis of each resident's financial worth. "Even with pensions and Social Security, most households have a relatively small amount of money available each month."

"But these are luxury houses, and everyone seems to have an expensive car."

"Right, so now the reverse mortgage deal on this house starts to make sense, though I'm still not sure why my sis and brother-in-law were taken in by what turned out to be a rotten deal."

"Scott," Holly asked, flipping a page in one of her files, "tell me your brother-in-law's name again."

"Chuck Westlake, why?"

"Charles was his real name, and your sister's name was Amanda, right?"

He nodded.

"Did she have pancreatic cancer?"

"How did you know that?"

"Was Chuck diabetic, and did they die in a motor vehicle accident on the road to Jerome, which the authorities declared a murder/suicide?"

"Yes; what on earth have you got there?"

Holly handed Scott the file.

"Wow, Jim's people have given us information that goes back years: the date Poets Corner was finished; people in, people out; illnesses; causes of death. It's an historical record of the community's involvement in the lives—and deaths—of a constantly replenished group of retired police and military personnel."

"What exactly does it all mean?"

"God knows I don't know, but we better start writing down questions, because I've got a boatload. I don't know what we've fallen into, but it's more like a nest of hornets than an innocent bird-watching club. And look, this just gets better—"

"Peterson again?"

Scott nodded. “He’s at the head of the company paying for health insurance, and financing cars . . . damn it, where did I put that sheet?” He rummaged through his files. “And all Poets Corner mortgages are held by an outfit called Ex Gratia, with our old buddy BP at the helm again.”

Holly looked at her watch and decided to change the mood. “Sweetie . . .” she purred, with a come-hither look. “I know we danced a little this afternoon—”

“A little? You nearly wore me out.”

“Shush, let me finish.” Her eyes twinkled as she walked over and locked the front door. “Are you up for a tango?”

“Damn, you are the most . . . I had bed in mind.”

She popped into the kitchen, took a can of whipped cream from the fridge, and led him to the bedroom. “So did I . . .”

Chapter Ten

When Jim arrived at Poets Corner the next morning, the Beemer's clock registered eleven-fifteen, and again, as he stopped in Scott's drive, the front door was open. This time, a bristling at the back of his neck told him someone other than his friends was in the house. Approaching cautiously, he paused at the kitchen window. Scott and an elderly lady were seated at the kitchen table.

Jim wasn't sure whether he'd ever get used to the open doors so common in warmer climates, especially considering what he knew about the dangerous situation his friends were in. "Hello," he said upon entering the house. "Anybody home?"

"Is that you, Michael?" Scott yelled out. "Come on through to the kitchen; I have a visitor."

Jim looked blank as he entered the kitchen.

"Charlotte," said Scott, "meet my nephew, 'Michael,' who just landed at Sky Harbor. He's stopping by on his way to the Canyon and all points north. Michael, this is Charlotte Messing. She lives on Keats opposite the clubhouse."

Jim smiled, understanding the name game, and offered his hand to the immaculately dressed senior. "Charlotte, nice to meet you. Any friend of Uncle Scott's is a friend of mine."

"Michael," continued Scott, "Charlotte has some questions about selling her house, and wanted to know what problems I'd encountered. Apparently, Ex Gratia, the mortgage company of record, is giving her a hard time. I told her you were a Realtor back east, and a much more appropriate person to talk to about problems in selling real estate." As Holly joined them, Scott spoke out. "Holly, look who's here. It's 'Michael.'"

Jim pecked her on the cheek. "Morning, Holly; it's been a long time. You look as beautiful as ever. The drive from Sky Harbor was a piece of cake. Straight lines, just like you said, and I made really good time."

Holly quickly understood the men were protecting Jim's identity. "Splendid, let me get you coffee. Anybody else want more?" She refilled cups.

*

Jim positioned himself next to Charlotte, a petite, fragile-looking senior, with a head of bluish-pink cotton-candy hair he imagined an avant-garde teen-ager would kill for. He noted she wore heavy makeup, despite the promise of ninety degrees later in the day, and supposed it was to cover what looked like rosacea still slightly evident at her temples. From her expensive clothes to the impressive diamonds adorning several fingers, it was clear to Jim that Charlotte was used to the finer things in life. "What seems to be the problem, Charlotte? I'll be glad to help in any way I can."

"Well, thank you, Michael. Like Scott, I want to sell my house, but I've also been told it's not mine to sell. I know the gossips are saying Scott can't sell this one because his brother-in-law owed a lot of money to the mortgage people, but that doesn't sound right to me."

"Did you know Chuck and Amanda?"

"Well, yes, they weren't here long, but Amanda and my husband Nathan had the same oncologist. We always seemed to be at the clinic on the same day. In fact, Chuck and I had a heart-to-heart in the waiting room just before their accident."

"A heart-to-heart?"

"Mmm, he didn't look his old self, and while I know cancer takes it out of everybody in the family, this look was different; sort of angry and uneasy. I'm not one to pry, but I thought I might be able to help, so I prodded him a little. He told me although he and

Amanda initially liked this community, something happened that didn't sit well, and he'd changed his mind about where he'd live after Amanda was gone. Said he missed the ocean and was going back to New England. Then when I heard they'd both died in that terrible car crash, and the police said Chuck had deliberately driven the two of them off a cliff, I didn't believe a word of it."

"You don't think it was a suicide, then?" asked Scott.

"I'm not entirely sure what I think. I only know when we spoke he was at peace with taking Amanda back east to be buried with her daughter. He'd also found himself a little job in Newburyport."

Scott raised an eyebrow.

"Oh, you didn't know! Anyway, being an ex-policeman, he was going to be a security guard."

"A security guard? He was a decorated officer." Scott barely hid his shock.

"Don't worry, my dear, it was very respectable; part-time at a wealthy family's summer cottage. I saw pictures; not a cottage at all but a grand place, right on the ocean, just like he wanted. He was going to live in the converted carriage house. He showed me pictures of that, too. It looked very nice: one bed, one bath, small enough for a single gentleman to maintain alone. Even had a garden so he could put in a few vegetables. He told me he missed decent veggies. Arizona is hopeless for a decent vegetable. It's the water, you know, can't get hardly anything worth eating. It's all shipped from Mexico, or frozen in east Oshkosh somewhere. I don't know what they do with veggies here. Oh, and the fish, don't get me started on that—"

Scott's discreet cough jogged her back to the present.

"Oh yes, sorry. I try not to believe everything I read and certainly ignore the grapevine here, though it's wickedly insidious. But when the newspaper reported the police had closed the investigation and not a single witness had come forward, I was mortified."

"How so?" asked Holly, offering more coffee.

"It sounds dramatic, but I know for a fact that someone from this very community was right behind them as they drove to Jerome."

The color drained from Scott's face. "Why didn't you say anything to the police?"

"Didn't know the person hadn't spoken up until I read the article, and by that time it was too late."

"Why would it be too late?" asked Jim. "Who was it?"

"Sarah Maitland."

Scott had seen the name on one of Jim's lists. "She lives here, right?"

"Used to, on Browning. She's gone now, pancreatic cancer, just like your poor Amanda. Ordinarily I'd have let things rest, but when that Cadillac hit you and nobody stepped forward to say it was Zoey Mitchell's fault, I saw red. She's practically blind, you know, has macular degeneration and can't see a barn door at arm's length. She's even had an operation and wears glasses like milk bottle bottoms, but somehow she keeps getting a license. It's criminal what some people get away with these days." Charlotte appeared comfortable venting and seemed to have forgotten the purpose of her visit.

"It will be a month tomorrow," she lamented, dabbing the corner of her eye with an embroidered hankie, "since my Nathan died. I can't live here without him; he was the one who brought us here. He loved it, said it was all the guys together, swapping war stories and getting together at the club. Frankly, it's way too clique-y for me, and I can't wait to join my daughter in Florida. Well, that was the intention, fat lot of good it did me. I tried to put the house on the market, and they told me I couldn't sell it."

Jim had begun taking notes. "Who's 'they', Charlotte?"

An exasperated sigh escaped the senior's lips. "The committee. It's always the committee. Swine, every last one of them. They make all the idiotic rules around here. You know I can't even have a dog. One little poodle, a yorkie, a pug might be nice, or maybe one of those adorable King Charles spaniels? But, oh no, they think I'm incapable of taking care of it, think I'll let it poop everywhere and spoil their precious walkways. Those buffoons don't know jack about anything."

"You've every right to be angry, Charlotte," said Holly swiping a hand across her face to keep from laughing, "but if you don't tell us what you want, we can't help you."

A drop of spittle escaped Charlotte's lips, and dabbing a hanky to her mouth, she composed herself. "I'm sorry I got carried away. These people make me so mad."

"So, take your time. What can we do?" asked Scott.

"I'd really love to know if you found a way around the committee. I've lived here two years, and I know real estate prices have gone down, but Nathan paid for the house and now they say I'm not entitled to a dime. I really hate this place, and I fear if I stay, I'll get sucked into some of the nonsense that's going on."

Charlotte lowered her voice to a theatrical whisper. "I'm not one to speak out of turn, but this community is good if you're one of those military people, you know the type? Takes orders without question and can follow a rigid set of silly rules that don't mean a hill of beans. Nathan was fine with that, but I'm not, and I'll tell anybody what I think. It's funny; people seemed tolerant of my views when he was alive, and now that he's gone, no one wants to associate with me. Except maybe Bill and Bubbles; such nice people. I've asked them if they've noticed odd things happening here, and even they tell me I'm paranoid. Then there's the cancer thing. Really, Scott, have you noticed how many residents have something seriously wrong with them? The turnover here is tremendous, and though we're all old codgers, nobody seems to last longer than a couple of years. But you know what's really scary? When one member of a couple dies, the other has to move out. I've had my letter, and though I want to go, I'm not letting the committee cheat me out of my house."

"There are some spouses living here," said Scott sympathetically.

"Those who belong, but look at yourself. I don't mean to be rude, but nobody has really accepted your being here, and you know I'm right about that. Well, I'm not standing for it. When I got my letter, I confronted them, and I'll do it again. Don't care if they call the police and have me taken away; I want my money. I'll get a gun if I have to and shoot somebody. That'll make 'em listen."

As a policeman, Jim had heard stranger things, but an angry septuagenarian wielding a gun was not normal by anybody's standards. He gently took Charlotte's hand. "No need for that, Charlotte," he said as his thumb traversed a gauzy frosting of skin over wasted muscles and tiny bones. "Did Nathan know how much you disliked it here?"

"Oh, yes, but he said he was obligated, and I'd have to make the best of it."

"Obligated?" asked Scott, remembering his sister had used the same word when describing her move to Poets Corner. "In what way?"

"I don't know, exactly; Nathan tried to explain things to me, but I've never been good with money, and the papers were so complicated."

"You mean mortgage papers, deeds, purchase and sales agreements—things like that?"

"There you go, just like Nathan. I left it all to him."

Jim frowned. "So you didn't co-sign any papers giving you joint ownership of the house?"

"I'm his wife; everything is automatically mine now that he's gone. I simply want to sell the house and get out of here. Can you help me do that, Michael?"

"I'm not sure, Charlotte. I'd have to know more about how you got to this point." Jim did his best to sound optimistic. "For example, why did you agree to move here, so far from your family? How did you choose your house?"

"I'm not sure I remember. It was all Nathan's department."

Scott smiled. "Just tell us as much as you can."

"Then if you don't mind, I'll have a little more coffee."

*

For thirty-five years, Nathan Messing worked with the Chicago Police Department. Because he never wanted to worry Charlotte, he didn't tell her exactly what he did. She lived in blissful ignorance, relishing her role as a homemaker, keeping the house in apple-pie order, raising four children, and acting as a leading light in local society.

Unfortunately, Charlotte's need to play Lady of the Manor had Nathan agonizing over the cost of every nut and bolt in their rambling house in the Chicago suburbs. Contractors performed all the home's expensive renovations, and caterers supplied the wherewithal for each *après* renovation party that Charlotte felt necessary to uphold her standing in society. And in addition to the house, Nathan's desire to please his wife meant vacations on the lake, huge family gatherings—which they hosted—as well as the burden of putting four work-shy youngsters through college.

For years Charlotte lived in her own little world, where Nathan brought home an overtime-boosted paycheck, and she spent money faster than he could make it. And as years of irresponsible over-commitment mounted, Nathan took out second and third mortgages. It wasn't until he was about to retire that their world began to crumble.

Arriving home tired and distressed after a day fraught with unproductive calls to a dozen financial institutions, Nathan finally sat Charlotte down to discuss finances. She learned that with his pension and Social Security, they would be receiving barely half of what they'd previously enjoyed, and they would have to downsize their life. At first, she behaved as always, flooding his shoulder with tears and attempts to reapportion blame, until Nathan sternly reminded her she'd never been embarrassed to demand gold or diamonds on every birthday and anniversary. And when he revealed that they still owed a great deal of money, and her extravagance and self-absorption had brought them to the brink of bankruptcy, she agreed to selling the house.

The couple spent weeks looking for somewhere smaller. Unfortunately, their freewheeling lifestyle had long since eaten into their house's equity, and even a miniscule home in the Chicago area would not fit their reduced circumstances. Faced with an uncertain passage into their golden years, knowing he could no more sell his wife's jewelry than rob a bank, Nathan scouted around for something else. An FBI colleague told him about Poets Corner, and it appeared to offer salvation.

At first, Charlotte was adamant she would not move further away from her two remaining children; Candy in Florida and Colin in Connecticut. In an effort to prevent a cross-country relocation, she asked them for help. She was curtly told they had their own lives and families, and could do nothing. Reality finally hit when Nathan returned from a hospital check-up for what he thought was a gastric upset and informed Charlotte he had advanced colon cancer. At that point, it was easy to convince her that not only would the dry mountain air of northern Arizona be better for him, but the perks associated with living in Poets Corner would allow them to maintain the lifestyle they'd enjoyed when he was working.

Liquidating everything of value, the pair paid their debts and wired their remaining one hundred thousand dollars to a mortgage company in Arizona. And after meandering across the country, checking out a dozen places they'd always wanted to visit, Nathan pulled to a halt in front of a brand new luxury home in Poets Corner. Charlotte never asked how they could afford such a big house, or where the money came from to furnish and maintain it; she was simply happy to move into an up-market community where she could resurrect her role as a seemingly affluent lady of leisure.

Nathan was instantly drawn into the community. Attending resident and committee meetings and organizing trips, it was as if he'd been part of the group for years. Over the months, when Nathan occasionally wanted to disappear for a couple of days, under the auspices of a boys night out, Charlotte indulged him. Nathan's popularity continued until he became too sick to participate in community business; then residents, with whom he'd had close ties, became distinctly cold. By the time he died, the temperature in Charlotte's small corner of the world had dropped to sub-zero.

*

"So that was my cue," said Charlotte. "I decided to move to Florida, which was what I wanted in the first place. However, when my Realtor said I didn't own the house, he suggested I contact the chairman of the Poets Corner resident's committee. Idiot said my deed clearly states that, upon Nathan's death, ownership of the house reverts to something called Ex Gratia, LLC."

"Who are they?" asked Jim.

"I was told they were the mortgage company."

"Did you actually see the document?"

"Yes, they gave me a copy. It's somewhere in Nathan's bureau."

"It's an important document, Charlotte." Scott could barely hide the exasperation in his voice. "It should be somewhere where you can easily find it."

"But I didn't want it out when I was doing my interviews, and I simply forgot about it."

"Interviews?" asked Jim.

"Didn't I cover that bit? I had this idea to get a roommate, which would allow me to save enough money to get a lawyer and fight the committee's decision. No one could throw an old lady out on the street as long as she is paying her way."

Scott smiled. "Sensible thinking. Did you find someone suitable?"

"No, Nathan hadn't been entirely straight with me."

"Nathan?"

"I don't know why he would've done this." Charlotte swiped a tear sliding down her cheek.

"Done what?" said Jim.

"When I received my first widow's payment, a letter from the administrator of Nathan's pension plan explained that because he had elected a higher payment when he was alive, my benefit was reduced to a third upon his death. Even with a roommate, I couldn't afford to maintain my house, so I decided to simply appeal to the committee at its next meeting."

Scott realized while he'd had his difficulties, he hadn't actually come across the committee. "Where does this committee meet?" he asked.

"At the café."

"The Eagle Lake Café?"

"Yes, down in the forest."

Jim's voice was casual and controlled as if talking to a child. "Do you mean the place with the observation deck overlooking the lake?"

"Have you eaten there?"

"I've just passed by."

"It's not such a nice place," whispered Charlotte.

"Food no good?"

"On the contrary, the food is wonderful. I just don't like the people they allow in there."

"You mean the committee?" asked Scott.

"Who else would I mean? And the woman who runs the place—Volder something—is in cahoots with the committee. I went there to make my appeal, and she wouldn't even let me in the dining room. Said it was a private meeting, and I needed to make an appointment with the community liaison. Nerve of the woman; I'd already tried that and got nowhere. Just because I'm old doesn't mean I'm feeble-minded. Besides, I was ripping mad, so I ducked around the side to sneak in the back way."

Holly had rejoined them and giggled again, imagining the old lady skulking in the undergrowth like a geriatric Emma Peel. "Sorry, all; don't mind me."

"I'd been there before and I knew you could get into the dining room from the observation deck. I went around back, saw where the drapes were pulled, snuck in and hid behind them. I was about to burst in when I heard a voice I recognized. It was Zoey Mitchell, the one who ran Scott down, and the casual way she talked about what happened sent chills through me. Anyway, I peeped through the drapes and she was standing at one of those white boards giving some sort of lecture; like at traffic school with diagrams of cars, and arrows showing the direction of vehicles. She was talking about mountain curves and what speed you could safely go, and when she paused for breath—and God knows I had to wait long enough—I jumped in to give them all a piece of my mind." With fists clenched, Charlotte jumped to her feet, and pumped the air.

"Whoa!" Jim ducked his head.

"Sorry, Michael, got carried away. Anyway, that's how I felt. I faced the devils alone and cussed out every last one of them."

"You didn't actually hit anybody?" asked Holly.

"Not for want of trying. That Colonel What's-His-Name grabbed me while somebody called the police. When they arrived, I was removed. 'For my own safety', they said. They're just rotten bastards, every last one of 'em."

Scott, Jim and Holly let out a collective laugh; it was a serious issue, but not without humor.

"Don't you youngsters laugh now." Charlotte pointed an accusing finger. "I want satisfaction. I want the money for my house, and if I don't get it, I'll make a ruckus that'll wake the dead."

The friends had no doubt Charlotte was serious. However, it was obvious she had no idea her amateur attempt to disrupt the committee could backfire on her.

Jim spoke first. "I'm not sure what can be done at this point, but leave it with me. I'm making inquiries on Uncle Scott's account, and if I get any news that might help you, I'll pass it on."

Charlotte's eyes shone clear with resolve. "I don't have long, young man. I want someone to help me make a stand, and I'd like to do it before I get hauled out of here in a pine box."

"I'll sincerely try, Charlotte, but you can't go charging about the place breaking in on private meetings; that's disturbing the peace. At some point, the committee will press charges."

"What about my peace? I've had none since Nathan died." She pulled out her hanky again and dabbed her eyes. "Bah, what do I care? What're they going to do, lock me up? Look at that Zoey character. She ran Scott down and what did they do . . . nothing. And why? Because she's a poor, defenseless little old lady. I'd lock her up right now, along with that Ben Watkins. He went through a store window, you know, and killed a man. And what about . . . what about . . ." The name wouldn't come to her. "Aghh, you're all the same, you youngsters have no guts. Why, in the trenches you wouldn't have lasted five minutes." Charlotte broke down in a flood of tears.

"We really will try and help," said Scott, draping an arm about the old lady's shoulder. "Let Holly walk you home and visit a while. I'm sure my nephew will think of something."

Charlotte wiped her eyes and rose to leave, and in passing Jim, patted his cheeks with her fine-boned hands. "You're a good boy, I can feel it. My number is in the directory; call me when you find out something."

Holly and Charlotte left the men to sort out exactly what she'd inadvertently told them.

"Christ," said Scott, "if I wasn't worried about the situation before, I am now. If she's not completely looped, it sounds like this place is full of old geezers making an art form out of getting rid of people they don't like."

"Sounds bizarre, but I think you're on the right track. Hang on a minute; I have something else to show you in my briefcase." He returned with a bunch of newspaper clippings. "I'm assuming you read the files, so I'll start at what I think is the beginning. If you have questions, jump in because this whole business is convoluted, and with Charlotte's contribution, it's about to get even messier."

Before anything more was said, Holly reappeared.

"That was quick," said Scott. "I thought you were going to sit with her a while."

"Didn't get beyond the corner. And she said something weird. Halfway across the road, she patted my hand, and said I should scoot home because it was dangerous to be seen with her. She said eyes were watching, and if she doesn't make it home, talk to Bill Sheffield."

"Bill Sheffield? Doesn't ring a bell," Jim said, "but I have seen a Sara Sheffield somewhere. You check the directory while I grab a file."

Scott pulled his directory from the drawer. "Here they are: Bill and Sara Sheffield, 1113 Shakespeare."

Holly moved to look over Scott's shoulder. "You think they're as crazy as Charlotte?"

Jim interrupted. "I don't think she's crazy. Look at this; Sara Sheffield, Alzheimer's, currently resident at the Sacred Heart Center. Formerly personal assistant to Major General Tremont Winthrop, president and co-owner of Abovo Consolidate Holdings, Cayman Islands."

Holly gasped. "How did I miss that? The only assistant I was aware of was his army liaison, Sandra Gibson. Actually, Captain Sandra Gibson. Who is this person, and what is Abovo?"

Scott scratched his head. "Another mystery. What the hell are we into?"

"I'm not entirely sure," Jim replied, "but I do know we're getting hopelessly bogged down. We need more help. I can call in more favors, but I need official backing."

"Will that be a problem?"

"That depends on how quickly we get this mess of information into some sort of order, how much help you two are with the million questions I have, and how good a case I put together to present to my Super'."

"Oh great, that'll be a piece of cake." Holly's sarcasm was unmistakable. "I can't get diddly belonging to my husband that might help. Scott is getting no answers from the mortgage company to clarify his issue. And we're surrounded by a bunch of people who'd as soon see us in hell as help us."

Jim spread out his file and retrieved the legal pad where Scott and Holly had jotted notes. "That often happens when you're dealing with a closed community. Fortunately you have me, and I'm pretty good at this, so let's go over what we know.

"It appears everybody in this community is connected through their job, be it career military, police or government agency. We also have evidence that every household has at least one occupant with an expensive long-term illness that, even with Medicare and secondary insurance, would render them broke in a matter of months. Contrary to that notion, everybody here lives very well, has a big house, an expensive car, and seemingly unlimited resources, which is definitely out of line with the list showing estimated pension and Social Security income."

Holly's charitable side had her leap to the residents' defense. "What if they made money on the stock market and have healthy dividend returns?"

"Good point, but the investment information I recovered shows that while a handful of residents have additional income, only three have enough to maintain the lifestyle this community enjoys."

Holly unconsciously smiled. Scott was one of those listed.

"As far as the reverse mortgage clause goes," Jim added, "I have someone looking into that."

"Because a surviving spouse can't ordinarily be kicked out of their home?" asked Scott.

"Right, but I think we've discovered there's nothing ordinary about the mortgage company or this community."

"So who exactly owns what in this cockamamie place?"

Jim flipped open a file. "I've pulled as much information as we currently have on Poets Corner and it seems three companies control everything; mortgages, car leases, health insurance, you name it."

Scott nodded. "And all those companies have the same principal officer: a man named Bryce Peterson, whose name is ringing all sorts of bells in my head. Give me time, I'll work it out."

"You may also have noticed this." Jim pulled out the Activated Operatives list. "My contact couldn't get much from the military, but these are the names of the intelligence types let loose on the world in January 1969." Jim pointed to Bryce Peterson. "There's the biggie for us. He's had his finger in a lot of pies since leaving the military, not the least being the three companies associated with this community."

"Did you get anything on them?" asked Scott.

"Some; the first is Internos, a private insurance company picking up residents' medical expenses not reimbursed by Medicare. The second, Ex Gratia, built the houses and has a financial hold on every property in the development. A colleague is working exclusively on that puzzle because it seems individuals buy into here for a variable fee."

"My brother-in-law told me he paid two hundred thousand dollars for this house."

"And Nathan Messing paid one hundred thousand, someone named Watkins paid one twenty-five, another paid three hundred, another paid two seventy-five, and on it goes."

"The house sizes do vary a bit," added Scott, "but not enough to cover the disparity in the dollar amounts. It seems certain people are being given a price break."

Jim nodded. "Certainly looks that way."

"Apart from jobs, is there anything else to link the buyers?"

Jim flipped to his notes. "The only constant that hit me was on each deed of record. It stated that when the single named homeowner dies, the property goes back to Ex Gratia awaiting another investor."

"Investor, not homeowner?" asked Holly.

"Right, every document we found refers to an investor."

"Well, whatever they choose to call themselves," said Holly, "I know enough about local real estate to ask why these houses are being sold for a quarter of their worth?"

"Because they aren't really being sold," Jim pointed to a paragraph on Scott's deed. "It's more like renting for the duration of one's life. See here, sub para 2 below the take-back clause: 'All household medical expenses, state and local taxes, vehicle and home repairs, and community maintenance costs will be offset against equity.'"

"Which means," said Holly, "no matter how much you put in, should you want to sell the house, it's guaranteed you'll never get anything back. But if the houses are never sold for their true value, and equity is used to pay expenses—which judging by the lifestyle of these people is probably enormous—where's the profit for whoever owns them?"

Jim shrugged. "Haven't worked that out yet."

Holly thought she had. "What about insurance policies? Say you take one out to cover the mortgage on a six hundred thousand dollar house, and then you die—or are killed—who gets the money?"

"You're right," said Jim. "Scott, did Chuck and Amanda have policies, and if so, who was the beneficiary? Wasn't you, was it?"

"Not that I know of. I received their wills, which simply

indicated they wanted me to have the house."

"When did you receive them?"

"The day after they died."

"Which means they were posted a couple of days previous. That's an uncomfortable coincidence," said Jim.

"I don't believe in coincidence," added Scott.

"Given what they, and now we, know about the take-back clause, why would they send their wills to you at all?"

"Maybe they were drawing my attention to their loss."

"So," Jim said, "Chuck is offered an irresistible deal on this house, and with the mountain climate good for Amanda and help with medical expenses, he buys in. They move in and appear happy, but when Amanda takes a turn for the worse, they decide that back east is where they really want to be. Figuring they've only been here a month and haven't chalked up any expenses to offset against equity, Chuck asks the committee for his money back. The committee tells him tough luck, and reality hits. No matter what they want, they're trapped. But Chuck refuses to let it stop there. He makes a stink and is pressured in the same way Charlotte has been."

"Jeez," said Scott, "you're making a quantum leap. Chuck was a member of the bomb squad; he didn't scare easily."

"Right, so forget scared. Suppose he sensed that in making some noise he'd put himself and Amanda in danger, maybe even expected something catastrophic to happen. He wanted to make sure the community's actions were brought to somebody's attention. Somebody he knew would continue to rock the boat until he got straight answers."

Scott smiled. "In that case, the appropriate boat rocker would be me."

Jim nodded. "Correct. And seeing as how the two of them died in a questionable car accident, and you received their wills so shortly thereafter, it's logical."

"But Chuck couldn't know I'd want to sell this house."

"I think he knew you wouldn't fit in here. Moreover, there's no doubt in my mind he knew you'd question the take-back clause and eventually get caught up in something more than selling a house."

Scott raked a hand through his hair. "Why didn't they simply leave, and do their own exposing from a distance?"

"That would've been safer," said Jim, "but we don't have any idea how much time there was between his realization and the accident. Maybe it was just long enough to throw their wills in the mail."

Scott was visibly shaken. "You think the committee had something to do with the accident?"

"Not positive, but they seem awfully tight with our mysterious Cormorant Club. And what you said earlier is nagging at me."

Scott looked puzzled.

"You said, 'This community seems to make an art form out of getting rid of people they don't like.'"

"You two are crazy," interrupted Holly. "You can't get away with killing people who ask too many questions."

Jim, the cop, took over. "Well you're correct in one respect; I have no proof Chuck and Amanda were killed. All I see is a police report determining their deaths were the result of a murder/suicide."

"That's bullshit." Angry realization washed over Scott. "Something most definitely screwy is going on here, and we need to find out what it is before someone else gets hurt."

"Now that I wholeheartedly agree with, but we had to talk this through to see where we're coming from and going to. There's no arguing that Poets Corner is a private development and can pretty much make up any membership rules they like. So what if those who live here are connected by a bunch of coincidences—"

"Because," interrupted Scott, "there are too many, and when

that happens, somebody is playing God."

"Hold that thought," said Jim, pulling another file, "while we look into the third company in the Poets Corner trinity, Absit Invidia. It financed all the cars you spotted at the café."

"What about that company with my husband as president; didn't you say it was in the Cayman Islands?"

"Probably just a tax loophole. That's very common, not illegal, and not particularly important in the big scheme of things. What is important is the common thread running through everything: Bryce Peterson. I have someone running his name, though so far he's a real enigma. He owns companies within companies, and appears to be doling out money like it's Halloween candy. Keep mulling his name over in your mind, Scott. Eventually you'll have one of those eureka moments. Now, let's look at something else." Jim took a pile of newspaper clippings from the file and spread them on the table.

"Most of these clippings refer to accidents in which an elderly person's foot got stuck on the gas, a senior driver was in reverse instead of drive, they had a seizure, dropped eyeglasses, were avoiding a dog . . . whatever. The outcomes, however, were the same. Someone was run down, pushed off the road, or T-boned, and—present company excepted—that person ended up dead. I also have accounts of seniors arrested for possession of unauthorized drugs at a customs checkpoint, the odd identity theft, death from heart attack for a senior with no prior symptoms, and the always spectacular, berserk employee with a shotgun. But for me, more perplexing than the seniors' connection in all these incidents is that not one was charged with a felony. Somehow, some way, through sympathetic doctors, smart lawyers, over-enthusiastic psychiatrists, and so on, every senior responsible was allowed to go home with a token punishment. Most paid piddling fines for offenses like 'operating a motor vehicle without due care and attention,' and the most serious repercussion was loss of a driver's license."

"Did you get the names of the lawyers involved in these cases?" asked Holly.

"Don't think so, why?"

"I'll bet money somewhere in the stink of things is an attorney called Marvin Shapler."

"Friend of yours?"

"My husband's. When Scott and I took a walk the other night, I saw him at the clubhouse with a group of people, and all the cars parked in the lot sported Cormorant Club stickers."

"I'll get my gal to check. In the meantime, look at these photos."

The photos were mostly police black and whites, and many were still gruesome enough to make even ex-nurse Holly wince. Scott flipped through the pictures quickly, then started slowly again at the beginning. "These colored ones are pretty graphic. How does anyone do this for a living?"

"You get used to it."

Holly leaned in. "I don't recognize the cars. This one has Florida plates."

Scott cleaned his glasses, and rubbed his eyes to aid focus. "Holly, can you get the magnifying glass from the right-hand drawer of the bureau, up top?" With the additional lens in place, Scott isolated an image, scrutinized several more pictures, and stopped at the one of his brother-in-law's car being pulled from a ravine. "Jesus H. Christ, this is unbelievable."

Jim was impatient. "What do you see?"

Scott's eyes misted, not because he'd been rudely reminded of his sister's death, but because Chuck's car exhibited a mark he didn't want to see. "It's a Cormorant sticker, and look at these," he pulled picture after picture to the fore. "Lots of the cars, fore and background, have stickers."

Jim placed a hand on Scott's arm. "I know they were your family, and you might not want to hear this, but I believe Chuck, everyone causing the accidents in these pictures, as well as everybody who lives here in Poets Corner, is a member of the Cormorant Club. And I have the distinct feeling not one of them is here to stalk birds."

Scott couldn't hide his pain. "It might look that way, but Chuck was a cop. Maybe he found out about all this and wanted no part of whatever madness we've uncovered. To keep him quiet, the club killed him."

Holly sympathetically stroked her fiancé's back. "Sweetie, there are a lot of cops living here."

"But Chuck was a good cop, an honest cop. I can't see him condoning any of this."

"Not even if it he thought it might save Amanda's life?" said Jim.

"I don't know, I still find it inconceiva—"

Holly put a hand on Scott's arm. "What if it were me?"

"I concede the point. Now look here," continued Scott, "some of these accidents are in other parts of the country. Are we to assume there's more than one club?"

"I'm not sure." Jim pulled one particular photo from the pile. "Pan that lens over this. It's a front view, so if there's a Cormorant sticker you won't see it, but this accident has a different connection to our untidy scenario. See if you agree."

It took a couple of minutes before Scott found the right spot. The photograph showed a Volvo with its front fender caved in, and the body of a man, bloodied and clearly dead, spread across and partially through the windshield. The picture's angle was such that you could see the hands of a cop taking notes, while a man Scott supposed was the Volvo's driver stood, arm raised, appearing to describe the victim's flight through the air. A crowd watched from the rear right of the vehicle. All appeared elderly, and their faces, though grainy, could be distinguished.

Jim disturbed the kitchen's quiet. "Am I right?"

"I think you are, if you mean that." Scott put his finger on a spot beneath the lens.

"Good grief, that's Charlotte!" Holly grabbed at the picture. "It says here the man driving is Arthur Levinson, 63, of Coral Gables, Florida. Doesn't her daughter live in Coral Gables?"

Jim nodded. "That's a coincidence even I can do without. She said her kids were Candy and Colin, but did she mention her son-in-law's name?"

"No, but I can call her and ask."

"Do it. Say we need to know because Nathan had him cosign her mortgage papers."

"I think she's smarter than she sometimes sounds," commented Scott. "Wouldn't she already know that wasn't true?"

"From her admission earlier, she didn't know much of anything financial her husband did. I think we'll be safe."

Holly's call confirmed Charlotte's son-in-law was Arthur Levinson of Coral Gables, Florida. "Why didn't she mention him this morning? She fingered plenty of residents here."

"I can only assume she was so upset about her own situation, she didn't put two and two together," said Jim. "God knows a move to Florida won't help her. She's going right out of the frying pan into the fire."

"Should we say something?" asked Holly.

"No, she's distraught right now, and she's likely to head off to the next committee meeting and blurt out something that will screw us up. So far, they've not taken her too seriously; I think we have time to let that game play out. You," Jim said, pointing at Scott, "are another matter. I don't want to alarm you, but unlike Charlotte, the group has already made its move on you. I think you're in more danger than either of you realize. You need to get away from here, and until you do, you shouldn't go anywhere alone."

Scott smiled. "Aren't you being a bit melodramatic?"

"If I am, and what I suspect is nothing, call me a drama queen. However, my advice is to distance yourself from Poets Corner."

"What about Ilse?" Holly asked. "She helped us get this whole thing rolling. If there is some sort of conspiracy, and people are watching us, wouldn't they have seen us—and you—with her at Eagle Lake?"

"Damn, I'm such an idiot. She told me last night that Mrs. Voldheim's husband died in a hit-and-run on the road behind her cabin. I've got to get her away from there. Scott, I know it's an awful imposition, but can she stay here until we ship her to Phoenix?"

"Murphy bed in the den okay?"

*

Within minutes, Jim called the café. Mrs. Voldheim answered the phone and curtly asked who was calling. Jim refused to give his name, stating he was Ilse's friend. All he heard was a haughty snort and the phone being laid down.

"Hello, this is Ilse."

"Hi," said Jim. "Say nothing. I'm coming for you now."

Though Ilse didn't know Jim well, the authority in his voice convinced her she should follow his direction without question. She reacted quickly when static indicated he'd hung up, but her escape wasn't to be straightforward. Mrs. Voldheim cornered her before she got to the dining room.

"Who was that?"

"Somebody wanting take-out."

The wily owner knew she was lying. "He said he was your friend."

"Liked my service last time he was here."

"I'm going to watch you very closely, *fräulein*. Now get back to work."

Ilse flounced toward the kitchen, knowing the woman she'd once seen as her savior but whom she now despised could no longer intimidate her.

*

Twenty minutes later, the formidable force that was Mrs. Voldheim reflected on the way her timid refugee had suddenly developed a spine. She returned to the dining room, but Ilse was nowhere to be seen. Neither was she in the kitchen or bathrooms. Striding purposefully back to the dining room, she stopped one of the other waitresses. "Where's Ilse?"

"Bathroom." Piled high with dishes, in no mood to handle a lengthy interrogation from the overbearing owner, the waitress tried to move on. A forceful grip held her back.

"I checked, and she's not there."

"Then I have no idea, but somebody better find her soon. If I have to cover all these tables much longer, something's gonna get really screwed up."

Cursing in German, Mrs. Voldheim lumbered off in the direction of the cabin. Given her considerable bulk, she didn't ordinarily move fast; however, she was on a mission, and her substantial legs powered her across the parking lot. As she unceremoniously burst into the cabin's living room, it was quickly apparent Ilse was not there. Advancing on the bathroom, Mrs. Voldheim's frustrated kick sent the door hurtling into the tiling, causing tinkling shards to fall. And upon opening the armoire, there was no doubt her possessions—and Ilse—were gone.

Letting out a string of obscenities, Mrs. Voldheim turned to leave. Propped against the microwave was a note written in German: "Going home; take out your perverted frustrations on someone else. Ilse."

Chapter Eleven

It was nine-thirty the following morning when the Morgan and the BMW roadster swept through the Poets Corner gates. A rippling of curtains in the unofficial gatekeeper's house proved at least one resident was monitoring their departure, and while Scott would ordinarily have proffered a mocking wave, today he was more concerned with putting the community behind him.

Both Scott and Jim were comfortable driving at high speed, and they behaved like kids in hot-rods the entire hundred miles to Phoenix. As they pulled into Poppy's drive, it was clear the chase-and-tag routine had done more for the guys than at least one of the women.

First onto solid ground, Holly wasted no time. "I swear to God," she scolded, "if we have to do another long run, I'm driving. The two of you are certifiable maniacs, and it's a wonder you didn't kill us all."

Sidling close to her, Scott draped an arm over her shoulder, and planted a kiss on her cheek. "But what a way to go."

When Holly approached the roadster, she found Jim and Ilse lip-locked in a world of their own. "Ilse," she said, tapping on the roof. "I know he probably has to give you oxygen after that hair-raising drive, but leave the beast. I want to show you around the place."

"You're just jealous," teased Scott.

Holly playfully pushed him away. "I'll deal with you later."

After Ilse's tour, Holly led everyone across the garden to what they thought was the pool's cabana. She unlocked the door, and ushered the group inside.

*

"Will I be living here?" Ilse asked, with eyes like saucers. "It's as big as a house."

Holly handed her the keys. "It's all yours."

"How will I ever be able to thank you?"

"Cook on the nights we don't go out?"

Ilse beamed. "Absolutely. It's a passion of mine, and the least I can do."

As Holly and Scott left, Jim took Ilse in his arms. "You didn't say cooking was your passion. I thought that was my department."

"You've yet to convince me of that."

"So do I go back to my lonely room in the main house, or bunk here with you?"

"I might be convinced to let you stay if I'm allowed a little taste of the passion."

Jim locked his lips on hers, and plunged his tongue deep into her mouth. She responded hungrily, and it was several seconds before they broke apart.

"I'll have you know," he continued, "my family owns some of the finest restaurants in Canada, and though I can't cook, taste is important to me. I have highly sensitive taste-buds."

Ilse didn't miss the innuendo. "I can tell, and that's good."

"How so, *fräulein*?"

"It means, in more ways than one, you need me."

"Of that, there is no doubt." With everything momentarily forgotten, Jim led Ilse to the bedroom.

Chapter Twelve

"Alone at last," said Scott, pulling Holly close. "Now what're we going to do with ourselves?"

"Find a bedroom. Follow me." She led him to an Indian-inspired oasis, dotted with sumptuous fabrics in pumpkin and gold set against dark mahogany furniture. And positioned about were a half-dozen Kama Sutra-inspired sculptures.

"Dear God," Scott said, angling one particularly erotic piece toward Holly, "I hope I'm not expected to live up to this."

She grinned. "All I ask is that you do your best."

"What on earth possessed Poppy to decorate a room like this?"

"You don't like it?"

"Like or dislike is not exactly what I was thinking. It's intimidating."

"We can move to another room if you'd rather."

"No, we'll give this one a try. But you have to admit, it's like being in a Vegas-themed motel."

"This room was inspired by a visit to the Taj Mahal."

"No kidding. It's a wonder she didn't install an elephant in the walk-in."

"Funny you should say that." Picking up a remote, Holly activated a cabinet mounted flat-screen, which popped up to reveal a film of elephants. As huge bulls charged, ears outstretched in a threatening stance, and small calves sheltered safely beneath their doting mothers' legs, the rest of a family group splashed happily at the watering hole. Then, as if on cue for their current conversation, the screen was filled with stunningly engorged pachyderms mating.

"Jesus," said Scott, "does this woman have no restraint whatsoever?"

"Poppy is very high maintenance."

Scott took Holly's hand, and kissed the palm. "I guess birds of a feather really do flock together."

Holly snatched her hand from him. "How rotten. I am not high maintenance."

Scott smiled indulgently, and chucked her under the chin. "Excuse me?"

"Okay, so maybe I am, a little, but I'm worth every penny."

He pulled her into his arms. "That you certainly are. Now may I escort you back to the patio where I have a fighting chance of being more outrageous than the furniture?" He looped her arm in his, and set off. "So where did you and Poppy meet?"

*

"At an embassy party in Washington. God, it was eons ago, around 1970; she was an old friend of Tug's, and when I say 'friend' I mean they were as close as you and I."

"Didn't that bother you?"

"Why should it? They were over each other. She was a flight attendant with TWA, and when she wasn't off into the wide blue yonder somewhere, we hung out together. She was so much fun to have around, and when Tug was away, I'd do the party circuit with her. That was how she met her husband. We were at a reception in Ottawa celebrating Pierre Trudeau's re-election in '72. Tug arrived late, as he had a meeting with some Canadian officials, and when he brought them over to apologize for keeping him, one of them was Jim's uncle, Oliver."

"Oliver? His name was Oliver Cromwell?"

"Cruel parents, huh? And from what Poppy told me, the name plagued him all his life. Anyway, it was a costume bash, and she went as Marilyn Monroe, albeit with red hair. That's why we call her Poppy, for the hair. Nobody uses her real name; it's a twelve on the yikes-o-meter and a booger to pronounce. Naturally, when

Tug introduced Ambassador Oliver Cromwell, Poppy had a field day with his name, but in spite of her irreverence and teasing, he completely fell for her. She told me they didn't get out of bed for a week, and when they did, it was to get married. He was very important in the Canadian government and that suited her fine, because they were invited to every social event on the calendar."

"Hopefully, she ditched the red-haired Marilyn Monroe."

"Not a chance. You should have seen her back then; she was a wild woman, and her antics were the talk of Canada. Of course, the press hounded them, as every week she got involved in some deliciously outrageous caper, but the more outrageous she became the more Oliver adored her. She was truly the yin to his yang. I'm sure you must have seen her; she went to every event I did and then some."

"I wasn't really Mr. Party Hearty."

"Were you at least at the Mardi Gras bash at the Brazilian Embassy when she turned up as Carmen Miranda? She had at least ten pounds of wax fruit on her head, and not much of anything on her body. Every society rag did a spread on her. All I got was slobbering Sam what's-his-name from the Stars and Stripes mooning over me."

Knowing how sensitive Holly was about some aspects of her past, particularly as they related to she and Tug's open marital arrangement, Scott said nothing. He knew Poppy wasn't the only wild woman back then, and the more he remembered of Holly in those distant days, the more he understood why. Despite knowing she was open to affairs, he'd chosen to maintain his distance. His decision might have meant wasted years, but he was thankful something deep inside had warned him not to make a move then. Had he done so, he suspected he'd have been one of many he knew she'd set aside to return to her husband. In her own way, she obviously loved Tug, whoever and whatever he truly was, and his tolerance of her peccadilloes proved he was also devoted to her. Now after spending time with her, Scott realized from where those feelings of devotion stemmed. Holly was an extraordinarily exciting woman, whose dogged passion for life brought out the best in those around her, and he, too, was now bound by chains no mortal could break.

As they exhausted small talk, the couple was comfortable enough with each other to let the metronomic clicking of the ceiling fan lull them into sleep. But even an afternoon of heat-induced sleep beneath the covered patio can be disturbed by the heavy mugginess of a monsoon rain. Not used to the spikes in temperature or pressure, Scott woke. With sinuses full and head feeling the weight of approaching pressure, he looked to the mountains beyond the garden where thick banks of clouds roiled. When a bolt of lightening, quickly followed by an extraordinarily loud thunder boom startled him, he reached for Holly's hand.

She woke with a start. "Bad timing. I was having the most outrageous dream about you and me at Mardi Gras."

"Was I good?"

"Divine."

He smiled, debating whether to take her indoors and break the spell. "I've loved you since Vietnam, you know."

Her fingers entwined his. "I know. You told me."

"I did no such thing. I was too chicken-shit to say anything once you flashed the wedding ring." He thought for a while, and called her bluff. "When did I tell you?"

"Sponge bath, way south of the 816th MASH unit, 17:46 hours, Christmas 1968."

She was deliciously outrageous, and he didn't think he'd ever get tired of her. "Enough, you brazen trollop." He pulled her to her feet, nodding at the approach of a towering cloud. "We better get inside before that dust storm hits. Besides, your smutty talk has made me hungry. Call the kids, ask if they want food."

*

Dinner passed pleasantly with no talk of danger or mutual difficulties, but as soon as the men cleared the table and loaded the dishwasher, Jim was all cop. "Sorry to ruin our pleasant evening with business, but that's why we're here."

Scott refilled wine glasses. "A little more wine shouldn't be too disruptive, so let's see what you have."

"The more I dig into Poets Corner, the more convoluted it becomes. And while I've cross-referenced and lain to rest as many coincidences as I can, certain events involving two characters keep bouncing out at me."

"Bryce Peterson and Marvin Shapler?" asked Holly.

"Correct. As you suspected, Shapler was the lawyer of record in many of the cases I researched, and he's also on the board of all the companies we had questions about. According to airline records, he flew into Sky Harbor the day before you saw him at the clubhouse. Bryce Peterson still proves to be elusive, giving the team in records and research the complete runaround. As to the other weirdness, particularly as it relates to the Cormorant Club, I've spoken to my superintendent and he agrees I may have enough of a case to request an attachment to the Phoenix Police Department."

"Which we can help you with."

"That's the plan; anything new pop out of the woodwork for you?"

Scott frowned. "I've wracked my brains over the information we've collected, and the only thing I can come up with is a theory that stems from conversations my friend Tim Bowman and I had in Vietnam. It's totally off the wall, but hear me out because my head has been buzzing since this whole thing started. My feelings aren't tangible; they're more like connecting a bunch of random dots to get an answer. I think my friend Tim Bowman was resurrected as Bryce Peterson."

"That's a pretty big bunch of dots," said Jim.

"I know, but with death recorded, signed, sealed, and delivered on

Tim, and Bryce Peterson emerging from the woodwork at that precise time, what else can I think? We've established Tim was working with Tug until just before the General supposedly committed suicide, and for me, this ball started downhill with that death. Holly, did you actually see Tim after his Medivac from Vietnam?"

"A couple of times in passing; he was with Tug."

"Did Tug call him by his name?"

"Not that I recall."

"So you could still know him as Tim Bowman, while the world knew him as Bryce Peterson?"

"Yes."

"We know that after Tug died, Holly saw stationery with a Cormorant logo fall from her safe," Scott continued. "It was a list of animals, which was undoubtedly a copy of the code Tim and I developed while in Vietnam. And for the sake of my theory, let's assume Tug recruited Tim, and military intelligence used that code for government covert operations."

"I thought you guys were developing the thing for fun," said Jim.

"We were, but there's no reason why it can't be used."

"It's that sophisticated?"

"Doesn't need to be, Jim—sometimes less is more. Anyway, simple or not, it was our baby, and I know Tim would've been tight-lipped about it, particularly the encryption parameters. He'd have shared the absolute minimum to get by; probably he, Tug, and I are the only people with full knowledge of its workings. Now, let's say the pair worked together, reaping whatever benefits they could from the system, until one day Tug decided to retire. This creates a huge dilemma for Tim. Does he let the General pass what he knows about the code to a subordinate, to be used as the government wishes, or can something more lucrative be done with it?"

"I don't know this Tim character," said Jim, "but human nature dictates he'd opt for drawing upon more benefits than Uncle Sam could offer."

"I know Tim, and that's exactly where I'm going. Let's say upon Tug's retirement, Tim suggests they transition into a business of their own, using the code, which in theory is unbreakable. It wouldn't be much of an emotional stretch to expand on what the government had been doing, and form their own company specializing in disruption and clean-up."

"You mean they'd be outside the government, but still setting up assassinations, coups, accidental deaths, that sort of thing?" asked Jim.

Scott nodded. "It's a very profitable business."

"Tug was a spy," snapped Holly, "not a common mercenary."

Jim cast a look at Scott. "I suspect in his case there was little separating the two."

"Then you don't know squat about service to—"

"Holly, stop," said Scott. "Jim is entitled to his opinion. We're all going to say stuff that rankles, but to get at the truth everything has to be on the table."

Jim put his hand over hers, as Scott continued. "I have no doubt Tug primarily oversaw Uncle Sam's problems, and would avoid doing anything that would discredit the United States. Let's agree that being a true-blue company-man, he said no to Tim's entrepreneurial endeavor; something we can safely assume did not go down well."

"Are you saying that because my husband wouldn't go along, he was killed?"

"Maybe. Military intelligence types are taught to think—and act—for themselves."

"So how do we get the bastard?"

"Slow down, Holly, this is all only a theory. We have mountains to scale before we tie in all this Cormorant stuff. So, Tug and Tim had been in the government's clean-up business for years, and Tug's retirement put Tim's forward movement in jeopardy. I'm speculating they had an agreement to work together for the betterment of each other, but after decades of making only marginal profit from the code, Tim now wanted to use it on more lucrative contracts."

Ilse was clearly fascinated by Scott's theory. "Now I see where you fit in. With Holly's husband dead, you're the only other person who knows exactly how the code works."

Scott nodded. "You got it. My gut is telling me Tim, Bryce, or whatever we call him, thinks I'll expose him. He can't move forward with his business until he gets rid of me."

Holly frowned. "What a creep. Well, I'm telling you right now, he might have killed one of my husbands, but he's not getting another. What do we do now?"

"The first thing is for me to fully reconstruct the code and show Jim how it works. Next, we have to prove that Bryce Peterson is Tim Bowman."

Holly was ready. "Pass over those lists, Ilse; I've met enough of Tug's business partners to recognize a name. Maybe we can pressure someone to help us."

Ilse paused on the first list. "This company name is Latin."

Jim smiled; she was as bright as he'd suspected. "I know; what the heck happened to good old English names?"

"It's quite clever when you think about it. It's not Internos, one word; it's *inter nos*, which translates to 'between ourselves.' Under the circumstances, it's pretty appropriate for a company paying bills for a select group of people."

Jim and Scott looked at each other, both having the same thought: *there are no coincidences.* Jim handed her all the data he had. "What do you read into the others?"

"Ex Gratia, the mortgage company, means 'as a favor, not as something owed.' This one, for the registered owner of the cars—including the one which ran you down, Scott—Absit Invidia stands for 'no offense intended.' How often is someone run down by a car owned by a company whose name means, 'no offense intended?'"

Jim took Ilse's face in his hands, and pecked her on the nose. Then he scribbled a note and handed it to her. "Try these."

"Alter idem? That's easy, 'alter ego,' and Abovo is two words actually, *ab ovo*. It can go two ways; like 'from the egg' or more practically for me, 'from the beginning.'"

"There's our link, people. Sit tight, I have to make a phone call." Jim returned in minutes and slapped the table.

"We've got him, Scott. We've nailed Bryce Peterson. I asked one of my colleagues to run a make on Bryce Peterson's personal investment holdings. They are managed by a company called Alter Idem, a subsidiary of Tug's company, Abovo in the Cayman Islands. This doesn't conclusively prove that Bryce Peterson is Tim Bowman, but 'alter ego?' He's playing mind games. I think the Latin translations in all this stuff provide the link between Tug Winthrop, Bryce Peterson, Poets Corner, a slew of dubious domestic and international companies and our mysterious Cormorant Club. A club, I might add, that has been photographed at the scene of an inordinately disproportionate number of seniors' related fatalities."

"Are you saying Bryce Peterson is behind the deaths, too," Scott asked.

"In good time, Scott, all in good time, I have to get all this on paper. If I add your theories and Ilse's translations to my report, I'll hopefully have enough circumstantial evidence to convince my boss and a half dozen skeptics that I have a case."

Chapter Thirteen

From his study, perched atop a mountain of the high desert, Bryce Peterson focused the telescope. As he panned the rolling dells opposite, the houses of Poets Corner filled the viewer. Bolstered by welling omnipotence, knowing little more than the crook of his autocratic finger could make any one of the unsuspecting seniors silently disappear, he followed his minions going about their—and his—business.

Until recently, residents had unquestionably done his bidding, but now, as he swept his spyglass to Keats Circle, the Cormorant Club's leader realized the failure of a simple run-down challenged the order of his well-oiled machine. He and his enterprise were on the verge of discovery, and being fully aware who led the insurrection, he intended to deal harshly with them. However, as he willed the object of his most major irritation into view, Scott Morgan's home appeared empty.

When the intercom squealed, disturbing the concentrated silence of the hidden observer's realm, he'd been thinking how many times the General had mentioned Scott Morgan's name over the years. And while the old soldier had wanted to bring the Vietnam vet into the military intelligence fold, Bryce never had confidence in the endeavor. He'd always assessed Scott as being too straight, too upright, too sanctimoniously all-American. The intercom squealed a second time. "Damn it, Janet, I said I didn't want to be disturbed."

"It's Wallis, Mr. Peterson. Said you wanted to know if anyone inquired about Alter Idem."

"Wallis, what gives?" Peterson said into the receiver.

"Unusual activity, sir. I've been tracking several inquiries into the network, usual stuff, board members, net worth, that sort of thing. However, about an hour ago, we received a phish from someone who turns out to be the Royal Canadian Mounted Police in Alberta, Canada. They're cagey, but requesting specific personal information."

"Canada—you sure?"

"Got it right here, sir. They only exhibited specific interest in Alter Idem account holder's names; do you want me to kick it back and establish a caller ID?"

"No, whatever game is being played, they'll be expecting that. We don't want anyone to know we're on to them, and I sure as hell don't want to mess with the Mounties. Take the back door in, and confirm whether the call was official or a general phishing expedition. Send your findings to Janet." He disconnected before Wallis acknowledged. "Janet, tell Rick to fire up the chopper, I'm going to Phoenix."

"Pretty bad dust storm threatening, sir."

"When I want a weather report I'll ask for it. Do as you're told."

*

An experienced helicopter pilot, Captain Rick Nyland kept well above and to the side of the rolling wall of dust approaching Phoenix. Nevertheless, as he swung wide, coming about over Sky Harbor to set the chopper down in the executive handling area, thick wind-driven powder filled the air. As the rotors idled, an asthmatic wheezing emanated from the air intakes, and though the pilot expected it, damage to his baby was always a serious issue. "Shit, boss," he said. "Sounds like we took in some crap, and that's gonna cost."

Peterson bagged his computer and angled from the cabin. "Whatever she needs, Rick, but don't tie yourself up. I need you to prep the jet for Cabo tomorrow."

Proficient on both rotary and fixed wing aircraft, Nyland was Bryce Peterson's fiercely loyal friend and confidante. In thirty years together, his flying pact with the same something inhuman that drove Peterson had helped the two of them escape death on more than one occasion. Moreover, he was one of only three people privy to what Peterson and the Cormorant Club did.

As Nyland stowed overnight bags in the trunk of a limousine parked beside the unmarked aircraft hanger, Peterson settled into the vehicle's back seat to make phone calls. Then, after alerting his mechanic that the helicopter needed service, and the jet should be made ready for the following day, the pilot returned to the limo, climbed into the driver's seat, and set off for The Saguaro, sitting in the shadow of Phoenix's Camelback Mountain.

Nyland drove directly to the rear of the resort's residential campus, pulling up at one of the discreetly situated private casitas. There, not wishing to waste a minute of his time, Peterson offloaded his own bag, allowing Nyland to continue on to make his pick-up.

Print IDs were used for those discriminating clients who required additional security, and as Peterson pushed his thumb against the electronic pad, the villa door swooshed silently open. Stepping into the cool, lemon-grass scented air of his most private retreat, Peterson dropped his bag in the bedroom before settling in the sitting room. As usual, Janet had called ahead and arranged for Cooksons, the resort's signature restaurant, to send over a selection of finger foods and two bottles of Cristal. After opening a bottle of the perfectly chilled champagne, Peterson picked up the phone and dialed a familiar number. "Rick's on the way; bring Karen Q," he barked.

Within twenty minutes, the limo was back at his door with the ladies, one for work, and one for play. Peterson greeted the younger warmly, led her into the bedroom and closed the door.

*

As the older woman remained in the sitting room sipping champagne, she impatiently flicked through the pages of *Vogue*. Waiting on his pleasure had become a degrading ritual for the once-ravishing sexagenarian, and she grew increasingly irritated listening to familiar noises emanating from the bedroom. She was never happy when Peterson was at play with someone else, on a bed she remembered so well, and as the uncommonly loud ticking of a carriage clock painfully reminded her how long her boss was entertaining, the woman rose and began to pace.

Stopping at an ornate gold-framed mirror, her hand, only slightly marked by age, brushed the smoothness of her cosmetically enhanced neck. She was still beautiful with an extraordinary figure, and while time and gravity made it harder for her to maintain her edge, neither had lessened her desire to perform the erotic tricks needed to inspire a partner. Sadly for her, she lived an empty life, for she alone could no longer satisfy the particular partner she craved. Taking a large swig of champagne, she cursed herself for a fool, and questioned why she tolerated any of the mental cruelty the man in the next room inflicted upon her.

As she circled the room, refusing to reflect further, a crescendo of well-remembered sounds drifted under the bedroom door. And cursing Peterson's insensitivity, and the other woman's youth, she emptied her glass. The one consolation; he'd soon be done, and his focus would be one hundred percent on her.

When the couple emerged from the bedroom, the waiting woman had drunk a second glass of champagne, and was pouring the next. She hated the eye-poppingly gorgeous hooker, baby-pink, and still damp from their shower, because she had once been that way. Now, no amount of surgery could emulate the dewy freshness of the hooker's skin. Moreover, the young woman, at least six feet tall, with the thighs and calves of a gymnast, probably achieved a level of carnal flexibility impossible for someone of her diminutive stature. She sipped champagne to hide her jealousy.

As Peterson's hand lingered on the hooker's ample breast, the elder woman dared not address his boorish behavior. Given their history, she knew she was crazy to put up with even a moment of transgression, but didn't all men of power, men fueled by obsessive drive and uncompromising spirit, have evil in them? He was merely more demonstrative than most. Besides, when it was her turn, he loved her with such tenderness, she soared; and when the occasion arose for the ferocious sensuality of the particularly exquisite pain he inflicted, nothing brought such joy to her being.

As she followed his movements, vividly recalling the heights to which he took her, she could almost feel the hardness of his body on hers, taste salt sweat as it dripped from his neck, and hear her own cries of ecstasy as he worked his magic inside her. But here, now, as the excluded party of the ménage, she resented his swaggering arrogance, and his blatant disdain towards her. It wouldn't always be that way. One day she would find the courage to move on. But at this minute amid the champagne, the memories, and the anticipation, she focused on him. Every fiber of her being craved him, and though it was no longer easy for her to worship a man she also hated, she knew, no matter what his perversions, there could be nobody in her life but him.

She was jolted back to reality when Peterson closed the casita door. He was together again, in control, all business, as if a switch had turned off any passion remaining, and the older woman smirked; even a talented hooker couldn't hold his attention longer than it took him to relieve an itch.

Peterson smiled as he replenished his champagne and angled the bottle to refill her glass. She hadn't seen him for several days, and as always, she melted under his naughty-little-boy grin. He pushed the tray of food in her direction. "We could be here a while. Eat something."

"It's not food I'm in the mood for."

He smiled that smile. "Sorry, love . . . not your day."

She winced at the casual way he affected a British accent to coldly mock her, and her discomfort wasn't lost on him.

"Wanted more of a challenge, and Karen is so . . . uniquely talented." He dunked his middle finger deliberately into his champagne, transferred the sparkling bubbles to his lips, and pushed the finger slowly into his mouth.

"That's not funny," she snapped. "I seem to remember you once thought the same about me."

Peterson took a seat opposite her, letting the robe fall from his lap. "Still might, love. I fondly recall the games we played—the equipment we brought to bear—and in the topsy-turvy world of *amour*, anything is possible."

"So you're not entirely immune to me?"

"Hardly, you're a woman, and I'm a man. When I have a minute or two to spare, who knows? After all, older women are so desperate to please."

As he sipped wine, fixing her with malevolent eyes, she squirmed; not always proud of the things they'd done, she knew at his command she'd do them again.

"Come now, love, don't be uncomfortable; you know I will continue to take pleasure from your more pedestrian skills whenever it suits me, but not today. Today, you are here so I can put you just a teensy, weensy bit in your place."

He could be remarkably vindictive, and as a distinctly uneasy feeling washed over her, she knew this was going to be one of those occasions.

"I wasn't happy about the botched Morgan run-down. If the Mitchell woman is no longer capable, I have people waiting in the wings."

"It wasn't her—"

"Just listen; it's time to move her out, do you get my drift?"

She nodded.

"And talking about moving out, why is Charlotte Messing

still around? I warned you if she started sounding off, there'd be repercussions, and that's exactly what is happening. I have to tell you, love . . . your performance of late leaves a lot to be desired. I want her and Bill what's-his-name, er, Sheffield, gone by the end of the week. Call your meeting: assign a person to the task."

"Having another meeting so soon is risky; we just met last week."

"Who the hell is going to care about a bird club meeting?"

"Well, somebody clearly did, or we wouldn't be in this mess." She'd never questioned his judgment before.

His smile was sadistic. "So, the worm thinks she can turn and become the head of the empire. I ask you to orchestrate a simple task, something I've successfully done a hundred times, and it's royally fucked up. Not only did the body in question walk away unhurt, but his meddling questions have brought a shit-load of heat raining down on my parade. All sorts of people, including a bozo police agency in Canada, are looking into the organization and my personal dealings, and I mean to rub somebody's nose in the resulting crap."

"Calling another meeting so soon could blow our cover."

"And you don't think it's blown now? What didn't you understand about the phrase, 'looking into my personal dealings?' We have to move fast. I want the Corner's loose ends tied up before I move on the next contract. How long do you think some of those old farts have left, because I have no intention of supporting their sorry asses without tangible returns."

"It's not as bad as—"

"I said listen, and shut the fuck up. Mitchell is clearly a chicken-shit who wavered at the last minute; that's why we're in this mess, not because I asked for an additional meeting. Let's get one thing straight; you no longer have authority to do anything unsupervised. I will call the shots; you simply have to listen, and do as you are told. Do we understand each other?"

She mumbled incoherently.

He took hold of her wrist and squeezed. "I said 'do we understand each other?'"

"Yes, Bryce, please let go; you're hurting me."

He flung her wrist aside. "Useless bitch. I should be in Cabo right now, meeting a potential home investor who might actually have some balls. But no, when our next contract should be in the bag, I have to stop here to clarify things with you. Have you any idea how pissed I am right now?"

"Bryce, I—"

Peterson leaped from his chair, and clamped a hand to either side of her jaw. "It pains me to be so blunt, love, since you have been such a pleasant diversion for me over the years. Nevertheless, now I expect you to earn the luxuries afforded you." He pushed her roughly away. "But I am not without a heart. Because of your devoted service I will give you an opportunity to regain a place in my good graces; deal with Messing and Sheffield—now."

He smiled as she massaged her jaw.

"One more thing; I hear from that useless kraut Voldheim that she's been assigning her club duties to a chippy she pulled off the street. Said chippy has since disappeared, and a little bird told me she left with a guy driving a BMW roadster. Find her and deal with her, too."

Nodding woodenly, the terrified woman expected the axe to fall further between her shoulder blades, but it did not. As her frightened eyes focused on Peterson, waiting for word that she could go, instead of a cold dismissal, he moved close beside her. Bringing his hand to her cheek, he caressed her lovingly the way she remembered. Then he kissed her tenderly, and as his lips and tongue caused a welling of longed-for emotion, she surrendered to his will.

Peterson recognized her submission as a sign of renewed loyalty and backed away. "Now, love," he cooed, "run along. And remember, I say these things for your own good . . . *absit invidia.*"

Breathless and brutally recommitted, she might have wanted more than he was currently prepared to give, but his small concession of tenderness meant she was still in his heart. She would do what he asked, and do it well. Then, when he wanted her back in his bed, she would rub his pretentious Latin phrases and holier-than-thou attitude in his face.

Chapter Fourteen

When the Cormorant Club booked an emergency meeting at the Eagle Lake Café, Mrs. Voldheim wasn't pleased. Not only was there no Ilse to set up, but she had bookings for a full house of diners she'd now have to divert elsewhere. Fortunately, the gas leak excuse had worked in the past, and a voucher for a free dinner would placate her customers.

That evening, twenty Cormorant Club members signed in, assembled in the dining room, and randomly seated themselves. Mrs. Voldheim had made it easy on herself by throwing open the bar, and a couple of the club members played barkeep. In addition, partially due to short notice but more because of her own laziness, she'd convinced the club's representative to forego a formal dinner in favor of a buffet. As she placed the last trays of shrimp and chicken on a trestle table at the far end of the room, she took a cell phone from her pinafore pocket, dialed her contact, and pointed the phone at the innocuous-looking gentleman seated with the club's crested silverware.

Ben Watkins had lived in Poets Corner for more than three years. His wife Florence had died of cancer eight months previously, and while he agonized every day over her loss, he was thankful for his Cormorant Club friends. Blessed with an uncommonly strong constitution, fortified by good food, exercise, and a lifetime of military discipline, Ben appeared stronger and more focused in his late seventies than many fifty-year-olds. And as he looked around the room noting the other robust seniors present, he knew that they, too, owed debts of gratitude to the benefactor who made the passing of their loved ones as gentle as possible.

A movement in the corner of his eye directed him to the dining room door where he saw the Voldheim woman train her camera phone on him. He hadn't spent a lifetime in the CIA missing details, and he was well aware she was transmitting his picture to someone. And from past experience he knew that later that evening, he'd receive his target instructions. Last time, it was a woman who'd given him the animal primer and a series of numbers, and he'd simply pulled a code sheet from his safe and transcribed the name and location of the person on whom he must focus. Then, having received airline tickets and traveling money from a courier, he went on his way. All he hoped was that after so grueling a mission in Florida, this assignment was closer to home.

As the dining room door closed, Ben smiled, and taking a large piece of chicken from the tray offered him, he dug into what might be his last dinner with friends.

*

Ben was home by eleven, dialed the "favors" contact number, and a recorded message said, "transcribe two, eliminate two." He wasn't sure whether it was age, or the extra brandy he'd had at dinner, but it seemed there were two targets. So be it. He was happy to repay his benefactor whatever favor was deemed necessary. He transcribed the primers and numbers, and referring to his code sheet, came up with two names.

Ben frowned. During his military career, he'd occasionally dispatched people he'd considered neutrals, but even his training hadn't prepared him to eliminate anyone he lived alongside and considered a friend. What on earth had Charlotte Messing and Bill Sheffield done to receive the ultimate censure? No matter, loyalty and unfailing allegiance were what the Cormorant Club demanded, and he would do as he'd always done; find the most efficient way of accomplishing his task. This was closer to home, but no different. Besides, he wasn't about to renege on the promise he'd made to the people who'd given so much comfort to his beloved wife.

Chapter Fifteen

Late July in Prescott Valley was a catalog of weather phenomena. One day, oppressive and overcast, the sultry sky filled with burgeoning monsoon clouds, rising black and heavy over the dormant volcano that was Glassford Hill. The next, sharply bright, the thin, altitude-lightened air yielding soft breezes and the heady fragrance of sandalwood. Today was such a day, and as Charlotte sat beneath her tiny piece of blue margarita sky, looking wistfully at distant mountains, she recalled the summers of her youth.

When the ringing phone fractured her melancholy, Charlotte hoped it was the nice young man she'd met at Scott Morgan's house. She was confident he'd help with her situation.

"Hi, Charlotte, this is Ben Watkins. I live on Wordsworth, behind the clubhouse; we met at Bill Sheffield's cook out."

"Yes, Ben, I remember; what can I do for you?"

"I hope you don't mind me poking my nose in your business, but I heard through the grapevine you're having difficulty selling your house. I'm seriously thinking about selling mine and wonder . . . could I come talk to you? I think something fishy is going on."

"You bet your life there is. Why, I tried to talk to the woman at—"

"Don't say anything now, Charlotte. I know it sounds foolish, but someone might be listening."

"How could somebody be listening?"

"Trust me," Ben reduced his voice to a whisper, "I was in the business for a long time. It's not difficult to listen in to somebody's conversation. It would be much safer if I came over and chatted with you."

"When?"

"How about now?"

"I have to be at . . . no, this is more important. Have you had breakfast, or can I get you coffee or something?"

He'd heard about her generosity as a hostess; it was one of the things that almost put her husband in the poorhouse.

*

Within minutes, Ben was on Charlotte's doorstep armed with a packet of McVitie's Chocolate Digestives. "Thought we might share a real biscuit."

"How thoughtful," she said, taking the pack. "My absolute favorite. Come on in, steam's almost up."

Following her into the kitchen, Ben was pleased to see an old-fashioned kettle whistling happily on a gas stove and an old Brown Betty teapot drawing warmth beside the burner. And, in true English style, as the kettle began its shrieking boil, Charlotte poured a measure of water into the pot, swirled it several times, and dispatched the warming wash down the sink. Then taking the teapot back to the frantically boiling kettle, she spooned in tea leaves from a carton of Typhoo, and flooded the leaves with boiling water. Giving the aromatic mixture a couple of turns with a spoon, she replaced the lid and popped a hand-knitted cozy on top.

"We'll leave it a minute to brew, then it will be perfect."

Culinary duties performed, Charlotte turned to Ben, flashing him a smile that lit up the room. He could see why Nathan had fallen for her so many years before. "Thank you so much, Charlotte. What a treat having real tea; I haven't had anything but those potpourri bags for ages."

Smiling at his humor, Charlotte wondered why she'd initially taken a dislike to him; he'd have made a lively addition at her last, somewhat lifeless, soiree.

"Where did you get real English tea?" he asked.

"There's a Union Jack store in Phoenix—59th and Commerce,

I think—and it sells all sorts of British stuff, even proper bangers. I got hooked on them and tea when Nathan did an exchange with a policeman from Scotland Yard. He was always fascinated by the British approach to crime detection; read too many Sherlock Holmes novels, if you ask me. The whole process bored me silly, all that sitting about in cars and getting fingerprint powder into everything. I was more intrigued by traditional English food. Do you know they make something called toad-in-the-hole?"

"Well, the French eat frog legs, so it's not too much of a stretch to imagine the English eat toads."

"No, silly, it has nothing to do with toads, although I, too, was skeptical considering the frog legs thing. It turned out to be sausage in Yorkshire pudding batter."

Ben, world traveler and consummate foodie, smiled at her indulgently.

"I'm sure being ex-military, you've been overseas; have you been to England?"

"Twice; first time with a security team helping the Brits clean up a base we vacated in Leicestershire, and then when I tagged along with the Coast Guard on a search and rescue mission to fish two of our fly-boys from the Irish Sea."

"So you haven't been lately?"

"Nah, way too expensive, and now being on a fixed income, I don't think I'll be traveling anywhere any time soon."

"I hear you, although Nathan managed a night or two away with the Legion here and there. Aren't you a member?"

It was apparent Nathan hadn't told his wife the true reason for his trips, or about his membership in the Cormorant Club.

"I am, but the bills from my wife's illness and running my enormous barn of a house take everything. I can't afford a day away, let alone a weekend with the boys. That's what I wanted to talk to you about."

"Don't want to borrow money, I hope."

Ben laughed, an easy comfortable sound, although Charlotte

sensed it was tinged with sadness. He probably still agonized over the loss of his wife. She knew exactly how he felt.

"I hope you don't mind me coming around bending your ear," he said, "but I'm at my wits end about this mortgage company take-back thing. I heard you tried to speak to the committee about it, and I thought we might share information, if you have any."

"Good idea. Grab a tray and bring the tea things into the den, I'll get plates for the biscuits." They settled into chairs like any couple at a Sunday social.

"Scrummy idea, chocolate digestives," continued Charlotte, "So much better than the plain ones. I had a slice of toast already, but visitors warrant a splurge. Isn't this room nice? It gives you a lovely view of the garden. Nathan loved it so, and worked very hard to get the best out of those irises. They're gone now, but you should see them in May. They're a blaze of color, and the roses out front—what wonderful fragrance."

Warming to Charlotte's inconsequential chattering, Ben took in her expensive clothes, her delicate hands with their perfectly manicured nails, and her artfully coiffed hair. She was patently high maintenance, and had probably never done an actual days' work in her life.

"I have noticed your garden. Will you keep it up now that Nathan's gone?"

"Oh, I'm not planning to be here another season. As soon as I get what's due me, I'm off to Florida." Charlotte adjusted the teapot cozy. "Must be nicely brewed now; I'll pour."

Ben accepted the tiny porcelain teacup on its dainty saucer, and though it looked incongruous in his well-worked hands, he managed to hold the perfectly brewed tea steady.

"Milk or lemon?" she asked

"Milk, thank you."

Charlotte added a dribble of milk. "Sugar?"

"No, thanks. I'm diabetic, so I have to watch my intake."

"Oh, I'm sorry to hear that. I prefer lemon in my tea with a little sugar." Gripping a sugar cube in the pincers of tiny silver tongs, she lowered it, with barely a ripple into the tea, and took a biscuit. "I do love chockie bikkies. That's what they call them in England, you know; chockie bikkies. So quaint."

Ben sipped his tea as quietly as the miniscule portion would allow. "You make a nice brew, Charlotte. It reminds me of my dear wife."

"I didn't mean to dredge up sad memories. How are you coping?"

"Good days and bad, you know how it goes." He finished his first cup, extending it for more. "May I?" She refilled the cup as he continued. "It's just that now I'm into this messy house selling business, I seem to be having more bad days than good."

"Can I help?"

"Maybe. Did you make any progress sorting out that reverse mortgage thing?"

"As a matter of fact I did, and between you and me, we're not the only ones having problems." She leaned conspiratorially forward. "Bill Sheffield, you know him, of course; wife has Alzheimer's, poor thing, and she's a resident at Carter House. Says it's costing him a fortune, though I always understood Internos Community Insurance paid all the bills. Anyway, he told me he took her some of that lovely clematis he has climbing all over the garage, but she doesn't even recognize him anymore."

She was prattling again, and Ben wanted her to focus. "The clematis is lovely; I see him stringing it most every day. Do you know he still drives that beat-up old Chevy? Why he doesn't take a company car, I'll never know."

As soon as the words were out of his mouth, Ben realized he'd said something that might prompt a question about an organization that to this point, Charlotte appeared to have no knowledge. Fortunately, she functioned in her own little bubble, and as her train of thought shifted, it was clear she wasn't nearly as sharp as Ben first thought.

"I'll have you know that car's a classic; at least that's what Bill will tell you. Don't care squat about cars myself. Nathan drove the same old Caddy for years until he passed it on to our pain-in-the-elbow son-in-law. Lives in Florida, which is where I'd rather be right—"

Ben dropped his teaspoon into his saucer, and the jangling shook Charlotte back on track.

"Sorry, Ben, you wanted to know about my confronting the committee about selling the house. Well, it's all about the deed. Apparently both mine—and Bill's, for that matter—say if our respective spouse dies, we have to give the house back, no payment or anything, simply give it back."

"Mine says that, too, and you know, that's just not right."

"I know, and I said exactly that to some friends who're helping straighten out this mess."

"Friends?"

"Scott Morgan down on Keats Circle; his nephew is visiting from back east, works in real estate, and knows about reverse mortgages. He said lots of seniors opt for them because they get a bunch of money to do with what they like. When they die, the lien holder simply takes possession of the house, sells it, and takes its share, leaving what's left for the kids. I didn't understand entirely what he said, but he was pretty clear the clause in our deeds is odd. They aren't supposed to take the house while a spouse is still alive."

"And the one in real estate—a nephew, you say?"

"Such a nice young man, can't remember his name. Getting old is a nuisance. He said he'd make some inquiries and get back to me. Holly was there, too; have you met her? She saved Scott's life, you know. Anyway, don't say you heard this from me, but I saw something between them; I think they're an item."

Her eyes twinkled as she relayed her juicy gossip, and this time Ben was happy to let her ramble. Instinct told him his benefactor would be happy to learn what she was saying.

"She lives in Phoenix," Charlotte continued. "She came all the way up here just to have lunch with him. She said—Holly, that is—that she and Michael—oh, that's his name, Scott's nephew, Michael. Remember I told you about him, he's in real estate, and he's staying at her house in Phoenix . . ." Charlotte paused for breath, looking confused. "Where was I going with this?"

Ben smiled. "Charlotte, it might be a good idea if we pool information. How about we get together with Bill Sheffield and our mortgage papers, and see what things are similar. We can go from there."

"What a good idea. Sometimes one needs a man about the place to pull things together. Taking advantage of a person in their senior years is not right, and I'll be damned, excuse my language, if a jumped-up nobody is going to cheat me out of what Nathan worked so hard to get."

"That's the spirit! Now, while I'm here, did Nathan leave a will, and maybe it has a codicil?"

"A what-i-cil? I never heard of such a thing."

"It's an appendix—"

"Appendix? Oh my, Ben; I'm not good with papers."

"It's an addition to the will; it might say something about the house passing directly to you after he dies."

"I don't know about any appendix or codeliseal."

"Co-di-cil. Maybe it's in a lock-box?" Ben was guessing.

"Lock box, what lock box?"

"You didn't know about that? I'm sorry, I thought Nathan would have told you."

She looked at him with a mixture of hurt and anger. "How come you know what Nathan had, and I don't?"

"It's a guy thing, Charlotte. All us military men have a box or a trunk. It's probably aluminum, full of mementos and documents important to us. Trade certificates, marksmanship scores, military discharge papers, medals, that sort of thing. I didn't mean to open a can of worms, but if he has one, it's probably in the space above the garage."

"Oh, that. Great big, ugly thing. I don't think there's anything of value in it; it weighs a ton. I can't even move it, let alone get it down to look inside."

"Would you like me to go up and look through it?"

"Do you have time?"

"For another cup of your lovely tea, you betcha."

After five minutes of small talk, Charlotte could no longer sit. Busting with excitement at the possibility of showing the woman at the mortgage company that the house was, in fact, hers to sell, she was eager to see if Nathan had one of the papers Ben spoke of. Leading Ben to the garage, she directed his attention to a ladder. And after placing the sturdy aluminum frame against the attic opening, he made his way aloft.

*

Charlotte held on to steady him until the blown insulation started to rain down on her head. "I'm going to leave you to it. That icky stuff is really coming down, and I have an appointment at the beauty parlor soon. Don't want them thinking I've got buggies in my hair. Come in when you're done."

"Leave me to it. I'll be fine. I'll take a quick look and be right back down. Turn on the other light, will you? I can't see anything up here."

Charlotte abandoned the ladder, flipped on another light, and retreated inside the house.

As Ben expected, the garage space held Nathan's trunk, a dozen boxes containing Christmas decorations, and a couple of inches of accumulated dust. Not wishing to dally any longer than necessary in a vent-less space, the old man swiped a dusty hand across his sweat-sticky forehead, and climbed down the ladder. What he'd actually come to see was in a cupboard in the corner of the garage.

Popping the cupboard door's catch, Ben found exactly the same water heater as in his house. Reaching inside, he flipped the lever to extinguish the pilot light. As the tiny blue flame flickered and died, he took a sliver of plastic from his pocket and held it across the gas aperture. He anticipated that when the pilot's emergency cut-off rod cooled and attempted to shut off the flow of gas, it would contact with the plastic and be prevented from closing. And as he bent close to the viewing space to check the positioning, the cooled connector rod clamped tight against the plastic, a perfect blocking mechanism. Smiling with satisfaction, he listened carefully. An almost imperceptible hiss accompanied the familiar smell of rotten eggs. Ben replaced the ladder on its peg and went into the house.

*

"Sorry, Charlotte," he said, joining her in the kitchen. "It's as hot as Hades up there. I didn't have time to go through everything, but I'd bet money he has what we're looking for. The only way to be sure is to haul the trunk down."

"Then we should do that and take a proper look."

"It'd take at least two guys. That thing's heavy."

"Well, we can't just ask anyone; you know the gossip around here. But Bill Sheffield's in the same boat as us, and I'm sure he'll help."

Ben nodded. "Call Bill, and ask if he can come this afternoon." He took more tea while Charlotte made the call.

"Bill will be over around one."

"Good. I'll join you both later." Ben stopped on his way out. "Charlotte, come here a minute; do you smell something odd?"

She joined him in the hall. "Can't say I do."

"Let me check one thing." Ben stepped back into the kitchen. "Yup, I smell something in here." He walked to the stove, leaned low over the hobs, and surreptitiously blew out the pilot. "No, not here." Then he stood over the sink, sweeping his arms from side to side. "When was the last time you cleaned the waste disposal?"

"Cleaned it?" Charlotte said. "I'm supposed to clean it?"

"Every now and then. Get a box of Disposal Care from Ace, throw it down, leave it a few minutes, and then swoosh it through with water."

"Good Lord, I don't do those things. I'll get a man in."

"Don't be crazy, they'll charge you an arm and a leg. I have some at home; I'll bring it back this afternoon. It'll take five minutes."

"That's so kind, Ben. Thank you."

"What are neighbors for? Now, don't use the disposal until I clean it. You could damage the mechanism, especially if there's a blockage in there."

With a look of almost childlike gratitude, Charlotte nodded her understanding, and turned to lead him to the door. As she did so, Ben palmed a couple of Zippo lighter flints and dropped them into the waste disposal. Plan B. If nothing else, Ben Watkins was a firm believer in a back-up plan.

"Remember, don't touch that disposal until I get back."

"I won't be doing anything," she answered. "I'm late for my beauty shop appointment. See you later, and thanks a million."

Ben couldn't resist. He walked back to her, took her hand, and kissed her fingertips. "Beauty shop is a waste of time; a lovely lady like you doesn't need any embellishment."

Subconsciously twirling the rings on her wedding finger, Charlotte watched Ben disappear down the hill to Wordsworth. "What a nice man," she mumbled to herself. "Those things I heard about him must have been malicious gossip after all."

*

When Ben observed Charlotte's return from the beauty shop, it was just after one o'clock. He could almost hear her humming as she carried groceries into the house, and even lugging supplies, she was immaculate. Her apparent self-absorption irked him, and as he mentally estimated how much she spent on beauty treatments, Bill Sheffield pulled onto her driveway. Charlotte was on her threshold, smiling broadly, and as she ushered him inside, Ben dialed her number.

"Put the kettle on, I'll be right over. And if you've got leaves, I'll have Chamomile this time?"

"Would I give an honored guest that other bark mulch?"

Ben laughed. Despite her faults, he liked her. Shame about that. "Crank up the stove, I'll be there in two minutes."

As he laid down the phone, Ben looked at the wall clock in his kitchen. He'd purchased it on a trip to Amsterdam; antique blue and white delftware, with a fine Swiss movement. It had cost him a small fortune and was his wife's favorite. It was a beautiful piece, full of bittersweet memories, and it kept impeccable time. Tick, tick, tick.

When a concussive draft of air followed a thundering boom, the clock fell off the wall and smashed into a thousand pieces. Ben smiled. He'd long since accepted that there were always innocent casualties in a war, and this time, it was his beloved wife's clock. As to his targets, his feelings were moot. He'd simply ensured the swift and decisive dispatch of a pair of misguided turncoats. As he hit the button on his coffee machine, thinking how much he despised the taste of tea, he remembered the Cormorant Club's support while his wife lay dying. He was again happy he'd been able, in some small way, to repay the favor.

*

It was three hours before the fire marshal declared the building safe enough to search, and he and the medical examiner watched as two bodies, appearing to be a male and female, were found in the wreckage. Someone had alerted Marvin Shapler, and in his capacity as lawyer and community liaison, he made a preliminary identification of the charred remains.

As the authorities buzzed around the wreckage of Charlotte's house and residents filtered back to their houses, Ben Watkins was speaking to the "favors" message machine. He confirmed completion of his task and mentioned Charlotte Messing and Bill Sheffield had elicited aid with their mortgage problems from Scott Morgan, his nephew Michael, and Holly Winthrop.

Chapter Sixteen

With the temperature in Phoenix hovering around one hundred and five degrees, one could do little outside but laze around the pool, so Scott and Holly played on their senior status, letting the youngsters deal with business. Jim was in the office sifting through e-mails, Ilse was preparing dinner, and when the phone rang, it was Poppy, checking on the progress of her new house sitter. She and Ilse hadn't spoken before, but as Holly walked into the kitchen to refresh drinks, the two were chatting like old friends. Ilse said her goodbyes and handed Holly the phone.

"Aah," said Poppy with a familiar sigh, "she sounds delightful, so young, so European."

Holly giggled. "And she can cook."

"Oh my heaven, hasn't one striven a lifetime to find a decent cook."

"Cool it, sister," smirked Holly. "It's been a long time since either of us had servants."

"I know, but don't you wish for those decadent times every now and again?"

"No, too many bad memories. Are you coming home soon?"

"Why would you want an old broad like me around? It sounds like the new girl is a distinct asset to your life. Must have gobs of young bucks flocking round, and at least one of them must have an eligible father you can charm the pants off."

"You're incorrigible; she's strictly here to watch your house and occasionally cook for us. You have to taste her *Wildpastete*—deelish. She serves it with a warm tossed salad. Heaven on a plate."

"She's German, then."

"Didn't I mention that before?"

"No, not that it matters. What does matter is you. Thought

you were staying in Prescott Valley with your new *amour*. Didn't that work out?"

"Things change," Holly's tone was defensive.

"Want to talk about it?"

"Not now."

"So . . ." Poppy made an abrupt switch, "How's the young thing getting on with you-know-who?"

"Jim?"

"Of course, Jim, he's my favorite nephew, and I worry about him. Wouldn't want him falling in with the wrong sort. Damn, if he wasn't blood, I'd—"

"Poppy, please, I haven't had my second cocktail yet, and I'm not sure I'm brave enough for one of your lurid dissertations sober."

"They are merely teaching opportunities—"

"For you or me?"

"Both, my dear, most definitely both. Now tell me, has he made a move on her yet?"

"Yet? I believe moves were made the first night they met."

"Oh, to be young and in full possession of one's muscle tone . . . He's a real catch, don't you think?"

"I do, and so does she. He's made quite an impression on her."

Poppy sighed again. "That's his style, although women never occupy his interest for long. His job has always been the most important thing in his life. Don't mean to be catty, but she'll be yesterday's news in a couple of weeks."

"We'll see about that. Right now they're getting along like a house on fire."

"It's sort of satisfying; someone is actually having sex at my house. Darn sure wasn't me. So, to recap, Jim is still there when normally he'd be out and about, and you're there when I expected you to be having some fun with your *amour* in Prescott Valley. What gives?"

"Something happened there, and I decided it would be better

to have my friend here a while. Hope you don't mind."

"*Mi casa es su casa*. Must have been pretty monumental; my house is big, but with a new relationship and all, I still thought you'd prefer to be alone."

Holly took a breath and whispered. "I'm not supposed to tell anybody, but you're family. Somebody tried to kill my friend outside his house. And if Jim has anything to do with it, whoever it was won't get near him again. Why didn't you tell me he was a Mountie?"

"Never came up in conversation. Besides, he was coming to Arizona on vacation. He deserves a break from work for a while."

"Well, he's back in the thick of it now. I can't say any more, Poppy; the men swore me to secrecy. But suffice it to say, Jim is proving to be very good at what he does."

"That's why he travels all over the world chasing criminals." Poppy had a strange hollowness to her voice.

The friends exchanged gossip and girl talk for nearly half an hour until Holly's laughing became so loud, it brought Jim from the office. With tears streaming down her face, Holly looked almost apoplectic.

"What's happening?" Jim was genuinely worried.

"Take her, quick, before I pee myself."

Jim looked quizzical until he learned Poppy was on the line. "Hello, dear," he said as he put the receiver to his ear. "What outrageous stories are you telling?"

"Dear sweet Jimmy, you never change. I invite you to Arizona to relax and have fun, and a little bird tells me you're already up to your eyeballs in it."

"What have you two gossip-mongers been cooking up?"

"*Moi*? I'm cut to the quick; besides who's cooking what with whom? I hear there's a certain epicurean *fräulein* who's commanded your undivided attention for several days. Is that some sort of record?"

"That's the pot calling the kettle black. If you're going to continue to be shameless, I'm not talking to you at all. God, when women get together, your mind is on one thing."

"And thank the Lord that it is; if it were left to your team, we'd be living in caves playing pinochle."

"Aunt Poppy, you're an impossible hussy. I love you dearly, but I'm changing the subject. When are you coming back to Phoenix?"

"Depends. How long do you plan on staying?"

"You know I said a month."

"Darling, I'd be happy if you stayed the rest of your life."

Holly returned from the bathroom and sat beside Jim. "You're an impossible monster and you know that. I'm through talking to you. Get back soon; I miss your twisted humor. Now take care, I love you. I'm handing you back to Holly. Don't keep her long, because I'm sure there's a certain somebody on the patio, busting for her company."

"She told me about your additional guest. Is he cute?"

"Not my type, but distinctly yours. See you soon, and behave yourself. Thanks for letting me stay."

Jim handed back the phone.

"Holly? You're right; he's got it B-A-D. I've never heard him so defensive about a woman."

Chapter Seventeen

After two weeks of opening all the mental doors the passage of time had closed, Scott recreated his code. Testing it using the incidents in Jim's files, he cross-referenced drivers and victims' names and addresses, and proved former Poets Corner residents were responsible for a disproportionate number of "accidental" deaths.

Unfortunately, most incidents were several months—and in some cases, years—old, and those who might irrefutably tie the Cormorant Club and Bryce Peterson to an event were already dead. But Scott was not giving up. Time might have slightly changed his code parameters, so he simply had to document those changes and reapply the cipher to recent events.

With insufficient conclusive evidence to move on anyone in Poets Corner, Jim's frustrations built like the thunder rolling over Piestewa Peak and Camelback Mountain. And as the White Tanks and Bradshaws cowered beneath dangerous lightning, rivers of water dropped on Phoenix. Old Arizonans welcomed the monsoon as a refreshing renewal to their parched state. However, with washes blown out, streets flooded, and trees strewn across thoroughfares, the intensity of such violent weather kept the newcomers inside. And as flash floods temporarily cut off Poppy's house in Paradise Valley, Scott and Jim retreated to the office for a lesson in code-making.

"Devising a code is easy," began Scott. "I'm sure at some point most kids play around with one in school. Breaking one depends on how many variables you have to deal with. The one Tim and I developed was pretty simple, and we chose animals as a base because they're easy to remember. At least they would have been, had I not had to drag 'em from four decades ago."

"But you did," said Jim. "Some of these animals are pretty funky, though. Where did you dig up cassowary and quagga?"

"I have a head full of useless information."

"What about X? I know that's not an animal."

"We couldn't think of one, so we used Xanadu."

"Like the Olivia Newton-John song?"

"Like poetry, by Samuel Taylor Coleridge. Tim loved that stuff, was always spouting something, and as we were in a hellhole dreaming of being home, Xanadu seemed appropriate. I'd initially forgotten Tim's love of poetry, until Milton's 'Cormorant' reference popped into my head, but now we have disparate pieces of this puzzle gelling. Something that has been staring us in the face makes perfect sense." Scott handed Jim the residents' directory.

"The residents' directory?"

"Right; apart from the fact that we're dealing with a secretive group called the Cormorant Club, which I'm officially establishing alludes to the Tree of Life in Milton's *Paradise Lost*, take a look at the inside back cover."

Jim flipped to a small map.

"Check out the street names," continued Scott. "Jeez, I must be getting old. I can't believe it never occurred to me before. As I said, there are no coincidences. This community is Poets Corner, and Shakespeare, Keats, Browning, Wordsworth, and Shelley all complete the circle that began in Vietnam with Samuel Taylor Coleridge. His Xanadu is the idyllic, beautiful place mentioned in the poem *Kubla Khan*; Poets Corner is Tim Bowman's Xanadu. Let's face it, every GI sitting in a foxhole with poisonous snakes and bugs the size of dinner plates wished he were someplace like Poets Corner. And every fiber of my being is screaming that Tim Bowman—Bryce Peterson, whatever we call him—is circling around somewhere."

"But a luxury development takes money, lots of it, and I don't think a regular banking institution would touch the mortgages, as we understand them. Where would anyone get enough cash to get this place off the ground?"

"Dubious real estate speculators are a dime a dozen, and whoever provided financing to build the community didn't do it for altruistic purposes. They were in it to make an ongoing profit. On the surface, we see an up-market development for retired gentlefolk, but it actually houses a highly trained, conscienceless—albeit aging—group of military and law enforcement personnel."

"Personnel who know exactly what they're letting themselves in for?"

"That'd be my guess, and while the speculators get richer from the old folk's deadly labors, said oldsters are content to spend their golden years living virtually worry-free in a paradisiacal place. It's exactly how Tim envisioned it."

"Until your uninvited presence caused a tiny crack in the fabric of paradise, and started a house-selling landslide that includes Charlotte Messing, Bill Sheffield, and who knows who else."

"Wasn't my intention; I had no idea the house wasn't my brother-in-law's outright. What's more, if the mortgage company had simply paid me its value, I'd probably have gone back to Boston and faded into the woodwork."

Jim laid down the directory. "Okay, so I concede somebody is pissed about you causing a mutiny. But why try to kill you for a forty-year-old code? Aren't there computers that can crack anything these days?"

"You've been listening to Holly, and as I said to her; sometimes more sophisticated is not better. Look what's happening in schools today. Kids use computers with calculators, spell-checkers, grammar programs, politically correct prompts, encyclopedias, let alone the Internet. Nobody has to know anything, retain any information, work out anything for themselves. They just press a button. Soon, there'll be no pencil-pushing, page-turning anything. We will have automated ourselves out of the basic education loop. This code is unbreakable, not because of its complexity, but because of its simplicity. It uses a random rotating animal primer, and the place where the receiving agent lives, governs encryption. An alternative animal, different house number, or the operative moving to another location, and the same word would be assigned a completely different series of numbers."

"Run that by me again."

"According to Ilse, at every Cormorant Club meeting, she took a camera phone and transmitted somebody's picture into the ozone. That picture identified the assassin, for want of a better word, and whoever received the picture looked up his, or her, street address. That person then randomly assigned an animal from the list."

"Sorry, Scott. I don't mean to sound dumb, but you're gonna have to break it down more."

"Okay, for the sake of the exercise, let's use the circumstances of my accident. We know Zoey Mitchell ran me down, and we know she lives at 1134 Shakespeare. The primer animal is Otter. Adding together the assassin's house number, which is nine, to the eleven digits in her street address equals twenty. Count twenty from Otter, on our list of animals and Gnu becomes your 'A.'"

Jim was following, with the help of a table Scott had drawn up.

"Aardvark A is number 1, follow through to Zebra Z at 26. Now, move down to Gnu and make that the first letter, or number 1 in your new alphabet, and spell out Scott Morgan. Use the second column I left for notes. It might be somewhat time-consuming for an all-singing, all-dancing spy like James Bond who can't spare a minute before the next adversary flies through the window, but for a bunch of veterans receiving minimal information for a future action, it works fine. You can pass on basic information, like a name, or if you have the time, write a book."

Jim was scribbling madly. "And because we're adding up the house numbers onto the number of letters in a street address, if I move a door or two on the same street, even with the same animal primer, the code numbers in my message would be different."

"Precisely."

"Dang, it actually works." Jim smiled. "So, now we have the code, we know who the bad guys are, and we're pretty sure we know who's behind the whole shebang. But the why is yet to present itself."

"Well, for our purposes, right now, it's money," said Scott.

"Agreed, but that can't be everything, the costs to operate a place like Poets Corner are too great. There has to be a bigger picture."

"There is, and it stems from Tug Winthrop's team. The military intelligence community is very incestuous. Everybody parlays with everybody else because they have to, and despite what a democracy might tell its listeners, nasty disagreeable shit-heads try to come between friends all the time. Somebody has to straighten them out, and half the time, with everybody buying and selling information, sharing resources and contacts, a target knows what's coming and can avoid the hit. My guess is, because no one could get into this code, Tug had a one hundred percent success rate with his assignments."

"So we're talking about him working for, or in spite of, the government?"

"Both."

"But you said the codes details are easy, so why couldn't the professionals crack it?"

"Sometimes intelligence whiz-kids get so wound up in their own self-importance, they don't see the wood for the trees. They probably heard about it, had even seen it working, but they underestimated its usefulness, and set it aside as kid's stuff."

"But the 'accidents' we're dealing with aren't major international players. They aren't despotic heads of puppet governments—they're ordinary people." Jim couldn't hide his exasperation.

"Right, but because we aren't able to dig deep enough, we've only seen the local picture. For the sake of argument, let's call what we've come across collateral damage: little people who knew stuff they shouldn't. Common everyday Joes who're talking out of place or old soldiers who've outlived their usefulness. Just because their death wasn't earth-shattering doesn't mean it has no ripple effect."

"I'm listening."

"Take it as a given that Tug and Tim kept the code to themselves since the sixties, and while legitimately working for Uncle Sam they developed a minor league clean-up business. Nothing that made a lot of money, which might rock some watchdog body's boat. However, when Tug wanted to retire and hand over even the small profits being made to the next generation, Tim balked. I know him; passing on a cash cow wouldn't have gone down well. He'd most certainly elect to bail on Tug, take the code, and develop his own infinitely more profitable entity. However, with no personnel, base of operation or large company infrastructure, he hit a roadblock. He needed Tug and his connections to get the ball rolling on that."

"Agreed," said Jim, "so, that's how they got a bunch of heavy-hitting investors and speculators to build out Poets Corner."

"Correct; there's no doubt they had an attractive package to sell, because the guys and gals living here would pay something to move in, and with the take-back clause, the money men wouldn't lose a dime."

"So far, so good," said Jim, rolling with Scott's theory. "And once the money was committed, Tim expounded on his idea for a geriatric assassination squad?"

"Right. It might sound preposterous, but I'm guessing he chose investors who had little regard for where profits came from and let him run with his idea. And I have to say, using old soldiers and an unbreakable code as a means for success is quite brilliant. There's no need to waste money on fancy equipment or special surveillance gear. The organization's biggest asset is a bunch of old geezers who owe the man big-time and are willing to pay back for their house, car, medical insurance, and whatever all else, by doing what they'd been trained to do."

"The investors simply sat back," added Jim, "and raked in money from individuals or governments wanting to get rid of this or that sleaze. Sounds like we might've hit the tip of an iceberg, because there must be a shit-load of accidents that've never been fully investigated because of the 'old geezer' excuse. Murder without consequence under the umbrella of patriotism and betterment of the human race. It's a once-in-a-lifetime quirk of imperfect logic, as well as a sweet return on an investment."

Scott smiled. "Makes you wanna cry, doesn't it?"

"Makes me want to do something, and crying's not my bag. But hang on; I thought you suspected Tug Winthrop was killed because he didn't want to be involved."

"I've been agonizing over that, but finally came to the conclusion I was giving Holly peace of mind. Think about it—Holly said Tug stashed millions. I know he was a major general, but Uncle Sam is not even close to being that generous, and if he was that good in the stock market, he'd have been up in lights with Warren Buffet. I hate to say it, because it means Holly loses, but Tug's money was definitely not legit. He had to be taking kickbacks from somebody—in fact quite a lot of somebodies—for a good number of years. My guess is, he and the other investors were full party to what was going on, but when handing over control to someone younger was proposed, Tug simply didn't want to step aside. In the end, it came down to who had the bigger clout; Tim simply outsmarted him."

"It's sad to think Holly spent her life living large on that sort of venality. She'll get nothing from her marriage. At least she has you to keep her going."

"I hope that's enough."

"How about we keep this revelation from her for now; I don't see any value in re-opening old wounds unless we have to."

Scott nodded.

"So," continued Jim. "You've established a basis for the

organization, and identified from where the funding came to get it off the ground, but why use seniors?"

"Because their needs are few, and they're inconspicuous. When was the last time you saw a bulge beneath an old guy's jacket, and said, 'I wonder if he's carrying a gun?' How many times have you seen an old lady weaving this way and that across a busy highway, and said 'I wonder if she's using that vehicle as a weapon?' Anyone over seventy is usually thought of as essentially decent and much too frail to do anything purposefully violent; ergo, they can get away with murder under a cover of diminished faculties."

"That's cynical. There has to be more to it than that."

"Why? All the residents in Poets Corner spent years living way above their means. Now at the end of their lives, when money is in short supply, they're offered everything for a token payment on a fabulous house. The actual signatories to those houses don't care that the money offsets the costs of living in the place; they know it's all part of recycling for the next brother-in-arms. And the investors know while a heap of additional money is being made through the seniors' nefarious adventures, with equity in the community as a whole building over the years, should the organization decide to actually sell they'll make a packet."

"It's a win-win," added Jim.

"Yup, and Bryce Peterson gets easy money and a certain twisted sense of godliness. Isn't that the ultimate high for most egotists?"

"So it's all about beating the system and getting away with it?"

"That's why we made up the code in the first place. It was a game. However, I'm sure Tim's time in military intelligence taught him that a lot of money can be made by eliminating certain undesirables. He simply tweaked our idea until he got to the art form we witness today."

"Bit of a disappointment, really. I'd hoped for something more noble."

"Maybe it was in the beginning. Under the umbrella of

benevolence and caring, Uncle Sam sends out operatives to rid the world of those who deserved to die. Now, you only have to read *Soldier of Fortune* to see there are plenty of ex-military types willing to deal with life's problem children, for no more nobler reason than cold, hard cash. Tim simply took a cheaper and more creative approach. He built an enclave, stocked it with willing workers, and bolstered their warped sense of belonging by picking up the tab for a bunch of expensive necessities, and allowing them entry into an exclusive ego-boosting club."

"Then it seems to me that without some sort of direct assault by Peterson himself, we can't prove diddly."

"Right," said Scott. "Holly said her house was stripped of everything, which is a pretty good indication there was something incriminating in the safe."

"You'll get no argument from me; I think we can safely assume it was proof of Tug's wrong-doing as well as the code. And whether it was the government, or Peterson's flock of Cormorants doing the stripping, it doesn't seem anything taken rightfully belonged to Holly. The government, whom Tug betrayed, provided the trappings of her life, and simply took them back. And the money, procured through his partnership with Peterson, was confiscated. Our victor, rightly or wrongly depending on your point of view, simply claimed his spoils."

"I know you're right," said Scott, "but I would have liked to recover something to make her feel whole. Then again, we're in our sixties, I'm comfortably off, and we have our health and each other. Maybe we should quit rocking the boat, move on and enjoy the remaining ride."

"What about justice for those killed?"

"'Til I know who they are, and whether their killing was justified, I can't say."

"So you believe some people deserve to die?"

"Don't you?"

"Umm." Although Jim was RMCP, dedicated to defending the law, he'd come across a number of miscreants who deserved to die. "But we're not God; we have a system."

"The system is broken."

"Nevertheless, given our general beliefs, it's the only one we've got."

"And that's why groups like the Cormorant Club flourish." Scott wasn't letting go. "Guys like Bryce Peterson know how to manipulate the system, and make no mistake, there are plenty of others waiting to jump in. Is getting rid of one man going to make any difference?"

"It's a start. Society as a whole has to work on eliminating the rest."

"Sounds like we're back to Xanadu."

Jim smiled. "It does, except our little corner of the world is no idyllic equitable place. We have a huge, out-of-control ego at work here. I'm betting Peterson tagged you the day you arrived. How could he not? The residents of Poets Corner think he is their financial and emotional savior, and it appears almost every one is committed to his cause. Look at the good old boy monitoring the gate; I'll bet money he lets Peterson know every time a stranger enters the community."

"So if he knew I was here, why didn't he talk to me? I think he knows I'd never fall in with him. All he had to do was lie, pay for my brother-in-law's house, and I'd have been out of his hair. Trying to kill me went way beyond ego. Christ, until Holly picked me up off the blacktop and we started talking, I was clueless about any of this Cormorant Club business. And even now, I don't understand how things became so convoluted."

"Maybe Peterson went on vacation," Jim suggested, "left someone else in charge, and when he got back, the shit had already hit the fan."

Scott smiled. "Convenient explanation and another of those coincidences I have a hard time with. I'd rather believe his ego is so out of control, when he saw me, he had to make sure he retained sole knowledge of the code. The man's an idiot. I wasn't any sort of threat; what happened in Vietnam was all but relegated to my mind's dead zone."

"That's why the wrong place at the wrong time theory bears thinking about."

"Ah, kismet Hardy." Scott grinned. "So when you convict him and his organization, what happens to the residents of Poets Corner?"

"Some are clearly guilty of wrongdoing, and will have to face the consequences."

"Point taken, but for a minute, put yourself in their place. Imagine you've spent your life in a highly structured military or service occupation, and are having a hard time adjusting to civilian life. For whatever reason, you've had difficulties with finances, and retire with a smaller pension and more debt than you imagined. And if that wasn't enough, your ailing wife of fifty wonderful years requires expensive medical treatment and exorbitantly priced medication, just to make it through the day. With little quality time left, wouldn't you want to show her how much you love her by giving her the best life has to offer?"

"That gives me license to go about bumping people off?"

"No, but hear me out. A smart operator comes along, been in the military himself, knows the ropes, has successfully worked the system, and totally understands how to fulfill your needs. He offers you and your wife a little piece of heaven in your declining years; nice house, fancy car, medical reimbursement, and a free vacation now and again. All you have to do is continue in the same line of business Uncle Sam trained you for."

"When you put it like that, it makes me want to sign up."

A wry smile crossed Scott's lips. "To the normal mind, this whole situation might sound crazy, but let's face it—when Tim and I put the notion together, our ideas were skewed by our circumstances. Our attitudes had a lot to do with being in a country that hated us, facing a bunch of folks who were making their best effort to blow our heads off. And like a lot of others over there, many of our actions were driven by ignorance, stupidity, and bravado. It seemed we were caught in an endless nightmare with no waking escape. Who the hell wouldn't want to find a cleaner way to resolve issues? I just had no idea Tim would actually follow through."

"Can we prove it?"

"All the evidence points to it. Damn it, Jim, nobody is going to put an eighty-year-old in the slammer for an 'accident,' no matter how tragic. And if they do, would that eighty-year-old care? He'd get three squares a day, health coverage, free teeth, visits from a social worker, TV room, gymnasium, and a library. U.S. prisons are holiday camps."

"They'd still be locked up."

"What hardship is that? A lot of them spend the bulk of their day indoors reading or watching TV anyway."

"Do I detect a creeping cynicism there?"

"I'm simply keeping it real my young friend. Look at Peterson, for Christ's sake; for over forty years he's been living like a king, having convinced me, his wife, and family, that he's dead. And except for a small pension, a flag, and an album full of memories, she got zip."

"That happened to a lot of families."

"Doesn't make it right. Besides, he didn't die. He copped a ride where he was the only one flying first class. He made a mockery out of love, friendship, duty, honor, and everything we fought for. And, if that wasn't bad enough, after Vietnam, he continued to kill on my tax dime, and now orchestrates more killing, for no other reason than to make himself a buck. If anyone deserves to die, it's him."

"He might get the death penalty if we can catch him."

"Sure, and by the time fancy lawyers, and Bible-thumping bleeding hearts have worked their magic, he'll have spent twenty-five years languishing on death row, still on my dime."

"Sounds like you got a bit of redneck in you, Scott."

"Didn't mean to come on so strong, but I can't remember being this rattled about anything."

"It's understandable," said Jim. "First you can't resolve your dead family's affairs, then you get hit by a car, find out the best friend you thought dead is alive, and what is more, that best friend is trying to kill you using a bunch of geriatric assassins. You finally get to live with the woman you've been crazy about for forty years, you help rescue a foreign damsel in distress, and drop yourself right into an episode of *Sergeant Preston of the Yukon*." He smiled, "That Yukon thing alone would unsettle most anybody."

Scott knuckled his friend's shoulder. "You're okay, kid; glad you're on my side."

"You know, I've been thinking about the newspaper clippings. Until we started digging around, nobody put the incidents together. All the cars clearly had Cormorant stickers, and if that fact was so completely missed, there are probably other connections staring us in the face. I need to talk to Charlotte Messing and Bill Sheffield to see if something is buried in their minds that will give us Peterson before anything else happens."

"You already sent your superiors more information to support your case. Wouldn't it be better to wait for an official sanction before investigating further?"

"Of course, but the first rejection took forever. How long can I sit on my hands?"

"Going it alone could be dangerous."

"It already is, but I've reached a crossroads. I can wait here hoping something more substantial comes along, or I can return to Poets Corner and schmooze what might be a case-making piece of information out of a resident."

"Then I should come with you."

"You're too conspicuous. No one really knows who I am yet, and even Charlotte thinks I'm a Realtor. I should be safe with that for a couple more trips."

"I don't like it, Jim."

"It's what I do, remember? By going alone, I'll be able to work faster, hopefully find someone who has dealt with Peterson face to face, and finally prove that Bryce Peterson is Tim Bowman."

"Shouldn't you call Charlotte, give her time to get her papers together?"

"Don't want to do that. If Peterson does have the level of control we think, he already knows she's not happy and may have tapped her phone. You're probably clear, because being here, he'll think you've been scared off."

"All sounds a bit iffy."

"Sometimes you just have to fly by the seat of your pants."

"They're your pants. But I don't have to like 'em."

*

As usual, the friends talked about the case at dinner, and the ladies hated the idea of Jim alone in dangerous territory. Nevertheless, once he reminded them his vacation was winding down, and he might soon have to return to Canada, they reached a compromise. Jim would drop into Poets Corner to pick up Scott's mail and check his message machine. If Charlotte approached him, he could ask her questions, but he agreed not to contact anybody else in the community until his latest appeal had official sanction. To make sure he behaved, Ilse would drive north with him, and so that nobody would be curious about an unfamiliar car coming and going from Poets Corner, Jim would take Scott's Morgan.

Chapter Eighteen

When dust began to kick up and billowing black clouds gathered, they had reached Dewey. "We better get to Scott's in a hurry," said Ilse. "The monsoon is unpredictable, and when the rain starts, look out."

"It's refreshing," protested Jim, as blustery raindrops splattered through the car window.

"Well, I've been here long enough to know it's going to pour any minute, so move it."

Within seconds, the heavens opened. Low lying road became a river, and fast-flowing gully-wash slowed them to a crawl.

Upon arriving at Poets Corner, they found the gate closed.

"That's odd," said Jim, hitting the remote affixed to the sun visor. "That doesn't usually happen until six."

"Maybe the wild rain knocked it out," Ilse suggested.

"But the roads aren't wet. It hasn't rained here at all. No sweat, let's pick up the mail and check Scott's message machine."

With a speed limit of twenty miles an hour, the car cruised toward the mailboxes situated in the clubhouse parking lot. Opposite, where Charlotte Messing's house had been, they found a five-foot high chain link fence. A huge dumpster surrounded by police tape sat alongside the rubble, and several men were lobbing in loose debris from the demolished building.

"Jesus H. Christ, will you look at this." Jim had attended a number of explosions, accidental and otherwise, but had never seen a house so precisely destroyed. "Now I know why the gates were closed. The community clearly doesn't want sight-seers."

"Did that house belong to someone you know?"

"Charlotte. Dear God, I hope she wasn't in it. She was our biggest lead."

"Can you call the police and find out what happened to her?"

"There's someone in the clubhouse; let's see if I can pick up a bit of gossip. Here, you get the mail; I'll go inside."

*

Fortunately for Jim, the woman making her way to the video library wasn't a permanent resident. And with little prompting, she told him Charlotte Messing and Bill Sheffield had perished in the explosion caused by a faulty gas line in the water heater. Moreover, she shared her opinion of the closed community, saying that despite the importance of her sister, Zoey Mitchell, a founding member of Poets Corner, she had been treated like an interloper. Jim sympathized, and as she appeared unaware he was fishing, he asked about Zoey. The woman told him her sister was so well thought of, she'd recently returned from an all-expense-paid week at The Saguaro Resort in Phoenix, courtesy of the community's owner. Jim bade goodbye to his garrulous acquaintance, his mind in overdrive.

With his main leads dead, he wasn't sure how he might gain further insights into the dealings of Poets Corner. All he knew for sure was that with one defining act of violence, somebody had disposed of the two people who could've brought him closer to exposing Bryce Peterson and solving the mystery surrounding the community. As he cruised sedately past the elegant houses, where nothing appeared untoward, Jim couldn't help admire the assassin's work. No matter what the authorities concluded, their deaths were most definitely not accidental, and with a crime investigator's morbid admiration for a person with such decisive skills, Jim knew he and his friends were now chin-deep in danger.

*

Jim pulled cautiously into Scott's drive, told Ilse to wait in the car, and got out. Seeing nothing amiss, he opened the front door and stepped inside. His police instincts, invariably activated by a tingling in the nape of his neck, detected nothing, so he moved to the kitchen. There, everything looked—and more importantly in light of recent events, smelled—normal. Jim noted Scott's message machine was flashing 3 and hit the play button.

"Scott, this is Charlotte. I think we have another ally, Ben Watkins. He came to see me today, saying he's also having trouble selling his house. He, Bill, and I are getting together this afternoon. I'll call you later and let you know what happened."

A cold chill ran through Jim as he let the tape run on.

"Mr. Morgan, my name is Bubbles Nyson. I have to talk to you. Could you call me any day between two and four p.m., or six and eight p.m.? We'll be able to talk freely because Duke is at his meetings."

The tape continued.

"Mr. Morgan, this is Autoworks. Your oil change is due. Call me to make an appointment."

When the messages ended, Jim opened the machine, and pocketed the tape. He got into the car deep in thought.

"You okay?" asked Ilse. "You look really mad about something."

"There's no doubt in my mind Charlotte and Bill Sheffield were murdered, and I have an idea who did it."

"Are you going to tell the police?"

"Not yet; I don't have enough evidence. Right now, we're getting out of here."

Jim hit the gas, and the Morgan sped up the hill to Route 69. The gates barely opened before he zipped through, and spotting a break in traffic, he gunned the engine, and shot toward Phoenix.

*

Approaching Mayer, it began to rain heavily, and passing vehicles kicked up intense road spray. He didn't notice a black Mercedes, three cars back, until he got to the Route 17 turn-off. Ordinarily, no car behind on this main drag to Phoenix would have particularly stood out. However, as Jim glanced in his rear view mirror, something about the imposing black-on-black vehicle made the hairs on the back of his neck quiver.

Jim knew that Route 17 dropped, in fairly short order, from nearly seven thousand feet in Flagstaff to just over a thousand feet in Phoenix. And the highway, while picturesque for sightseers, had places where canyon drop-offs and road overhangs made for a heart-pounding drive. Scott had warned him that one such area occurred on the steep winding portion between the Bumble Bee and Crown King turnoffs. And that stretch of road was a machismo-fueled drag race for every suicidal trucker and brain-deficient yahoo in Yavapai County. Jim couldn't miss the numerous slashes and dings in the road's rock walls and barriers, and as he proceeded south amid two lanes of traffic, the expected yahoos zipped by him in excess of eighty miles an hour. He motored cautiously, the sane side of a barely existing hard shoulder on the brink of a sheer drop; nevertheless, it wasn't anywhere near his idea of a relaxing drive. And it didn't help when the vehicle he'd been watching moved up so close behind, he could've plucked the bugs from the radiator grill.

Slowing to allow the blatantly reckless driver by, it was quickly clear his follower had no intention of passing. Jim reduced speed further, having no interest in playing games on a slick road. The driver behind took the hint and dropped back. It was several miles before traffic thinned to just the Morgan and the tailing vehicle. Jim picked up speed. The car behind also accelerated but did not pass. Then, as the guardrails ended and the partial shoulder resumed, the solid blackness of the massive Mercedes moved alongside and hovered dangerously close to the much smaller Morgan.

Fearing for Scott's paint job, Jim drifted into the hard shoulder. It hadn't rained this far south, and dust billowed and stones spit noisily about the low-slung car's chassis. Jim bore down harder on the accelerator, banking on the momentary forward spurt of the lighter car. The gutsy maneuver saw the Morgan fishtailing back onto the blacktop. A glance in the rear view showed the Mercedes driver was momentarily outsmarted, but it again pulled up close to the Morgan. Jim wasn't sure whether he could outrun the powerful sedan on the straightaway. But he took off. The Mercedes followed, and Jim slowed. The Mercedes held fast, advancing to within inches of the Morgan's bumper. Jim's every move was countered. And when the Mercedes cat-and-mouse game rankled, Jim slowed the pace, flipped on the emergency flashers, and drifted into the breakdown lane. The Mercedes followed.

Almost before the Morgan came to a complete stop, Jim unfurled from the bucket seat, and advanced on his tormentor. He could see no one through the visored windshield. But Jim strode on as the Mercedes engine raced. The driver's foot continued to tickle the accelerator until Jim came within a couple of yards. Then, with gear engaged, rubber caught on asphalt, and the Mercedes breezed past Jim into the fast lane. He couldn't see the driver, but it didn't matter; as the car blasted into the distance, there was no mistaking the plate number: 2321512. And even if Jim hadn't recalled the odd seven-digit number plate, a familiar Cormorant sticker adorned the bumper's edge. It was the car that Scott said belonged to Bryce Peterson.

Hustling back to the Morgan, Jim disengaged the emergency lights, slammed the gears, and gave chase. Now the game was personal.

The sports car was fast, and handled well on the grade, but it was clear at the onset of every curve, the other driver had the benefit of weight and familiarity with the road. The chase was hurtling toward Black Canyon City when Jim glanced at Ilse. He couldn't miss her knees wedged tight to the dashboard.

"What the hell are you trying to do?" she pleaded, fear in her voice.

"I think that car belongs to Bryce Peterson, and if that bastard thinks he can force me off the road, he picked the wrong guy."

"Are you crazy? You'll kill us. We have to call the cops."

"My thinking exactly. Pull the phone off my belt."

She unclipped the tiny phone. "Who am I calling?"

"Dial 911, and ask for the Highway Patrol. The operator will connect you."

She flipped open the phone casing but heard nothing. "No dial tone. Your battery is out."

"Can't be. I charged it last night. It must be these damn mountains. Just keep trying."

They were past Black Canyon City before Ilse got a signal.

"Tell them you're calling for Sergeant Cromwell of the Royal Canadian Mounted Police. I'm pursuing a man I think is a murderer, and he just tried to force us off the road. We're on Route 17, heading south past Black Canyon City. Tell them we're chasing a black Mercedes and give them the plate number."

Ilse repeated Jim's words exactly, and after several seconds of silence, she let out a disgusted snort.

Jim didn't take his eyes off the road. "What did they say?"

"It was a guy. He said 'Ten-four, Car fifty-four, where are you,' then hung up. What did he mean?"

Jim slapped the steering wheel. "Jesus H. Christ—"

She might have no clue, but he could see the absurdity of it all. The dispatcher obviously thought he was receiving a crank call. Understanding didn't make Jim's frustration any less apparent. "Shit. Freaking morons, give me the phone." He tried to drive and dial, but the car's speed and sensitive handling made his attempt suicidal. Reluctantly conceding to good sense, Jim eased off the gas, and watched the Mercedes disappear into the distance. "Shit, shit, shit. Would you believe it; that's why I need official backing."

As they eased to a more comfortable speed, Ilse put her hand on Jim's thigh. "What happened, Jim? Why did the police hang up on me?"

"I guess when that cute accent of yours said you were with a Mountie, they thought you were joking."

"Don't you policemen have a secret password or something?"

Her naïveté was adorable, and he didn't want to burst her bubble because he could see she was scared. "I'll get one when they officially assign me to the Phoenix police department."

She had no idea he was joking. "Good, then you'll get the bastard."

Chapter Nineteen

When Holly heard the front door open, Ilse entered looking like death warmed over.

"There was an incident on the way home," Ilse said. "Jim will tell you. Could I have a brandy or something; I don't feel well."

Holly felt her forehead and pulse, and checked her eyes. "My goodness, you're in shock." She moved to the office to find Scott. "Darling, could you get Ilse a shot of brandy and open the wine; I think I'm going to need one."

When Jim came in, he told them about the explosion and his brush with Peterson on the highway.

"Why would somebody try to kill you?" asked Holly.

"Charlotte's the only person you met," Scott added, "and she thought you were a Realtor."

"We had the top up the whole trip because of the rain. I don't think the Mercedes driver knew who was in the Morgan until they sped past. My guess, they thought I was you."

"So again I'm a target, this time in a marked car. Whatever next?"

"Don't vent your outrage yet," said Jim, removing the cassette tape from his pocket. "I've got more. I stopped by the house to get your messages, and pulled this off the machine. " Everybody followed Jim to the kitchen where he inserted the tape into Holly's machine. He hit play and even the refrigerator appeared to cease humming as the messages reverberated around the kitchen.

"Correct me if I'm wrong," said Scott. "But it sounds like this Ben Watkins might have had something to do with the explosion."

Jim nodded. "That'd be my guess, and as soon as somebody in Canada gives me permission to move on this, I'll run him through the wringer."

"So who's this Bubbles Nyson, and what's her story?"

"I know her," said Holly. "She's married to Duke Nyson."

"Why would you know that?" Jim asked.

"I was delivering a package to him the day Scott was run down." From her friend's raised eyebrow, Holly knew she needed to impart more information. "It was his airline ticket, hotel voucher, prize money, stuff like that."

"You often hand out such goodies?" asked Jim.

"Poppy is a full-service travel agent, and I often make deliveries when she's away."

Jim heard, but didn't quite understand. "Why do you have to deliver anything? Isn't all that done over the web or at the airport?"

"Poppy's office transmits the tickets and vouchers, but my deliveries always include a fair amount of cash. I take whatever Poppy tells me from the safe and deliver it."

"There's a safe in the house?" Jim couldn't hide his surprise.

"Behind the Stubbs reproduction in the living room," explained Holly. "Lots of luxury homes have a built-in safe."

"But they don't pay out money like an ATM," said Scott.

"Well, thank you for your insight, Mr. Thinly-Veiled-Sarcasm. What exactly are you getting at?"

"Guys, guys, hang on a second," interrupted Jim. "Let's take a step back; you're missing the big picture here. Two people willing to help us are dead. Charlotte said she was being watched, and it's therefore logical to assume, given what we suspect about the community, she would encounter animosity. What no one anticipated—least of all me, the professional—was that an explosion would silence her."

"Don't blame yourself," said Ilse. "How could you know?"

"It's my job to read signs and interpret situations. God knows there was enough weird stuff floating around. And now, finality of the explosion notwithstanding, we receive a cryptic message from another lady who sounds like she wants to bare her soul."

"Do you think this Bubbles knows something about the explosion?" said Scott.

"All we know for sure is she wants to talk to us without her husband knowing; a husband who recently received an airline ticket and a substantial wad of cash. Holly, the ticket was for him alone, right?"

"Right."

"So, suspecting what we do about Poets Corner residents, what do you think the tickets and cash were for?"

"Are you suggesting they were payment for disposing of Charlotte and Bill?" asked Scott.

"No, my gut is telling me the timing isn't right. Besides, Charlotte's message said she, Bill Sheffield, and Ben Watkins were getting together that afternoon. The first two are dead, but I've heard nothing about Ben Watkins' demise. Shouldn't he, too, have been in the house when it blew?"

"Maybe they haven't found him yet," added Ilse.

"Don't think so; those fire teams are very thorough. My guess is he's alive, and right now he's on top of my list of murder suspects."

"Well, I don't know him," said Holly, pouting. "I only delivered an envelope to Duke Nyson."

"Perhaps Nyson was setting them all up to be together," suggested Scott, "Watkins got there after the explosion, and now he's too scared to speak up."

"That might be a possibility. But hang on," Jim went to the office and returned with a file. "Look at this."

Scott took the file. "Well, that blows the 'too scared' theory out of the water."

"Come on, you two, share. What gives?" Holly took the file. "Benjamin Watkins, CIA Special Ops. I see what you mean; somehow, I don't think he's the nervous type."

"It gets better by the minute," added Jim. "He might be my first suspect for this event, but Nyson isn't off the hook. Something about the contents of the envelope you delivered is bothering me. It's not unusual for a travel agent to dole out airline tickets and hotel vouchers, but why would anyone get money from my aunt?"

Holly sprang to Poppy's defense. "Poppy told me I'm delivering to competition winners who request their prize money in cash so they can avoid paying tax."

"Convenient excuse," mumbled Scott.

"What is wrong with you, Scott? Everything I say today seems to—"

"Behave you, two," snapped Jim. "You're bickering like a couple of kids."

Holly scowled, turned her back on Scott, and addressed Jim. "Then you tell Mr. I've-Never-Done-Anything-Just -Because over there to quit trying to shoot the messenger. Poppy's my friend, she pays me to live in her house, she asked me to do her a favor, and damn it, I'm guilty. I did it. But may I remind you, had I not been delivering that package, he and his sorry ass might still be spread all over the blacktop."

Suppressing a laugh, Scott put on a contrite face and laid his hands on her shoulders. "Sweetie, I'm sorry. I wasn't criticizing; it was simply a shock to hear Poppy had you delivering something to the enemy."

Jim jumped in before they could start again. "Let's not jump to conclusions. Nyson could have won a trip, and his wife wasn't invited, in which case she has a perfectly legitimate gripe. Maybe she wants you to call her because she knows you're a friend of Holly's and might have her phone number so she can talk about it."

"You believe that?" asked Scott.

"Not a chance, but I'll go with it until I have proof otherwise. Now kiss and make up."

Holly stayed put. "Not sure I'm interested in kissing."

Scott took a couple of cherries from a bowl and dangled them in front of her. "Got some goodies," he said, and kissed her neck.

Giggling, she turned and cuffed him. "Fool, gimme that fruit."

"Holly," Ilse said hesitantly from the background, "Poppy is rarely here. Why would she keep large amounts of cash in the house?"

"She keeps money for the company's competition winners."

"What company?"

"I see what you're getting at," said Scott. "She doesn't work for a company. According to all accounts," he turned to Holly, "she's had the same private client for over ten years."

Jim picked up the drift. "A client who travels so extensively he needs a personal travel agent, and who she's reluctant to talk about, even to her best friend; right, Holly?"

She nodded.

"A client who may or may not know she is moonlighting as paymaster to a bunch of ex-cops and military personnel who have been involved in suspicious criminal activity."

"Hold on, Jim," said Holly. "You're making your aunt sound really bad."

"Maybe, but I'm a cop, I go where the clues point me. I hate to say it, because she's my aunt and I love her, but she might very well be involved in some of the weirdness that's been going on. We need to find out more about Poppy's client, and clarify exactly who does what for whom. Maybe there's something in the safe that will help. How about opening it, Holly?"

"I haven't committed the combination to memory; it's kept at the bank."

"Why the bank?"

"Poppy didn't want it in the house, in case of robbery. She not only keeps a lot of cash; there's a bunch of personal stuff in there. When she needs something, I get the number from a card in her safety deposit box, use it, then destroy it."

"You also have access to her safety deposit box?" asked a surprised Jim.

"I'm her best friend, and I look after her house. It's not so unusual."

Jim smiled. "I suppose not. She needs somebody trustworthy

to look after her affairs. Still, this handing out money bothers me. Tomorrow I'll pull another favor and request searches on Nyson and Watkins. You'll go to the bank first thing?"

"Sure, no problem," said Holly. "Darn it, I hope you're wrong Jim. I'm sure a phone call would clarify everything. Let me call her."

"No, please don't contact her until I tell you it's okay. Aunt or not, I have to handle this like any other investigation."

"You're the boss, but I think you're barking up the wrong tree. Now, it's been a long day with way too much of the wrong type of excitement. I really need to get some shut-eye. I'll say goodnight to you two, and come, Mr. Morgan, I have something I'd like to discuss with you." She took Scott's hand.

Bowing his head in mock submission, he shuffled beside her. "Are you going to punish me for arguing?"

"Oh yes, my dear, I'm going to punish you very badly."

Chapter Twenty

When Holly's phone rang at eight a.m., the friends were taking coffee on the patio. Jim answered and, smiling satisfactorily, simply said, "Thanks a million, Stu."

"You look pleased," said Holly. "What gives?"

"As of noon today, I am on loan to the Phoenix PD. I report to a Captain Ryan, who can spare a couple of people to get this thing really rolling."

"All right, Jim," said Scott, high-fiving his friend. "One for the good guys. What do we do now?"

"For the moment, we don't do anything. Let me gather the paperwork, and take it downtown. After I lay out the case as I see it and get their input, we'll take it from there."

"I'm out of the loop?"

"Just temporarily. When I get home this evening, we'll brainstorm. However, given the tight-knit composition of Poets Corner, you're going to be invaluable there. Having said that, we might get into some serious—and possibly dangerous—cage rattling, so sorry ladies, you're taking a back seat."

Holly scowled. "Just when I was beginning to like this Sherlock Holmes stuff."

"Speaking of the master," Jim added, "he solved crimes with an overwhelming wealth of knowledge, so I need you to hustle off to the bank and get the safe combination. I'm hoping to find something that will help us."

As Holly retrieved the roadster keys from the kitchen, she spotted the mail Jim brought from Prescott Valley. "Hey Scott," she called out to the patio. "You never opened your mail."

"It's probably junk. Throw it out."

She dumped the bag on the table and flipped through. "You want me to pitch everything in the garbage?"

Scott snuck up behind her. "You really are going through my mail?"

"I'm an almost wife, that's what we do."

"Okay, so keep dividends, bank statements, checks, and toss the rest."

Holly held on to one piece, a greeting card-type envelope, written in a woman's hand. She sniffed it, and tapping it against her fingers, gave him the scorned wife scowl. "This one smells suspiciously like an invitation. From whom, Mr. Morgan?"

"Not a clue. Open it."

She tore it open. "Lucky for you, it's just a wedding invitation."

Scott looked at it quizzically, his memory finally jogged. "Damn, that's it."

"That's what?"

"Let's go outside and show Jim . . . hey, Jim, you know the something that was bothering me about the name Bryce Peterson? Well, this is it."

Jim took the card. "What? Did you get an invitation to his wedding?" He read through the folded card. "Mrs. and Mrs. whatever request the pleasure of yada, yada, yada. Pretty standard stuff to me."

"It reminds me of the first time I met Tim Bowman's wife and family. It was at their wedding."

"And?"

"Tim Bowman's mother and father are Dolores and Peter. Tim's mother's maiden name is Bryce."

Jim grinned. "I guess he never imagined the law would have you on its side. Mother's maiden name is Bryce, and he's Peter's son—Bryce Peterson. Add it to the pile my friend; we so have a case."

Chapter Twenty-One

When Scott and Holly returned from the bank, Jim immediately locked onto the wad of papers protruding from her purse. "What did you do, rob the joint?"

Jim took the papers, and they all moved to the living room safe. But when Holly opened it, the cavity was empty.

"The last time I was in here, there was money, lots of it, jewelry boxes, papers, folders, all sorts of stuff."

Jim peered in. "Well it's empty now, Poppy must have come by and collected it."

"And didn't tell me."

"Maybe she was in a hurry and forgot."

"Jim, we're best friends. She tells me everything."

"Not everything, I think." He fanned the papers Holly gave him. "Have you looked at these?"

She nodded. "That's why I brought them."

Handing Scott the documents, Jim drew his attention to a certificate whose second page listed the partner's names: Bryce Peterson, Persephone Collins, Marvin Shapler, Douglas Aitkin, and Tremont Winthrop—the same names listed for the Poets Corner companies.

"I'm no lawyer," said Jim. "But that seems to indicate that each partner has a twenty-percent share in something called Abovo Consolidated Holdings, which is forfeited back to the group upon an individual's death. Why would Aunt Poppy have these papers?"

"As I told Scott," said Holly, "once upon a time, Poppy knew my husband, er, very well. Maybe she was looking after them for him."

"Why wouldn't he leave them with you, his wife?"

"He was in the business of covering his bases, and in light of the fact that someone stripped our safe of everything valuable, I'd say he did a pretty smart thing."

Jim stared intently at the page, unconsciously rubbing the back of his neck. "I'll buy that for now, but look at this: Douglas Aitkin. Aside from board memberships, I know I've seen something else on him. Where are those black-and-white photos?" Retrieving his file from the office, Jim spread the pictures on the lounge coffee table, pulled a grainy photograph of a car through the window of a restaurant, and read aloud. "Local businessman Douglas Aitkin was killed today in a tragic accident when an elderly driver mistook the gas pedal for the brake. Benjamin Kent Watkins, 78, of Prescott Valley, Arizona, was vacationing in Florida when the accident occurred. Sobbing in the ambulance, he told this reporter he was distracted by the recent knowledge that his wife Florence had been diagnosed with inoperable cancer, etc, etc, etc. Oh, this is just too sweet—"

"That's a heck of a coincidence," said Holly.

"Aitkin being run down by Watkins?"

"No, that." She pointed to another of the names.

Scott leaned in. "You know Persephone Collins?"

"No, but Persephone is Poppy's real name. What are the odds of that monstrosity of a name turning up twice in one person's lifetime?"

Scott looked at Jim and raised an eyebrow.

Jim blushed. "What? I've always known her as Poppy. My whole family calls her Poppy."

Scott turned to Holly. "Why didn't you say something when we mentioned the names before?"

"You guys were losing me with the code thing, and I wasn't really paying attention. Though in my defense, I did tell you she had an unpronounceable name. It's moot, though; she's not Collins."

"Oh, damn, she might be." Jim unclipped his cell, and dialed Canada. "Hi sis, it's me. Yes, I'm at Aunt Poppy's. Quick question, then I'll have to call you later. Do you know Aunt Poppy's maiden name?" A pause. "Know any of the family who might? Cousin Shelby? Who the heck is he? Oh she, yes, yes. Can you get hold of her? Good. Call me back. But Sis, make it quick, I have to be out of here in fifteen minutes." Severing the connection with a please-don't-let-my-cop-instincts-be-right look, Jim turned to Holly. "Now madam. It's truth or consequences time."

Holly dipped behind Scott.

"Have you been telling Poppy what we've been doing, where we've been going, like that?"

"A little snippet here and there."

"This is no time for coy," said Scott, reaching back and pulling her forward. "How much is a snippet."

"Okay, I told her everything. She's Jim's aunt, and my best friend. We gossip, we laugh, we share. Why shouldn't I brighten her day with news from home? She's in Guatemala or some God-forsaken place, and she needs to feel connected."

Jim didn't want to play bad cop to Scott's good, but it was necessary. "Did you tell her Scott was going north to collect his mail?"

"My God, I did, but I said we—me and Scott—were going. She's supposed to be my best friend, why would she . . . I don't believe she'd have anything to do with running the Morgan off the road."

Jim shook his head. "I hate my job sometimes. If this damn hackle on my neck is right—and it usually is—Persephone Collins is Aunt Poppy, and Bryce Peterson has been one step ahead of us since we started, because she's been feeding him information she's getting from you. Jesus H. Christ, how could I not see something like this coming?"

"Don't beat yourself up," said Scott. "You know as well as I do some of the worst crimes in history have been perpetrated right under the noses of unsuspecting family."

"They weren't highly trained professionals." Jim's cell rang. After a few non-committal sentences, he hung up and clipped the cell back onto his belt. "Collins—her maiden name is Collins."

Ilse came alongside and laid a hand on his arm. "Jim, remember Scott suggested every person in the organization knows a small piece of the Bryce Peterson puzzle? Maybe Poppy is a silent partner who simply books vacations and hands over spending money."

"I appreciate the thought, but my gut is telling me otherwise. She has these incorporation papers not because she's holding them for someone, but because she's a bona fide member of Peterson's organization. But that's not the most disturbing thing; it's finding that of the five members listed here, two are dead. Who's next? This is one mess I'm not going to enjoy sorting out."

"But you will sort it out." Ilse kissed his forehead.

"I will, so for now, I'll add this lot to my case and report downtown. Nobody leaves this house 'til I get back. Understand?" As Jim loaded the mountain of paperwork into the car, he turned to Scott. "Look after them, buddy. I'm counting on you."

Chapter Twenty-Two

At the Phoenix police department, Jim met the individuals that would comprise the investigative team assigned to what was being called "the Cormorant Club conspiracy."

Captain Mark Ryan, a twenty-plus year police veteran, had handled every type of case imaginable and was the anchor to the team. His contacts were many, his knowledge of Arizona history legendary, and as he was due for retirement, he requested he be allowed to work his final case with "the Mounties."

Carol Whitman's special skill was interrogation. With an advanced degree in psychology, she applied her prodigious memory and hypnotic manner to draw things out of people they wouldn't tell their priest. Moreover, of medium height, with shoulder-length brunette hair and pleasant features, her demeanor gave off nothing that said "cop."

Bob Black, a computer savant, barely twenty-one and typical geek-next-door, had been chosen to work with Jim not only because he possessed the best hacking skills in the southwest, but because he was a licensed pilot. With the distinct possibility that Peterson, as the head of a multi-million dollar conglomerate, traveled by private jet, Bob's flying connections would allow him to ask questions without sending up red flags in Arizona's tight-knit aviation community.

*

As the team gathered in an interview room, Jim was satisfied his Canadian colleagues had forwarded copies of the accumulated Poets Corner and Cormorant Club information, as well as the military records of Daniel "Duke" Nyson and Benjamin Watkins. And after handing out additional sheets highlighting seniors' accidents occurring since the initial information was collated, Jim explained how Scott's code worked.

"So, Jim," Carol said, as the meeting wound down, "we've had time to go over your paperwork and from what you said, it seems someone has already accessed your aunt's house and removed articles from the safe. Wouldn't it be smart to move Scott, Holly, and Ilse to a safe house?"

"I thought about that, but Poppy has had such a loose dialogue with us all, I'm sure she'd be suspicious and would no doubt pass on her concerns, should all her houseguests disappear in such a singular fashion. Instead of relocating, I propose an officer be placed in the house for the women's protection."

A shadow crossed Carol's face. "Just the women's protection?"

"I'd like Scott to accompany us north to follow up on leads in Prescott Valley."

"Even with Mr. Morgan's unique knowledge of his subject," added Carol, "I'm not sure Captain Ryan would go along with involving a civilian."

"I think he'll understand my reasoning," said Jim. "In a closed community like Poets Corner, every stranger stands out. Neighbors are used to Scott and have even seen me about. If you pose as my girlfriend—"

"A German chick is mentioned in dispatches," interrupted Bob. "Thought she was your lady?"

"I'm a single guy playing the field. Who's to know?"

Carol shook her head. "If you've quite finished with the testosterone fest, we can get on. Where will I sleep? I'm not a friend with benefits."

Jim laughed; he liked these two. "Scott's place is pretty big, so you'll have your own room. But I need you as my girlfriend to talk to Bubbles Nyson and anyone else who might come forward."

"Thought they weren't forthcoming to outsiders?" Carol pointed out.

"That's why I need your unique talent. So far, our Chatty Cathies have been elderly ladies; you'll get them to open up a lot better than I did."

"Sounds reasonable. So, Bob will play with his computer and feed stuff to whoever Captain Ryan can spare to work local leads, and we have a number of guys who'll be glad to pull overtime on a babysitting gig. Paradise Valley mansion, you say?"

Jim nodded. "Nice cushy detail."

"Dude," said Bob, pulling a PDA from his shirt pocket. "Wish I could get some of that gnarly gig. But it's just me and . . ." he patted his computer. "How far back do you want us to go with the data search?"

"Two years. The RCMP pulled in a boatload of historical stuff, which is good back-up, but doesn't help us on-going. I'd like you to work off the current resident list; interrogate every transportation database you have and match anything countrywide, to seniors' related accidents. Also, as Peterson undoubtedly has several centers of operation, use your aviation expertise, start with companies listed in the file, and expand to any flying entity with a poetic, Latin, or animal name. Isolate and track all private aircraft in and out of Prescott's Love Field, Phoenix's Sky Harbor, and any local fields you know about; I want to know the who, what, and why of every aircraft movement."

"No sweat. Anything else?"

"Not for now. Carol, do you happen to know anything about The Saguaro resort?"

"Not much, although a couple of months ago I remember one of the beat guys retired and was taken on as their head of security. I imagine Captain Ryan will know exactly who."

"Good, I'll ask him if he can make a phone call; getting anything on Peterson's activities there might help. So Bob, get to it. We'll be in touch."

"Ten-four, kemo sabe. I'm smoke."

Jim smiled, and turned to Carol. "He always talk like that?"

"Pretty much."

"Good, I like it. Let's head out to my Aunt's place."

*

While Scott and Holly were welcoming, Ilse was nervous that Jim arrived with an attractive female cop. And when Carol, Jim, and Scott decamped to Prescott Valley, she wasn't entirely thrilled to learn Carol would be assuming the role of Jim's girlfriend.

Chapter Twenty-Three

While Jim was at Prescott Valley police department retrieving copies of reports relating to the explosion at Charlotte's house, Scott familiarized Carol with Poets Corner. And just before two p.m., the pair completed their third circuit of the community's meandering walking trail when Jim joined them. Reminding Scott that Bubbles said she could talk freely between two and four, the trio hustled back to the house.

Scott had already formulated an excuse to speak to Bubbles should her husband answer. He need not have worried; she picked up the phone and said her husband was away for a couple of days, repaying a favor to a friend. He arranged for Carol to pick up Bubbles in the Crown Victoria she was using, and if a neighbor should subsequently ask who the stranger was, Bubbles was to say Carol was the girlfriend of Scott's Realtor nephew, Michael.

Within minutes of strapping into the car, Bubbles was chatting to Carol as if she were a long-lost daughter. And knowing Scott was observing from his window, she swept slowly by Keats Circle before powering up the hill to the main gate. Seeing Carol pass, the men climbed into the Morgan to rendezvous in Prescott Valley's Plaza Square.

*

Scott took a direct route and arrived first, and when Carol pulled alongside, the men climbed in to conduct their meeting on the move.

"Mrs. Nyson," began Scott, "I'm sorry to be so secretive, but I think you know how gossip gets around. I didn't want anyone to see us together."

"Thank you very much for your consideration, Mr. Morgan. I knew I was right to trust you."

"These are friends of mine. Carol, you've already met, and this is my nephew Michael. They're helping me sort out this mortgage business. Would you mind if they asked you some questions?"

"Oh, you're the young man who spoke to Charlotte. Is Carol the cop?" Bubbles wasn't as empty-headed as her name suggested.

"Would it bother you if she were?"

"No, I was hoping someone would have the guts to do something about the goings-on. You know Charlotte was such a lovely person, and although I didn't know Mr. Sheffield too well, nobody should die that way."

Carol's voice expressed concern. "What do you mean 'that way,' Mrs. Nyson?"

"Bubbles, my dear, you must all call me Bubbles."

"Thank you, Bubbles. You don't believe the explosion was an accident?"

She made a derisive noise. "That's why I left the message on Mr. Morgan's machine. Charlotte and I were very close, and she confided in me that he was helping her. Now she's gone, and somebody needs to look into what nobody will talk about. Well, I'm not afraid to speak up. It was that vile man, Ben Watkins. I can feel it in my bones. He was at her house, you know. I saw him there, bold as brass, the morning it happened. Then I saw Charlotte in the afternoon as I was going into the beauty shop. She was leaving and said she didn't have time to talk—normally she'd talk your ears off. She loved to gossip, and goodness knows she would go off at a tangent until you didn't know whether you were coming or going. Goodness, listen to me. I'm doing it myself.

"Anyway, this day she was in a positive tizzy, said she had to rush home because Bill Sheffield and Ben Watkins were coming over for tea. They were going to pool information and give it to Mr. Morgan so he could stick it to the mortgage company. Can you really do that, Mr. Morgan?"

"With my friends' help, I'm going to try." Scott placed his hand on the old lady's shoulder and proceeded. "Why do you think Ben Watkins had something to do with the explosion?"

"He wasn't found in the wreckage, was he?"

"Maybe he was running late."

She let out another disgusted snort. "Scott, really . . . may I call you Scott?"

He nodded.

"If he was on his way over, why wasn't he in the crowd that gathered after the explosion? Shouldn't he have been right there, horrified like the rest of us? More horrified in fact, because he was supposed to be in the house! He wasn't in the street or at the clubhouse residents meeting when that horrible lawyer Shapler spoke to us. Do you know that pompous turnip said he was going to speak for the community, and nobody was to say anything to the police? Well, I stood right up and mentioned Charlotte told me she was having tea with Bill Sheffield and Ben Watkins, and they'd most likely find three bodies in the house. That devil screamed at me right there in front of everybody, and said I was to say nothing, about anything, to anybody. Who is he to tell me what to do? That's why I called you. I'm curious to know why Ben Watkins was so conveniently absent, and why he hasn't been seen since the explosion."

Carol tried to placate Bubbles. "Sometimes life's just like that."

"My dear, I'm eighty-one. I'm not in the market for platitudes. All I know is there are fishy things going on in Poets Corner. It always was a bit of a closed community, but lately, it's been a war zone. Look at Scott there, knocked down right outside his own house, by a woman who said she didn't see him. Now I don't mean to be rude, but how could anyone with half a brain not see a big strapping man towing a dog the size of a pony?"

Scott and Jim exchanged an amused look.

"I want you to have these papers," Bubbles handed over a large manila envelope. "I stole them from my husband's desk. Don't think he'll notice they're gone; he's been so very sick lately and doesn't have the energy to keep up with the community's pettifogging paperwork as he once did. You know he's kept every one of our papers since we lived in Florida, and if there's something in there to get people like Charlotte what they're due, I'm glad to help."

Scott glanced at the wad of official-looking papers and placed the envelope between himself and Jim.

Bubbles continued. "Duke has prostate cancer, you know. Like most men, he wouldn't get the tests, although the community pays for it. I told him he was stupid, but he'd heard some nonsense from the other guys about what the doctor does. Said no man was going to stick . . .oh, excuse me . . . that was probably more information than you needed on the subject. No matter, it's too late now. He's critical and not expected to live beyond a couple of months."

Carol squeezed the old lady's hand.

"He's been told to rest, enjoy what time he has left," Bubbles continued. "But gosh darn it; I can't keep him away from his meetings. I've resigned myself to letting him go on until he keels over at one of the silly things. He's eighty-two, you know, had a good run, and make no mistake, he still tries to be active. In fact, as I said earlier, he's off doing something right now for that nice Mr. Peterson."

Scott reacted first. "Mr. Peterson?"

"Have you met him? Hardly anybody has, except my husband. He thinks very highly of my Duke, does Mr. Peterson. He's such a nice man, and looks after us so well. The men don't like us ladies getting into community business, but I know Mr. Peterson is very powerful locally, so when Charlotte spoke to me about her problem, I called his office to see if he might help. His assistant called me back that very day, and said he'd talk to some people and see what could be done; that was a couple of weeks before Charlotte died. Sadly, anything he might do will be too late for her."

"You say Duke knows Peterson well," Jim probed. "Do they meet in the community?"

"Oh no, he never actually comes to the Corner."

"Any idea why?"

"No, and that's rather strange; it never occurred to me until you said it, but considering he owns most of the houses, you'd think he'd want to show his face now and again."

"You know for sure he owns the houses?" said Scott.

She lowered her voice. "When Duke has a drop or two of the hard stuff, he talks about this or that person in trouble. Usually one of a couple passes, like Charlotte's husband, and the other doesn't have enough money to pay off their mortgage. Don't mean you, Scott; I'm sure your problem is different."

"What about you and Duke?" asked Carol. "Do you have a mortgage?"

"My goodness, no. Duke took care of all that a long time ago; our house is all paid off, though I can't remember for how much."

"Do you know which houses Peterson owns?" Jim pressed.

"Most of them." She closed her eyes, making little motions with her finger as if she were running down each street. "Two on Shakespeare, the houses on the upside of Keats, all of Browning and Wordsworth. And would you believe, Mr. Peterson gave the house two doors down from Charlotte, God rest her soul, to the Prices. Er, Austin and Jill . . . Jane . . .no, Joyce. They come from somewhere back east, lived in a mobile home, and now have a beautiful big house, for nothing."

She lowered her voice again. "I think she drinks . . . in the morning. Not for me to criticize, you understand, I like a glass of white wine myself with dinner. But she's unsteady on her feet after breakfast. Why, only two days ago, she and her husband were strolling along the trail, and she almost fell into my rose bushes. Austin caught her before she hit the ground; he's wonderful, such a gentleman. Another military type, you know."

Jim was frantically scribbling notes. "When did they move in?"

"Couple of days after poor Charlotte passed, and you know something else?" Gesturing for the men to move closer, she lowered her voice to a rasp. "Neither of them is yet fifty-five, and that's supposed to be a hard and fast rule here. Nor did they pay a single penny for the furniture."

"How do you know all this, Bubbles?" Scott asked, "I've always been given the distinct impression the residents in this community are under a gag order."

Bubbles, tapped Scott's hand. "Silly boy, not for those of us invited here. Sorry, that sounded awfully rude."

"I've gotten used to being the outsider. What else do you know about the Prices?"

"Well, while Austin and my Duke were swapping war stories, Joyce—who'd had a drinkie-poo or two—told me that Mr. Peterson paid for everything, because Austin will be working for him as his personal bodyguard. Imagine, a bodyguard; what is the world coming to? I wish he'd helped us out like that. We paid a hundred and fifty thousand dollars for our house. There you go; amazing what pops into your head when you least expect it."

Even given the time Bubbles and her husband had resided in the community, it was clear they had paid only a small percentage of their luxury home's worth. And as Jim made a mental note to add the Prices to Bob's database searches, he steered Bubbles back to his original line of questioning. "Has anybody you know been to Mr. Peterson's house?"

"I should imagine the committee members."

"Do you know who's on the committee?" interrupted Scott.

"Carl Wright—nice man—was a Colonel, never been married; I can't think why, he's so very handsome and dashing. Allie McCallium, she's single too, and very, shall we say, opinionated and independent. Not the marrying kind, if you get my drift." Bubbles winked at Scott. "Then, of course, there's the lawyer Shapler, horrible creature, and another lady and gent who I don't know; think they're from Mr. Peterson's office."

"Peterson's not on the committee, then," asked Jim.

"No, but he can probably see everything that goes on from Mount Olympus."

Carol laughed. "Mount Olympus, strange description."

"Well his situation is similar. He lives on the hill overlooking the community. Must look down on us like a Greek god in that movie, can't remember what it's called, has that English actor in it, John something or other." Bubbles scowled, searching her memory for the actor's name.

"Do you know where the house is?" asked Carol, pulling Bubbles back on track.

Bubbles pointed at Glassford Hill.

"Have you and Mr. Peterson ever met?"

"Not to have a proper conversation, only in passing at the chamber of commerce."

"What would you be doing there?" Jim asked. "Do you own a business?"

"I'm an ambassador." She sensed the next question; people always asked. "We help out at the meetings. When a new business joins the chamber, they throw a welcome party for other business owners and chamber members, and we, the ambassadors, act as hosts and hostesses. We set up the reception, sell raffle tickets, help give out prizes. We have a lovely time."

"Why would Mr. Peterson be there?"

"His business interests, of course; he owns lots of things around and about, housing developments, clubs, restaurants, and he's often at the meetings."

Jim was more excited than he dare show. "Can anybody attend?"

"Not really, they're for chamber members only. A member can bring a guest, of course, but the point of the meeting is for local business owners to introduce themselves and their product to their peers, network, swap information, things like that."

"When's the next one, Bubbles?"

She pulled a small diary from her purse. "Oh my goodness, it's this evening. How fortunate you said something; otherwise, I might have been late, although my friend Bee usually calls to remind me. Lord, look at the time, I must be getting on. If I'm not there when she calls, there'll be all sorts of panic. Meetings start at five-thirty. Tonight is a reception at the Hassayampa for a company called . . . can't read my own writing . . . looks like koo-ua-vadiz."

"You mean Quo Vadis?" said Carol.

"How clever you are, my dear, Quo Vadis, yes, I suppose that is how it's pronounced. Anyway, I know it's a swishy day spa and fitness center, because we ambassadors have already received a huge basket of toiletries from Mr. Peterson. Such a thoughtful man."

"What time does Peterson normally get there?" asked Jim.

"Who notices. Mr. Peterson's events are always catered, and they're such a crush. Now my dears, enough, we've had a lovely chat, but I really must be getting home."

Jim was ecstatic. Bubbles had not only inadvertently imparted a slew of valuable information, but had also suggested a means of confronting Bryce Peterson. "Carol, drop Scott and I, then take our guest wherever she'd like to go; we'll meet back at the house." Jim reached and took the old lady's fragile hand in his. "You've been an enormous help, Bubbles, and I'm sure once we review your husband's papers, we'll be able to help everybody in trouble. If there's anything else you need, call Scott. We'll talk again soon."

Carol returned the men to their car, and as she slipped the Crown Victoria in gear and pulled away, Bubbles blew a kiss to her new friends. Dropping a hand gently on Carol's arm, she giggled mischievously. "What a nice young man my dear, and so handsome. You make a lovely couple."

Carol smiled and drove Bubbles home.

Chapter Twenty-Four

As the men drove back to Poets Corner, Jim pulled out his phone. If the Chamber of Commerce required accompaniment by a member for one to be a guest at their meeting, he knew exactly who to ask.

"See you then," said Jim, disconnecting from John Neverson at The Grapes of Wrath. Next, he dialed Prescott Valley's police department and requested that the liaison officer assigned to the Cormorant case log and research owners of all vehicles attending the evening meeting.

When they arrived at Poets Corner, the gates were again closed, and Carol was parked on the slipway's outer edge. As the Morgan came alongside, Jim rolled down his window. "You okay?"

"I had no idea the gate would be closed. Bubbles bailed out and walked home."

"And no one has come by since?" asked Jim.

"Do you have any idea how hard it is to get in here? Four cars came out, but not one of them would buzz me in. It's quite funny really. Bubbles was in one of the cars with another woman, and winked as she went by; I think she's enjoying her role as a secret agent. What's not funny; the whole time I've been sitting here, I've had the distinct feeling I'm being watched."

"Scott said the old boy in the first house fancies himself the gatekeeper, and he logs everybody coming and going."

"That's probably it. I tried to call your cell, but it was busy. What gives?"

"Had to set up an invitation to a soiree."

Chapter Twenty-Five

From atop his mountain retreat, Bryce Peterson's telescope not only focused on the plate number of every car going into the community, but the high-powered camera attached, took photographs. For days he'd been identifying visitors, some of whom were proving very unwelcome, and he'd already pegged the Mountie with Scott Morgan. Now, he anticipated the meddling duo's new addition was a female cop.

As he watched the Poets Corner gate close behind the cars, Peterson knew the assassin he'd dispatched to Paradise Valley was in position, and he could do nothing to stop what was going to take place. He didn't allow field operatives to carry phones, but was confident Austin could assess the changed situation and use his wits. Very soon at least two of the interfering busy bodies, plaguing his erstwhile smooth-as-clockwork organization, would be eliminated. No bother; he would simply regroup and deal with the others later. What did bother him, however, was that Poppy had relayed no word of Morgan and Cromwell's foray north. Nor had she mentioned an addition to the investigative team. As her friend Holly had been forthcoming to this point, it was now apparent that the allegiance of his former mate was in question. That fact posed no problem either. Knowledge was power, and Bryce Peterson still had that, aplenty.

Chapter Twenty-Six

When the Chamber of Commerce gathered at the Hassayampa Inn, more than a hundred and fifty local business owners plus guests packed the ballroom to eat, swap horror stories, and share suggestions on improving their lots. As people mingled and chatted, Jim circulated the room, noting the locations of entry and exit doors. After checking a board listing the evening's sponsors, he and the team gravitated toward a table stacked with door prizes. And casting his eyes over the usual assortment of gift baskets, electronics, and kitchen gizmos, Jim noticed two vouchers: one for a weekend getaway at The Saguaro resort, the other an all-expense paid week for two at the Palacio del Toro in Cabo San Lucas, Mexico. His hunch about connections had been right, and the prickling at the nape of neck confirmed that whatever track he was on, it was the right one.

Meandering about the ballroom's perimeter, it was decided the best vantage point to survey the entire room's comings and goings was behind the buffet area, and as the evenings presentation was about to commence, Carol and Scott took up a static position there. Jim and John, from The Grapes, made the stage area their beat, but by six-thirty, when no one had identified their man, it looked like Peterson wasn't going to show. Then Scott's eyes were drawn to a tall, impeccably dressed man at stage right, standing in the shadow of the entertainment area's velvet curtains.

He hadn't seen Tim Bowman in over forty years, and while people change a lot in that time, Scott was sure he recognized the general outline of the man hidden in shadow. Tapping Carol's arm, he indicated for her to follow him, and the pair slowly made their way along the ballroom's perimeter. Although Scott stopped opposite the man, his view of the face still wasn't clear. This man appeared no heavier than the Tim Bowman of so many years ago, but the hair Scott remembered as a flaxen bristled army buzz was now dark, sleekly shining and frosted with gray. As Scott stared, he willed his old friend to look in his direction, but he did not. And as he stood, attempting to translate Tim's boyish features into the matured face before him, Scott felt the presence of, rather than saw the figure of, Tim Bowman. Nothing beyond Scott's gut feeling distinguished the man or set him apart from any of the businessmen present, and Scott feared too many years had passed for him to recognize his old friend. Then the man moved his arm, and Scott was transfixed.

Making a fist, with wrist bent, the man brought the back of his hand to his mouth, so the hairs atop it ran across his lips. As the hand hung there, right arm balanced on the left, wedged tight into his body, the hand panned slowly across his mouth. Once, twice, three times and more, Scott watched the delicate brushing of hair against lips. It was a gesture anyone could have made, a nervous tic in moments of pensive oblivion, but the way Tim did it was something else. It was almost sexual, a self-gratifying, pleasurable movement that Scott had teased him about a million times. He recalled his words "make the most of that, bud, it's as close as you're getting to foreplay tonight." And now, because of all that had recently transpired, the camaraderie jiving borne of true friendship translated as hollow and painful. Then, it had been guy stuff; lonely testosterone-pumped, guys-in-foxholes stuff. It was innuendo, it was crass, and it had held the men together. Now, it divided, and ultimately hurt. Remembrance and anguish always hurt. Betrayal and lies hurt more. No matter how many years went by, there was no mistaking that gesture; it belonged to Tim Bowman, and Tim Bowman was Bryce Peterson.

Scott took a deep breath and looked around for Jim, who was looking straight at him. He'd watched Scott's progress down the room and noted when he'd become transfixed. All Scott had to do was nod his head; but all Scott could do, was return his gaze to the man. To stare at his friend, lost a lifetime ago, and feel a mixture of love and hate pound in his chest. Those feelings emitted intangible, inexplicable vibrations, which invariably hit their mark. Peterson turned, and his eyes and Scott's connected.

Dropping his hand, Peterson flashed Scott a boyish grin. But as quickly as the smile came, it disappeared. And with eyes shining black, hard, and over-shadowed by something indescribably malevolent, he lifted his hand and fashioned his fingers into a gun. Pointing directly at Scott, his concentrated glare emitting pure evil, he flicked once in a chilling gesture that indicated he'd aimed and taken his shot.

Blood pounded in Scott's temples, paralyzing him with something darker than fear, and with his mind in limbo, he fought to understand his friend's decline. It forced him into action. He nodded at Jim, and the two muscled forward, powering through the crush. Jim clattered onto the stage with Scott close behind, and pulling aside the curtain, they were just in time to see a figure darting toward a door behind the stage. The men burst onto the corridor with the staircase that went up to the lobby.

Jim hurtled to reception, three steps at a time. Turning left to the Marina Street exit, he saw no immediate movement in or around the parking lot, and charged back through the hotel to the much more congested Gurley Street exit. Jogging down the street, Jim saw nothing familiar either rolling down, or hovering to exit from the tightly packed curbside spots. He had underestimated his quarry and been beaten again. Jim vented adrenaline in a frustrated curse, and returned to the lobby where Scott was waiting.

It was several seconds before Jim caught his breath. But Scott's age had ensured his flight up the corridor's stairs had been at a more sedate pace. He asked the receptionist if anybody had just passed.

The clerk pointed at the Marina exit and said, "Mr. Peterson."

Jim shook his head and turned to Scott. "Jesus H. Christ, what is this guy—smoke? I went there first, and there was no movement, no people. Shit, shit, shit."

"Can't be helped," said Scott, "but at least we confirmed Bryce Petersen and Tim Bowman are one and the same."

"Small comfort if we can't get our hands on the bastard."

"So what do we do?"

"Same as always, regroup and start again. Let's rejoin Carol and John."

*

Winding their way through a departing crowd, Jim and Scott found their friends had been busy. After the commotion, John spoke to people and was able to confirm what Jim and Scott already knew, the man who'd been on stage was Bryce Peterson. Moreover, after Carol spoke to the raffle's prize winners, she learned their getaways included air transportation in Peterson's private jet. Jim was heartened; his instinct about aircraft had been right.

The team returned to The Grapes of Wrath, reluctantly conceding that while they might have lost a round, Bryce Peterson was their man, and he was now on the defensive.

Chapter Twenty-Seven

Paradise Valley, north of Phoenix's Camelback Mountain, is everything it purports to be. With high-end environmentally friendly homes surrounded by sensitively landscaped gardens, the whole area sits under a timeless blue sky, quietly oozing tranquility. Except during the monsoon.

During that time, clouds build, roll to thundering fullness over the mountains, and ahead of the rain, violent winds kick up swirling frenzies of blinding dust. Dust that Mother Nature capriciously lifts and dumps into the pristine swimming pools of the pampered and prosperous.

As Duke Nyson and Austin Price sat quietly in the landscaper's truck waiting for the storm to vent its fury, nobody could imagine the mission on which they were engaged.

The household Austin was to deal with lay a hundred yards ahead, and though he could barely see the building through the dust, his mind had a detailed picture of its layout. His instructions were simple and conclusive: Dispose of the two couples inside, and quietly return to Poets Corner.

Taking the line of least resistance, he decided to first tackle the retirees, staying in the main house, and then move across the garden to clean up the youngsters in the guest cottage. Austin's driver and lookout was Duke, and under the guise of the landscape crew, he would drop his partner at the house, retreat to the arroyo at the far end of the development, and wait until dusk. If Austin did not rejoin him by six-thirty, it meant the mission was on, and he would stay in a local motel for the night, then collect his partner in the morning.

Duke pulled into the target house's cul-de-sac, and Austin exited the truck. Armed with gardening equipment he pulled from the Toyota's flatbed, he proceeded to Poppy's house. Rain or shine, a gardener arrived at the same time every two weeks, although this week, a couple of hundred dollars had persuaded the regular guy to loan the team his truck and call in sick.

Under a still-threatening sky, Austin casually walked to the back of the house, setting his equipment at the far end of the patio. The wind had deposited plenty of dust and debris for him to clean up, so diligently wielding rake and broom, he made a circuit of the house. At strategic points, he'd made noise, and while he expected somebody to challenge him, there appeared no sign of life. It crossed his mind to abandon his mission, until he backed into the pool area, and Holly tapped him on the shoulder.

He swung around so fast he dropped his broom. "Dis culpa me, senora," he mumbled, stunned as much by her presence as the realization that his formerly razor sharp senses hadn't heard her approaching.

Smiling sweetly, Holly picked up the broom. "Here, I didn't mean to startle you."

Austin looked at her blankly.

"Do you speak English?" Holly asked.

Austin averted his eyes as a menial might. "Si, senora."

"Does the pool need cleaning?"

"Si, senora."

"Can you do that today, or do I have to wait until tomorrow?"

"Si, senora."

"Which?"

"Si, senora."

"Aqui, senor, venga a . . ." Holly grabbed his arm and led him to the pool. There she mimicked vacuuming by making swooshing sounds.

Austin nodded. "Si, senora, si . . . okay, okay."

Holly smiled and retreated into the house.

Busying himself about the garden, Austin passed the kitchen window and spotted the younger female. Disposal of the women would be easy, as neither looked particularly strong. However, with neither male present, he was, once again, torn about continuing. His mind reset to mission mode when a man came onto the patio and lit a cigarette. Seeming to be in his early thirties, tall and dark with an athletic build, he fit the description of the younger woman's boyfriend, and though fifteen years Austin's junior, he knew a professional's knife to the throat while sleeping would quickly eliminate any waking advantage he might have. Weighing the odds, Austin figured the older man was inside, and he elected to move forward with his assignment as planned.

*

By five-thirty, Austin had completed as much work as he felt the regular gardener would do, picked up his tools, and went round to the side of the house. Passing through a small courtyard, he pulled out a key and let himself into the utility room attached to the garage. His briefing said it had a stocked kitchenette and recliner, on which to wait for nightfall, and all the electrical systems he needed to deactivate were in a boxed panel on the wall.

Using the code number he'd been given, he turned off the night-light motion detectors, then identified the phone line he'd cut before embarking on his mission. He then locked the door, switched on the ceiling fan and helped himself to a cold drink. The fan barely dispersed the heated air of his confined space, and lulled by the circulating blade's hypnotic ticking, Austin drifted into an easy sleep.

He woke, in pitch-dark and deathly quiet, his watch-light indicating eleven-fifty-seven. Cautiously opening the utility room door, he peered out. Detecting nothing but the muted glow of the main house's internal nightlight, he dipped back into the storage room. Quickly locating the taped wire in the electrical box, he pulled a knife from his belt-scabbard and severed the phone wire. Then he flipped off the power.

With the nervous anticipation he'd enjoyed so many times during his former life, Austin left his makeshift hide. And, after pausing in the courtyard for his eyes to adjust, he worked his way to the front of the building. Using a master key to open the front door, he headed directly to the alarm panel. Expecting to see the auxiliary battery had kicked in after he cut the power; he noted the system had never been activated. Austin smiled with one thought in his mind. "People with such a cavalier attitude to personal safety deserve to die."

*

Despite his age, Austin Price still moved like a cat, and measuring every step, breathing long and slow, he planted his feet firmly and silently, approaching each downstairs doorway. He was told the older couple was in one of the bigger rooms upstairs. Nevertheless, he was trained to believe only what he saw, and checked the bedrooms for himself. He then made his way to the stairs, and hugging the left rail to avoid a sculpture on the right lower newel post, he slithered up the stairs like a fog.

*

Austin was skillful and deadly silent, so when Holly saw the shadow above her, it was too late. The weight upon her was crippling, and accompanying the constriction in her chest was searing stifling heat. She struggled for breath, tasting soap and steam iron, and knew a cotton pillowcase was the shroud about her face. She knew someone was trying to smother her, and she knew she wasn't ready to die.

Desperately clawing at the body atop her, the more she flailed, the heavier the pressure on her chest, and the harder it was to draw anything life-sustaining into her lungs. She gasped into the pillow getting nowhere, for only carbon dioxide remained, and the pressure from her impossibly strong assailant increased.

Panic quickly gave way to despair as Holly's oxygen-starved brain dropped her into mind-numbing blackness. Then she saw Scott. He was young again. As was she. They were in Vietnam but now it was he who was ministering to the wounded. He told the soldiers to relax, be strong, and focus their pain elsewhere. And then he took her hand, his eyes shining with devotion. "Do as I say," he said, and it made her try. But it wasn't easy. She went limp, floating like she was dead. And she was at peace. She was in a better place, and nothing could hurt her again.

Then from somewhere below, she heard him; his voice more powerful than Tug's had ever been. He was telling her to fight because he wasn't ready to let her go. And when she did as the love of her life asked, her fighting forced blood to her temples.

Life throbbed, excruciating painful, behind Holly's eyes, and she thrust her body upward in a last attempt at salvation. It seemed to unseat her attacker and dislodge the pillow just long enough for her to take a breath. And as she drew up her knees and kicked for her life, she struck something with give; flesh, not bone. And as she fought, she repeated to herself, "You can't beat me today, you can't beat me today." Her nails wracked the hands that held her. Whoever won this fight, Holly determined that no one would escape unmarked. She fought hard, tearing as much flesh as her perfectly manicured nails could gouge.

What power Holly suddenly possessed came from Scott, from the knowledge that he loved her and she him. But her resurgence was short-lived. Her assailant had unlimited air and she did not. He was atop her again, in control, dead weight pressing down, and everything went black. And then she was floating above the bed again, looking down, spent, done, exhausted, and could fight no more. It wasn't that he was more determined; he was simply too strong. Bone-crushing, heart-stopping, life-taking strong. And with her impossibly heavy legs, lead-weighted and cramping, Holly ceased to kick. And as her hands dropped, and black empty nothing enveloped her body, she was heading somewhere she really didn't want to go.

Chapter Twenty-Eight

Sergeant Al Burton completed his check of the property's perimeter, and as he emerged from behind the guesthouse, he noticed the nightlight in the house was out. Moving swiftly across the garden, he radioed for backup and proceeded inside. As he stepped silently through the patio door, Burton got the weirdest vibe. Moving deliberately forward, he drew his pistol.

A quick review of the area had it looking undisturbed; however, the feeling of foreboding wouldn't leave him. Then, as he made his way to the stairs, he noticed one of the doors leading to a downstairs bedroom ajar. He absolutely knew he'd closed the doors when he did his last walk through, so he cocked his pistol and continued to the second floor landing. There he stopped. Holding his breath to better assess the quiet, a muffled sound permeated the silence. It was a squeaking rasping noise he'd heard before, from a dozen movies, in an assortment of scenarios. Somebody was being smothered.

Burton knew Mrs. Winthrop was sleeping at the end of the corridor to the left, and compelled to the door of the far bedroom, he paused. Taking a deep breath, he eased the door open with his foot. And although his eyes had adjusted to the meager light coming through the house's skylights, here was pitch. He knew he'd be shooting blind. He balanced, aimed at what he felt was an appropriate height, and yelled, "Stop, police!"

*

When Austin heard the order, he knew it was a cop. Cops had a way of saying things that really pissed him off. Pseudo-macho-fascist assholes. Nothing, once you took away the badge and the gun. Couldn't hold a candle to anybody who'd been in combat, and this one was no different. And Master Sergeant Austin Price knew that no two-bit, hick cop was going to stop him from accomplishing a mission.

Feeling the woman go limp beneath the pillow, the ex-Marine drew the knife from his belt and in one movement of lightening reflex, spun around and launched it at the voice. The last thing Austin heard was a pop, and someone saying, "Oh, shit."

*

A series of what sounded like car backfires broke into Ilse's sleep, but it was the sound of breaking glass that had her jumping from bed. She knew Sergeant Burton was in the house, and immediately assumed someone had gotten by him and was trying to get to her through a window. Keeping low, as Jim had instructed her, she reached for the phone. It was dead. She attempted to turn on the lights; no power. And as her brain worked a mile a minute, she remembered everything Jim told her. "Stay low, use the cell to call 911, and say Cromwell is in trouble." Feeling her way to the kitchen, Ilse pulled her cell from the charger, and though its charge light was still blinking, she prayed it had enough juice for one call. She dialed.

Upon recognizing Jim's name and the panic in Ilse's voice, the operator told her Sergeant Burton had called in and help was on the way, and she must find a place to hide until the police arrived. Ilse grabbed the biggest knife she could find, and with her cell still connected to police dispatch, locked herself in the bathroom.

Within minutes of taking position, someone knocked on the bathroom door. But Ilse only came out after an ID slid under the door, and she confirmed the officer's identity with dispatch.

As Officer Sally James led her across the patio, Ilse could see someone had restored the house's power, illuminating a whole team of officers photographing, fingerprinting, and tooth-combing the crime scene. And while she knew little about police procedure, she'd seen enough cop shows to know that the bustle of activity meant something more dreadful than broken windows had occurred.

"Officer James," she asked, "is Holly okay?"

"Not too bad," the young cop replied before lowering her voice. "A man tried to suffocate her. She's pretty shaken up."

"Can I see her?"

"I'm sure that'll be fine; she's receiving medical assistance in an ambulance out front."

"And the man—you arrested him?"

"No, he's dead. Sergeant Burton had no choice but to shoot him."

"Oh my God, is he still in the house?"

"He will be for a while, until forensics are done."

Ilse looked around. "And Sergeant Burton? I don't see him."

"He's at the hospital. The assailant threw a knife and hit him in the abdomen. It's quite serious, but they expect he'll make it."

"What about the other one?" asked a nervous Ilse.

"Other one?"

"He tried to get in my window."

"For now, we think the dead guy was acting alone. Sergeant Burton was covering his bases, thought there might be another attacker, and was trying to get to the guesthouse to protect you. When he realized he couldn't, he had the foresight to alert you by firing several rounds through the window."

Ilse tracked a vermilion trail from the house to its coagulation at the guesthouse side of the pool. "Don't think about that," Officer James cut into her thoughts. "Let's go see your friend."

"How could anyone lose so much blood and survive?"

"Don't worry, Burton's a tough cookie. Come on, I'll walk you to the ambulance."

*

When Officer James opened the ambulance door, Holly had an oxygen mask covering her face. She looked in poor shape; however, as soon as she heard Ilse's voice, she attempted to get up. The EMT held her back, and Ilse climbed into the ambulance beside her. As they were transported to hospital, Ilse recounted the evening's events as she'd been told.

Holly wasn't prone to drama, and it took a lot to break her shell, but at the end of the story, she began to cry. She tried, but took no comfort from Ilse's soothing words. One man was dead, a young policeman was seriously injured, and she was scared out of her wits. It was too much, in too short a time, and she couldn't understand what had happened to her world.

A deluge of her tears began to fall. But not tears of relief for those who survived, and God knows not for the sick, twisted individual who was dead. They were selfish, and hers alone. Never in her wildest dreams could she imagine why someone wanted her dead.

Chapter Twenty-Nine

Jim and Ilse were waiting when Scott wheeled Holly from the hospital. They had wanted to return to Poppy's house, but it was a hive of forensic activity that also had become the focus of intense media scrutiny. The news was reporting the incident as a home invasion for the purpose of robbery, but the team knew otherwise. And while Jim suggested they remove to a safe house, Scott argued that, as Holly's assailant was most probably a member of the Cormorant Club; the eye of the hurricane was the safest place from which to observe and investigate Peterson's organization. He further asserted that security can more easily be maintained by monitoring Poets Corner residents and visitors, as the community had but one way in and out.

*

The team had been back in Poets Corner less than two hours when a delegation of Bubbles Nyson, Joyce Price, and Sandy Beech appeared at Scott's door.

"Welcome back, Scott," said Bubbles. "Apologies for intruding so soon, but we had to come see Holly and let her know she has a support group."

"How nice, she'll be glad to hear that. Holly, Bubbles and her friends are here for moral support."

"Hello, ladies," said Holly. "Thank you for coming. Can I get you coffee?"

"Thank you," said Bubbles, "if it's no trouble."

The ladies sat quietly, seeming to wait for Bubble's lead.

"Is everything all right with you, Bubbles?" asked Scott. "You're unusually silent."

"It's delicate; I'm not sure where to start."

"The beginning's good."

"Of course," said Bubbles. "The ladies and I have urgent concerns about our futures and only you can help us."

"What concerns, Bubbles?" asked Jim.

"We all need to get out of Poets Corner as soon as possible."

"Did something happen while we were gone?"

"As a matter of fact, several somethings. I hope you don't mind but I told Sandy and Joyce about what you all are trying to do and we agreed you were the only ones we can trust." The other ladies nodded. "For my part, being here is a continuation of our previous conversation, except this time it's not about if I leave, but when. My dear Duke returned from his trip in such pain, I had to take him to the emergency room, and the Doctor said he's pretty much done for and will go anytime. We talked about it, and I'm leaving this awful place as soon as I can. Sandy is of the same mind. Her husband is in the final stage of Alzheimer's; he doesn't know her anymore, and she sees no reason to trek to the nursing home getting upset about something over which the doctors have no control. She's already been symbolically thrown out of her house—"

"Who's being thrown out of their house?" Holly had returned with coffee.

"Last week," said Sandy, "I returned from visiting Joe, that's my husband, and found one of those terrible committee people in my house. He was taking measurements."

"Measurements?" asked Jim.

"Yes, he said that another couple would be moving in soon, and I should make arrangements to vacate. Have you ever heard of anything so rude? My Joe isn't even dead yet."

"You know about the take-back clause, then," asked Scott.

"I do. That doesn't mean I agree with it. But I thought I would be able to stay until—well, you know." Tears flooded Sandy's eyes.

"There, there, Sandy," said Bubbles. "Scott will do something, I know he will. Joyce, you tell him about your problem."

"I don't want any trouble. I mean, my Austin wouldn't like a fuss made, but it's because I've only got him, and he just up and disappeared." Joyce slurred slightly, the result of a breakfast with Jim Beam. "I've only been here a little while and don't know why my husband would leave and not come back. Bubbles said Miss Carol was with the police; I thought she might find out if he's been in an accident. I'm told they happen a lot around here; accidents, I mean."

Jim was sympathetic. "When did he leave, Joyce?"

"Day before yesterday, I think."

"Did you file a missing persons report?"

"I don't even know where the police station is; besides, Austin isn't missing. Something bad happened to him."

"Why would you think that?"

"Because I have no idea how we got the money to get here, why we were given this fancy house, or who the man is that he's guarding. All I know for sure is he promised if anything happened to him, I'd be looked after. He used to say that every time he got assigned by the military. Lately he's been acting like a Marine, exercising, eating special stuff, laying off the booze, and he spends a lot of time doing God knows what in the garage."

"Maybe he's just getting fit so he can guard his boss properly," said Carol.

"You think what you like, Missy, but he knows what I think about him going back into the military, so he's keeping it to himself. He's doing something for Special Services, I can feel it."

"Isn't he too old to re-enlist?" asked Jim.

"Once a Marine, always a Marine. Something is going on, I tell you. What about the lady who called me and said Austin's situation has changed, and it would be good if I go back to live with my kids?"

Jim motioned for Ilse to get him a pad and pen. "What lady?"

"I don't know," continued Joyce, pulling a piece of a paper from her bag. "Sounded like one of them hoity-toity bitches I used to talk to when he was in the Marines. Didn't tell me squat then, won't tell me anything now."

Jim motioned toward the paper Joyce was holding. "Is that her phone number?"

"No, like I said, it was a couple of days ago. I woke up, and he was gone. I found this on the kitchen table."

She handed Jim a note, which read, "Just as promised, babe, I always look after you."

"The note was with a key." She pulled a bunch of papers from her bag. "Turns out it was the key to his military trunk. I expected he might have some money, but all I found was this load of crap."

Jim glanced at the documents and handed them to Scott. "These are your mortgage papers, Joyce."

"I know. They ain't worth squat to me."

Scott noted that in company with others, the deed had the death clause. However, there were highlighted spots with dated notes alongside: "Check this with P," and another dated two days later, "Okay with P, will send amended paperwork."

"Are these notes in Austin's writing?"

"Yes." Concern etched Joyce's face. "What does it all mean, Mr. Morgan, and what's to become of me? Is Bubbles right, does that paper mean what it says?"

"That if anything happens to Austin, you must vacate your house; yes, that is what it says. It looks like he tried to have the wording changed, even spoke to someone about it and got a verbal okay, but unless you actually received a signed amendment—"

"I don't have anything else." Tears filled Joyce's eyes as she appealed to Jim. "Bubbles said you know people; can't you help me?"

"I can promise if you leave your papers with us, we'll look into things. Was there anything else in the trunk that might help us?"

"I'm not sure. I've never been in it before. It looked like a piece of his equipment was missing."

Jim's interest piqued. "What sort of equipment?"

"I don't know. He kept all that military junk to himself. Something oblong, like a box, about a foot long."

"What did your husband do in the military, Joyce?"

"I heard him talk about Special Operations. I just know he left me alone, went to places he couldn't talk about, and never even called while he was away. Left me home with screaming kids and not enough money. I was glad when they let him out; it drove me nuts not knowing where he was."

"Do you have a recent photograph of him?"

"Got one of him with the grandkids last Christmas; will that do?"

"Absolutely. Carol, could you take Joyce home and get that picture?"

Carol helped Joyce to her feet and led her to the car.

"Ladies," said Holly. "They'll be a few minutes, so how about more coffee? And maybe a cookie—Ilse made them herself."

"Oh my, how lovely," said Sandy. "But before I do, I'd like to get rid of this." She handed Jim a grocery bag bursting with papers. "I couldn't make heads or tails of these papers. My husband took care of that side of things, and now he doesn't even recognize me, let alone know what all this trash is. Sixty years together, and he doesn't know who I am. That Alzheimer's is wicked; I can't wait to get away from it."

"Wouldn't you feel better if you waited a while?" asked Carol gently.

"Don't have much choice in the matter, according to the measuring guy."

Carol smiled thinly.

"Besides," Sandy continued, "to the committee he's as good as dead, and I know the speed they work in this place. My husband was chairman for a while; that bag contains all sorts of messages and notes from members at various meetings. I'm not waiting around for their axe to fall; I'm leaving tomorrow to go live with my daughter. Bubbles said those papers might help others, and I feel it's my duty to help all the widow women."

"Thank you, Sandy, they might well prove useful," said Jim.

"I don't even care about selling my stuff. I'll leave my address, and after you sort things out, let me know to get someone in."

Bubbles began to fidget and handed Jim another bag. "I found more of Duke's papers," she said as she opened her purse and pulled out a bankbook. "And this."

Jim opened it. "One hundred and fifty thousand dollars. Goodness, Bubbles, this is a lot of money."

"I know. Isn't it wonderful; Duke left something for me after all."

"You didn't know about the account before?"

"No, he gave me the safe combination and said he'd left a present. He was hiding it because I'm not very good with money. So, like Sandy, I don't need the sale of my house to start up elsewhere. I'm off as soon as I've seen the people at the bank."

Jim looked at the dates of deposit, the last within the previous week. "Would you mind if I took a photocopy?"

She patted his hand. "Long as I get it back, you go right ahead."

Jim gestured for Scott to follow him into the office. "You thinking the same as me?"

Scott nodded.

"Let's see if Bob can find out where Duke got a hundred and fifty grand, I also told him to freeze the funds. While I take this back, will you watch it all go through?"

By the time Scott rejoined the group, Carol and Joyce had returned, and Jim was looking at a Polaroid Joyce had brought him. He'd seen many missing person pictures, often indistinct, years younger, leagues healthier, or shown in a way the family wanted them to be remembered, and this smiling Christmas jester was no exception. Nevertheless, ignoring the extra pounds, and accounting for the surprised look he'd last seen on the Phoenix corpse, Jim had no doubt the face grinning out at him was Holly's attacker. He handed it to Carol, who nodded, and took it into the office for transmission to Bob.

*

"Okay Joyce," she said, on her return to the living room, "I've sent the picture to a colleague in Phoenix. I'll keep it if you don't mind, and if I hear anything, I'll call you."

It wasn't long before the ladies had set aside their immediate concerns, and were sipping coffee and chatting as if nothing untoward had happened. That cordial atmosphere allowed Scott to canvas them about hiring a policeman to monitor the front gate.

"What a splendid idea," said Sandy. "Then if we have any more trouble, someone will be right there to deal with it. What do we need to do?"

"Call a resident's meeting and take a vote," said Scott, "and if we get approval, the gate will be closed, and everybody will be subject to having their comings and goings logged."

"Oh, that sounds so . . . *Miami Vice*," said Bubbles, giggling. "How many votes do we need?"

"According to your regulations," said Jim, having checked, "at least two committee members must be present, but if the majority of those attending agree, it's a done deal."

"Won't it take a while to organize a policeman?" asked Bubbles.

"A police presence could be organized almost immediately." Jim had already set a roster.

"Then I'll be responsible for stirring the troops," added Bubbles. "If we work quickly, we should be able to organize a meeting for later today. And you know, Scott, there are actually quite a few people who think you got a raw deal over that business with Zoey Mitchell; I'm sure you'll get enough votes to pass the thing."

*

Within a couple of hours of leaving Scott's house, the diminutive but extraordinarily aggressive Bubbles had whipped pro and con residents into a frenzy. Some didn't want to get involved, fearing reprisals from the committee. However, when she told them the police were now involved in the investigation of their mortgages, a flood of people attended the clubhouse to find out what was going on.

The meeting began at five o'clock, with the two members of the committee, who actually lived in the community, positioning themselves on a raised table at the forefront of the meeting. It was a deliberately intimidating ploy, set up to remind the wavering how things are done in Poets Corner. However, after a heated back and forth, the vote carried by a margin of two, and Scott could almost feel a sigh of relief from the room.

Chapter Thirty

When Scott, Jim and Carol returned to the house, Prescott Valley's police liaison had transmitted the list of cars and owners attending the Chamber of Commerce meeting. As Jim expected, several were registered to companies with foreign names. He recognized three of the four as Latin, and asked Ilse to help with translations. She told him Abextra was "from outside," Nolens Volens meant "whether willing or not," and Judice, which she suspected was short for *me judice*, roughly translated as "I being judge." He transmitted the information to Bob, requesting company profiles; then turned his attention to the paperwork he'd received from the Poets Corner ladies group.

Separating each collection and adding them to what they already had from Charlotte Messing; the team each took a set and compared them to Scott's papers.

"Well, guys," said Scott, "it seems all the houses we know about were initially 'purchased' for less than a fifth of their actual worth, and all monies were paid to Ex Gratia Mortgage LLC."

"With the exception of Austin Price," interrupted Holly. "He received his house for a cash settlement of one dollar. If, as Joyce said, he was Bryce Peterson's bodyguard, I'm thinking payment for services rendered."

"Sounds reasonable," added Jim, "so let's set him aside for the moment and concentrate on the rank and file. These papers universally confirm that upon the death of the single named homeowner, the spouse gets zip."

"Exactly what happened to me," said Holly, "I so feel for these women."

"But you have me now, sweetie."

"And I thank you for that, my darling."

"So," said Carol, "we can't really do anything for them, housewise. Are you going to break it to them?"

"Not yet," added Jim. "Nor am I mentioning my suspicions about Bubbles' newly acquired bank account."

"What's this?" asked Ilse, picking up a small black notebook from under the table. "It must have fallen out when I emptied my envelope." She handed it to Jim.

"Will you look at this," he said, flipping the pages. He passed it to Scott.

"These look like meeting minutes."

"Hold that thought, I'm calling Bubbles." Jim dialed, and she answered immediately. The call wasn't to be as quick as Jim had anticipated, and as he sunk under a weight of platitudes, he shot Scott the "help me, I'm drowning look." His friend simply shrugged and chuckled.

"Bubbles . . . I know . . . one question. . .yes, I understand. You said Duke attended a lot of committee meetings. Did he keep the community minutes? Unofficially . . . I see . . . a lady you don't know, pretty, with red hair. Somebody from the bird club. Okay, thank you so much." He put the phone down to laughter from his colleagues. "Let's see you do better—one of you gets the next call. So, we discover a couple more things: Persephone Collins—and we know who that is—appears to be the community secretary and takes the minutes at all the meetings. However, Duke, the old stickler, wanted an accurate record of what he heard, and jotted down his own observations after every meeting. My guess is we'll find some useful stuff in that little black book."

"Well, far be it from me to come between a man and his little black book," said Holly, "but Ilse and I have to be the responsible ones and make dinner. You need us, yell. Come on Ilse," she grabbed the youngster's hand.

Scott smiled and went back to scanning the logbook. "Duke seems to have developed his own form of speedwriting, but it's easy to decipher. He's got meeting dates, attendees, and notes accompanied by a place name; could that be where an incident was to happen?"

"Let me see," said Jim. "The back is probably the most recent stuff. Umm, this is interesting. Exec Conf Cabo atop a bunch of names. Carol, pass that list we just sent to Bob." He stared at names: Guillermo Rialto, Patterson Booth, Fiers Antipove. They were noted in Duke's book along with Persephone Collins and Marvin Shapler.

"Wasn't a trip to Cabo one of the Chamber meeting door prizes?" asked Scott.

"Right, at the Palacio del Toro," agreed Jim. "I'll lay odds the conference Duke mentioned was held there too. Seems we hit the mother lode of connections here."

"Let's hope so, but something is still bugging me," Scott added. "We started this whole thing rolling after Holly noticed Cormorant stickers on a bunch of cars. Then you brought the pictures of senior-caused accidents, with more stickers. Why didn't anyone pick up on the bird connection before now? It might have saved some lives."

In defense of fellow police officers, Carol responded. "How could anyone make the connection unless they have all the information and pictures bunched together like we do? Most everybody has some decal or other on their car, so it's not something an investigator would find particularly unusual. Plus, these incidents are all over the map, in all sorts of jurisdictions, and for the most part appeared to be accidents."

"Carol's right," added Jim. "If the authorities found anything they suspected was criminal, they, like me, would have gathered information from anywhere and everywhere with even a remote connection to the incident. But all the seniors involved in our cases explained their position, and admitted guilt. They subsequently went to court and took their punishment, ergo, cases closed.

Accidents just don't warrant the kind of far-reaching investigation a criminal matter does."

Scott frowned. "But there are so many."

"Not in the big scheme of criminal things. The Cormorant Club conference in Cabo is a prime example of seeming innocence, because there's absolutely nothing unusual about a bunch of folks meeting at a resort in Mexico. It happens all the time, all over the globe. However, in light of what we're investigating, it's a big honking something."

"When you put it like that, I guess I'm reaching."

While Jim was talking, Carol had pulled the accident pictures and was putting them in chronological order. "Don't stop challenging though, Scott, because it's easy to miss things, especially when they're right under your nose. Take this, for example." She pointed at the dates on the pictures. "Now that we know what we do, this becomes useful. See, there's a pattern. Each is about a month apart."

"Pull out the picture of the Chuck and Amanda Westlake accident," said Jim, "and see if we have anything on Scott's tussle with Zoey Mitchell's Cadillac."

"Here's the Westlake picture, but I can't find anything on Scott. Tell me again, when was your accident?"

"I'm already with you," answered Scott, flipping through Duke's log. He found the nearest meeting date to his accident, then isolated two other meetings that quickly followed.

"Hold those pages," said Jim, stepping to the office door. "Ilse," he yelled, "when did you say the Cormorant Club met?"

"Once a month," floated in from the kitchen. "Now quit slacking and get back to work."

Smiling at her rebuke, he retook his seat. "Remember when I first met Ilse, she was annoyed Mrs. Voldheim dumped all the club set-up on her, especially as it was so soon after the previous meeting."

Scott nodded.

"Note who is at the meeting just before you were hit. And for the sake of argument we'll assume one of them got photographed with the magic knife Ilse told us about and was assigned the dubious pleasure of running you down. Then check the following two meetings that came within a month. If my hunch is right, Zoey Mitchell, at the very least, will be front and center."

"Carl Wright, Ali McCallium, Duke Nyson, Ben Watkins, Susan Josephs, and Zoey Mitchell; taking out the committee leaves us Josephs and Mitchell, and Ms. Mitchell sports a small red asterisk at the last two meetings," Scott reported.

"My next guess," said Jim, "is that Mitchell didn't warrant one of Duke's asterisks at the first meeting because at that time nobody knew she was the assassin. But by the second, it was known she'd botched her mission—big notable disappointment—and at the third, which was entirely out of synch with the monthly schedule, the committee was reading her the riot act, maybe even telling her to do something to make things right."

"Okay," said Carol, "isolating and pointing the finger at Mitchell is easy, because Scott is alive to tell the tale. And while Duke's dedication to accuracy helps us establish approximately 'when' crimes were committed by the club, we'll get nowhere without the 'who' to match with the 'did what.'"

"Agreed," said Jim, "so here's my thought. We send all this paperwork to Bob. He can put together a computer program into which he'll feed Scott's code parameters, and all residents' names and addresses for the past couple of years. Using Duke's notebook, he can factor in meeting attendees, and any other information he finds useful, then add dates and places of the incidents photographed here and in the databanks. And as we have the victims' names, tell us who, did what, to whom."

Scott shook his head. "Just the code won't help."

Jim looked quizzical.

"You need the animal primer to back-track the assassin. Even having a victim's name won't establish where your alphabet's 'A' is."

"Then he'll have to input every animal, for all past and current residents, and cross reference those to every incident we have recorded."

"Christ, that'll take weeks," said Carol.

Jim nodded. "It has to be done; I don't see anyone coming forward to tell us they participated in a murder."

"Point taken, but even if we isolate our murderers, how do we prove an irrefutable connection to Bryce Peterson?"

"Weight of evidence, we confirm one fact at a time, then join up the dots."

"You're the boss." Carol started to collect up papers. "I'll put the package together, and take it down to Bob tonight."

Chapter Thirty-One

Scott took Holly's hand and led her to the bedroom. "I thought they'd never leave."

"They've gone out for dinner, Lochinvar; what did you have in mind?"

"A little champagne and a lot of debauchery."

"Umm," she ran a finger down his cheek. "Will that come with true passion, or are we going with empty carnality?"

He smiled. "Had a yen for empty carnality, followed by true passion."

"My, aren't we being a bit ambitious. They'll only be gone a couple of hours."

"No, they won't."

"How so?"

"They're staying the night at The Hassayampa."

She cuffed him. "You little devil, how did you all hide that from me?"

"It was touch and go, especially when you spotted Ilse's overnight bag."

"Which she said was dry cleaning to be dropped off."

He pulled her closer. "You are so trusting, I worry about you."

"Well, don't. I'm no shrinking violet."

"Now that, I know."

She pushed him back. "What's that supposed to mean?"

"Whipped cream and a 'tango'?"

"Oh yes, wasn't that delicious."

"It was, in more ways than one, which is why I have planned several surprises in that very direction."

"That very direction, you say?"

"I do say. But first, there is a small formality to take care of."

"And that would be?"

Scott pulled a velvet box from his pocket. "If you hate it, you can change it. But it was so you, I couldn't resist it."

Holly opened the box to find a diamond ring set with onyx and emeralds in the art-deco style. "My God, Scott, you remembered. It's perfect."

He slipped the ring on her finger. "It's a copy of a ring purchased by Isadora Duncan in 1924."

"Do I get the Morgan ride, too?"

"Oh yes, my darling, you are going to get a very long Morgan ride."

"I love you so much."

He smiled. "I know."

Chapter Thirty-Two

It was Saturday evening when Carol called Jim from Phoenix. "Hey, boss, forensics finished working on Poppy's house, and with the help of your photo, we positively identified the man who attempted to smother Holly. No surprises there; ex-Special Forces Master Sergeant Austin Price."

"Gotta love this Peterson guy," said Jim. "Doesn't even have to pay his mercenaries the going rate, just offers them free room and board. At least we solved the mystery of Joyce's disappearing husband."

"Want me to come up and talk to her?"

"No, I'm going to hold off. From our last conversation, it seemed she was pretty heavily into the bottle. I don't want her mouthing off; she might blow everything if she starts garnering sympathy around the community."

"You think that might happen? I thought Scott said gaining acceptance from the residents was difficult."

"For us normal people. I'm sure by now everyone knows where Austin Price fit in, and Joyce is riding his coat tails. Whatever Peterson said to suck these people in, it's so deeply entrenched, they feel he's untouchable. I don't want somebody alerting him to how much we know."

"So you're not concerned about escalation?"

"I'm concerned that he seems to be conducting business as usual, knowing we're right on his doorstep. That attitude of invincibility tells me he has a solid escape plan. How much do you know about airplanes?"

"Dated a pilot once, took me up a few times."

"That's a start. We know Peterson has a chopper and a jet. Ask Bob for a down-and-dirty Aviation 101, and work the airfields while his databases are cross-referencing. I want to know what type of aircraft is flying Peterson around, how much runway it needs, its range, and where it has flown in the last six months. Get me the name of his pilot and what flight plans he's recently filed. I need to know where his aircraft is, where it's planning to go, and when, because the tingling in the back of my neck tells me that once it sinks in his pet assassin is toast, he'll come after Scott himself."

"You think he's still local then?"

"Yeah, he's on a mission; won't be going anywhere until it's complete. His ego is out of control, and after three failures on Scott, his next attempt will be right in our faces."

"You need back up?"

"Not yet, the community gate monitoring is working pretty well. Officers are getting used to residents' faces and vehicles, and apart from a couple of complainers, everything appears back to normal. Anything starts brewing, I'll call for help. Did you talk to Poppy's neighbors, anybody see anything out of the ordinary?"

"There was a pretty nasty dust storm the afternoon of the incident, but one of the neighborhood watch members spotted a landscapers truck parked in an arroyo at the end of the development. Thinking the driver was in trouble, he volunteered his help, but the old guy inside said he'd broken down and was awaiting a tow-truck. Couple of hours passed, nobody arrived, so the neighbor went back out with water. He said the landscaper, who had to be in his eighties, looked really sick, so he invited the guy to wait inside his house. Apparently, the oldster declined, saying something like, 'don't count old Duke out yet.' Neighbor thought nothing more and went back inside. By six-thirty, truck was still there; neighbor wasn't happy and called the landscaping company. The owner said their guy had called in sick that day; that's when the neighbor called the cops. By the time our people arrived, the truck was gone."

"Bubbles said Duke was in Phoenix around attack time. I'm sending his picture now; run it by the neighbor, let's see if we can tie up another loose end. Anything else?"

"Bob's kicking ass on the computer, but you requested so much stuff I hope you don't mind that I followed up on a few things for him."

"Hey, we're a team, good initiative."

"Thanks. Anyway, pal of Captain Ryan's heads security at The Saguaro where Bryce Peterson has a permanent casita. He was last there day before the chamber bash. Our contact says he's been known to invite 'lady friends' over, but has never given any trouble, tips well, is considerate to the staff, and pays his bills on time."

"Just an all-American good guy."

"Right, and I'm Angelina Jolie roughing it."

"You got her smarts, C, and you can kick ass."

"Bite me!" She heard him laugh down the line. "Next, the hotel in Cabo San Lucas was more difficult. Those local cops don't like talking to us."

"No kidding; try and get an extradition from there."

"Like you suspected, Peterson keeps a suite at the Palacio del Toro, swanky place, lots of high rollers. I got no help from their spokesperson, however, I got chatting to a receptionist whose sister lives in the town I was born. She told me on the QT that Peterson's last visit was three or four weeks ago, and his guests were a Mr. and Mrs. Price. According to her, he often entertains foreigners. They always stay on his dime, and the receptionist's friends are regularly asked to supply, shall we say, personal services to his VIPs. I told her the names we registered at the Chamber meeting, and Guillermo Rialto and Patterson Booth rang bells because they were really big tippers."

"Damn, so here we are, back in the same gene pool—heads of Abextra and Nolens Volens, right?"

"You got it. And while Bob's initial research had them listed as American companies, some fancy finger-work—don't ask what he did—found the base for Abextra is Sicily, and Nolens Volens is in Australia. They're both incorporated in the Cayman Islands. Bryce Peterson is listed on the boards. Bob dug deep into both and on the face of it, they look upstanding enough; government contracts in waste disposal, insurance, and risk management, even found a couple of backwater newspapers. Then once I cast a new eye over his research, I recognized offshoots in gaming, munitions, and pharmaceuticals."

"Man," said Jim, summarily impressed. "You two have been cooking; anything on Duke Nyson's hundred and fifty grand?"

"Still working on that. What about you and Peterson's house on the hill?"

"Nothing much by the time we got there. We did find a telescope with fancy camera attached, sort of a 'gotcha' for us; it was trained on Poets Corner. He didn't even need the crippled old gatekeeper in the end house, probably took our pictures as we waited for the gates to open, ran 'em through the wringer, and identified us for what we are. There was a control for the gate too; he could close it whenever he wanted. That's about all I have for now. Hey, Carol, really good job. Be careful out there."

"Back at ya, boss."

*

When Carol called Jim forty minutes later, she confirmed Duke Nyson was in the landscaper's truck. But he succumbed to his prostate cancer before anyone could question him.

Chapter Thirty-Three

Zoey Mitchell wasn't accustomed to receiving mission instructions during a routine phone call, but when Allie McCallium called, the out-of-favor senior was eager to work back into the committee's good graces. Her instructions were simple. At one-fifty, she was to leave the community, and proceed to the highway side of the Main Street parking lot in Prescott Valley. There, she would hand over her car to Mr. Peterson. She could sit in the car or drive somewhere, but under no circumstances was she to return to Poets Corner until after two-thirty. At that time, she would park Mr. Peterson's Mercedes in the clubhouse parking lot and go home. She would be advised when and where to reclaim her Cadillac.

At precisely one forty-eight, Zoey pulled up at the Poets Corner gate, impatiently drummed her fingers on the steering wheel, and mumbled about the imposition of checking in and out. The officer on duty calmly checked her plate number against his log, entered her name on his clipboard, and mentally flipped her the bird as she swooped through the gate. At the very least, he hoped she'd have the decency to stay out until he signed off, letting some other poor schlub receive a dose of her misery.

*

The parking area was busy, but Zoey quickly spotted the large black-on-black Mercedes she was expecting at the lot's outermost edge. She parked as close as she was able and made her way to the other vehicle. She was three cars shy of her target when a man she assumed was Peterson climbed from the back seat. Handsome in a hawkish sort of way, hair slightly graying and eyes black as jet, he looked aggravated. She'd heard about but never met her mysterious benefactor, but when he came alongside and Zoey proffered her keys, he ignored her and swept by.

When someone tapped her shoulder, Zoey was startled, and turning abruptly, she faced the committee secretary. "Keys," she said curtly, and Zoey handed them over. "Do not return to Poets Corner before two-thirty."

"Wha—"

"Two-thirty, do you understand me?"

"I resent being spoken in that—"

"Do you understand, old woman?"

Zoey nodded woodenly, and watched her car disappear.

The Mercedes looked even more imposing close up, and as she slid behind the wheel facing more buttons and knobs than an airplane cockpit, she realized she had no idea how to start it. "Where the hell," she mumbled to herself, "is Peterson's snooty-ass, know-it-all assistant when she could really be of use?" She was forced to take off her wrap-arounds, revealing milk-bottle bottom spectacles, and after converting the computer to key mode, she fired the engine.

*

At ten minutes after two, the Cadillac pulled up alongside the officer monitoring the Poets Corner gate. Peterson was hidden beneath a blanket in the rear, and with sunglasses on, and hat pulled low, the driver gave her name—Zoey Mitchell. Checking the plate number against his clipboard, the young officer saw Mitchell had registered out. However, while he wasn't yet familiar with the faces of all the oldsters who came and went, something about this lady didn't feel right. Returning to his cruiser, he consulted his directory, then re-approached the driver and asked for her address and phone number. The driver smoothly answered with the correct information; nevertheless, the cop recalled previous encounters with Mitchell at 1134 Shakespeare and expected a lot more back talk. He continued to hesitate processing her entry until the arrival of a second car into the gate space. With no wish to cause undue inconvenience, he noted Zoey Mitchell's return and buzzed the Cadillac into the community.

Having the distinct feeling the cop wasn't convinced who she was; Poppy drove the Cadillac sedately down the hill, and hung left as if going to Zoey Mitchell's. Then, she doubled back to Scott's house, and parked directly across from his front door. Peterson emerged from the Cadillac's back seat, strode purposely forward, and was ringing the bell before Poppy switched off the engine.

*

Holly opened the door to feel Peterson's extended hand pushing her roughly into the house. "Back up quietly," he ordered. "Keep out of my way and you'll be all right; I'm here to see Scott."

"He's not here," she replied, standing stiffly in an attempt to stay his forward motion. "And who are you anyway?"

Peterson muscled Holly aside. "Poppy," he demanded. "Make yourself useful and take this one to the kitchen. I don't want to hang around here any longer than I have to."

Upon seeing her friend, Holly gasped, "Poppy, what the—"

"I said, take her away now, and keep her quiet."

Holly took a step toward Peterson. "You can't just come—"

"I can do whatever I like. Now shut up or I'll make you."

Before Holly could formulate a reply, Scott emerged from the office. Face to face with his old friend, conflicting emotions flooded through him. "I thought I recognized the voice," he said. "What the hell are you doing here?"

"Scotty, Scotty," Peterson smiled malevolently. "Always on the defensive. Now what sort of a greeting is that after all these years?"

"Holly, dear," said Poppy, trying to alleviate the tension. "You always wanted to meet the man in my life, so I brought him to see you. I'd like you to meet my friend, Bryce Peterson."

"Friend," Holly snapped, pulling her arm from Poppy's grasp. "You don't know the meaning of the word."

Poppy looked puzzled. "Why do you say that, Holl? I've always been your best friend."

"Until you and this . . . this animal tried to have Scott, and then me, killed."

Peterson grabbed Poppy's arm. "What didn't you understand about get her out of here?" He tried to push her forward. "Now go."

Poppy stood her ground. "What are you talking about, Holly?"

"Don't play innocent, you damn bitch. Have you seen the state of your house?"

"My house? You know I haven't been home in weeks. What's my house got to do with anything?" It was clear from her expression and the genuine concern in her voice that Poppy had no idea about the attempt on Holly's life.

"Shut up, both of you," interrupted Peterson. "Screw the house. I have business to conduct with Scott, then we'll be gone. Poppy, get her into the kitchen."

Scott moved protectively in front of his fiancée. "She goes nowhere."

"So, Scotty, nothing's changed. Still the Eagle Scout, so gallant, so—predictable," said Peterson. "No matter, though it's your brain I want, I can still find a use for that kind of integrity."

"Integrity, that's rich; you can shove it up your ass."

Peterson smiled again. "Oh my, such vulgar language, and in front of the ladies. I stand corrected, you have changed."

"But you haven't. You're still finding ways to take the easy way out, just like you did years ago."

A tic fluttered beside Peterson's eye. "Not so, and you know it. I tried to do the right thing. You seem to have forgotten how hard I worked, schlepping sacks of corn in a feed store ten hours a day to support a wife and kid I didn't want."

"Whose fault was that? You had a good mind, and could've gone to college if you'd quit whining long enough to apply yourself."

"Instead, Uncle Sam drafted me."

"He drafted us all. That didn't mean we turned into psycho killers."

"But we did, my friend. To one degree or another Vietnam made us all that way; some of us simply took to it a little more enthusiastically. And now here you are all righteous indignation with your lady friend behind you. By the way, Holly dear, how are you coping after all that nastiness with dear old Tug?"

"Why, you despicable piece of—"

Scott felt Holly tense as she moved by him, and held firmly onto her wrist.

"She can be a sassy little thing, can't she? I remember Tug saying he so liked putting that spirit in its place . . . until his accident . . . tough on you, eh Holly?"

Holly lunged forward. "You stinking perverted bastard."

"Shut up, you stupid bitch; precisely what harm do you think you can inflict on me? Keep hold on her, Scott; unlike you, I'm not averse to showing a woman who the boss is. Believe me, this one is way overdue."

"Leave her out of this; haven't you caused her enough pain?"

"Pain? You have no idea—"

"Whatever you want is between us, but don't make the mistake of thinking I'm even the remotest bit like you. Then, or now."

Peterson's eyes flashed anger and recrimination. "You can protest innocence all you want, even give me the 'I-was-only-doing-my-duty' crap, but you felt exactly the way I did when we were sitting in a foxhole in Suoi Dau. None of us knew why we were there getting our heads blown off, while the fat cats' kids stayed home in cushy desk jobs, raking in the cash. You could've gotten out, lived high where the sun shines, just like I did; you were simply too chicken-shit to make the commitment. Christ, is your memory that short?"

"I wanted to sleep at night."

"Oh, make no mistake, I sleep—real good, in the best hotels, with beautiful women who are attracted to a winner."

"Yet here you are, busting into my house like a common criminal."

"Your house? I believe your family and I already debated that point, and your side lost."

"Screw you! Say your piece and get out."

"You know, I think any piece I have to impart might be wasted. Let me simply assure you, once a man develops a taste for the finer things in life, he quickly realizes what is worth fighting for. And I, for one, do not intend to abandon my lifestyle without a fight. Whatever you think, and at this point I'm not sure I give a damn, I have merely been taking care of business." Peterson pulled some papers from his pocket. "But enough bickering. I came here in the spirit of our long-lost friendship to make you an offer. It's not too late to join me; it'll be like old times, an unbreakable code, you and me. I've made my millions, and the least I can do is cut the co-author in on a share; I have the papers here to make it legit."

"What about your wife and kid? Do they get a share? What compensation do you think they deserve for everything you put them through?"

"Grow up, will you? I barely knew either of them before I was shipped out, and I'm sure my so-called wife didn't give a rat's ass what happened to me as long as Uncle Sam gave her a few bucks compensation for my untimely demise. This is real life; this is now, and I've been doing what I do, because there's a market. I don't make the situations; I simply solve other people's problems."

"Solve this . . ." Scott reached for a table lamp and flung it. But it was plugged firmly into the wall, and jerked a couple of yards before smashing into a hundred pieces on the hardwood.

Peterson didn't even flinch. "Now that is simply rude. I came here with a genuine offer, an olive branch you might say, and you attack me." With eyes menacingly black, and demeanor ice cold, Peterson returned the papers to his pocket, removed a gun from inside his jacket, and fired. Scott slumped to the ground clutching his chest, pained betrayal bathing his face. Holly hurled herself at Peterson but was swiped aside like a rag doll. "You two really are causing me a monumental amount of trouble," he rasped, "and frankly I've had enough of it." As he pointed his gun at Holly, Poppy leaped into the path.

"No, Bryce," she pleaded. "You said you wouldn't hurt her, you promised. She won't say anything." Poppy frantically turned. "Holl, you won't, will you? Tell him you didn't see anybody, tell him, Holl, please, God, tell him."

Holly was cradling Scott, tears streaming down her face. "Go straight to hell," she spat at her former friend. "Both of you."

Sensing Peterson was about to fire, Poppy swiped at his arm. She deflected his aim, but the bullet hit its target, slicing along Holly's temple. He took aim again, but the sight of her long-time friend motionless incensed Poppy. She kneed Peterson full-force in the groin, and he dropped to the ground.

"You bastard," she screamed. "You promised." And with strength and tenacity belying her years, Poppy clawed maniacally at his face.

Peterson shielded himself from forces only one as evil as he would understand. And regaining his composure, he pistol-whipped the tiring arms raining blows on him.

Poppy was stunned, her mind flashing to happier times when she'd blissfully encouraged her lover's sexual violence. But as the pain began, and the full measure of his brutal disdain hit her, the anger, and frustration of years dancing to his tune, brought out in her an uncharacteristic surge of audacity. She grasped the gun's barrel.

Peterson had never experienced such boldness from Poppy, and in another setting, he might have found it enjoyable. Now, the tantrum of a former diva was emotion he had neither the time nor inclination to explore. Smiling coldly, he squeezed the trigger, and let fly a bullet. It slashed up the inside of Poppy's arm, hit bone, and deeply embedded itself in her abdomen. As her body constricted in pain, she dropped before him. Her hands remained clamped on the gun, and with her dragging weight threatening to rip off his trigger finger, he let it go.

Rising slowly, he viciously kicked Poppy aside, and surveyed the carnage. The two he intended dead were down, and dealing with a turncoat was a satisfactory bonus. Re-buttoning and straightening his jacket, he brushed off his clothes, ran blood-spattered fingers through his disarrayed hair, and calmly walked to the door.

*

At the sound of gunshots, the gate's police officer assumed the worst, radioed dispatch for back-up, and went directly to Scott's house. With gun drawn, he cautiously approached and pushed open the door.

Peterson saw the cop through the door's sidelight, and as he ducked toward the hall powder room, a single shot from behind zipped past his head. It hit the cop squarely between the eyes. Seeing his opportunity, Peterson jumped over the fallen officer and fled. A second bullet ripped past his hip, and in a blinding whoosh, ignited the gas tank of Zoey Mitchell's Cadillac parked out front. For a microsecond, the billowing cloud of explosive flame enveloped him. Then, as the flame sucked back to its power source, it engulfed the car, allowing Peterson to walk on with little more than a singed Armani. Elated by the fortunate turn of events, ego-boosted, feeling invincible and more casual than anyone had a right to be, he climbed into the police cruiser and flipped open his cell.

"Rick, total cluster fuck here. Fire up the jet, I'll be at Love Field in twenty-five minutes." Engaging the cruiser's gears, he peeled away from Scott's house as choking smoke and orange flame violated the sky. He anticipated five minutes before the whole area became a blockade of emergency vehicles, and headed for the community's collapsible fire exit, which let out onto the highway.

*

With his foot to the floor, Peterson blasted up Keats Way, and as he expected, the sound of multiple sirens brought a company of his ancient puppets scurrying from the clubhouse. He also saw the Mountie running from the pool deck, and headed straight for him.

Jim could do little but hurl himself sideways. Nevertheless, the car clipped his hip, sending him tumbling backward onto the clubhouse lawn. He came to rest with his leg impaled on a sign saying Keep Off the Grass. He cursed loudly, and ignoring all medical advice to the contrary, yanked the offending signage from his thigh. It was with no satisfaction he stood, the condescending sneer of the man driving the cruiser at the forefront of his mind. Bryce Peterson was again escaping out the back door.

Taking a deep breath, Jim ignored his pain, and hobbled on towards Scott's house. He'd gone about a hundred yards when Ilse came up beside him and tugged at his shirt. He turned to face her.

She noticed his pallor, and his favoring one leg. She looked down. "Dear God, what happened? You're bleeding!"

"It's nothing, grazed my leg." He placed his hands on her shoulders. "I want you to stay here. I have to get to Scott's. Something very bad has happened."

"Are you crazy? You can barely walk; lean on me."

"I said stay, and I mean stay. It could still be dangerous. Peterson just ran me down."

"What if he comes back? I'll be defenseless." She knew that would get to him.

"Shit, come on then."

"First, let me do something." Unclipping her bikini top, she knelt and tied it as tightly as she could around his thigh.

He couldn't help smiling. "You're not walking around here with your top off. You'll give these old men heart attacks. Take my shirt. Now, I'm going to lean on you, but if I say hit the dirt, you will drop. Do I make myself clear?"

She nodded, and they headed off down the hill.

Chapter Thirty-Four

Seeing Cromwell fall spurred Peterson on, and without hesitation, he flipped the cruisers siren and barreled through the flimsy fire gate. He expected people to move aside when they saw him, and a Dodge Ram heading south swerved violently to avoid his sideswipe. Several other vehicles veered to the shoulder and screeched to a halt. Not so a black-on-black Mercedes, speeding toward Poets Corner at more than sixty miles an hour.

Zoey Mitchell was angry at Mr. Peterson and the witch Collins. Now, with the sound of sirens behind, in front, seemingly all around her, and cars swerving every which way, she felt something akin to panic. And in that microsecond of distraction, she looked down to indicate her turn into Poets Corner. Peripheral vision was something Zoey Mitchell had been losing for some time, so she didn't see the cruiser hurtling at her from the side-road. And she barely felt an impact as it T-boned into the Mercedes, sending it across two lanes.

All she felt was a seductively warm, velvet fog engulfing her. It was surprisingly pleasant, and looking out the window, a sign greeted her, in slow motion, quite poetic, like a ballet dancer. She smiled, and the inevitability of what was happening somehow comforted her. Then, as a wailing alarm assaulted her ears, the air bag hit her chest. She knew that this was her time. Her fate was in the hands of a higher power. But as the luxury automobile came to a crushing halt, pretzeled around a signpost, it dawned on her. Now, she would have to pay for her past transgressions.

*

Metallica blared as the beat-up F-150 driver re-ignited his roach. And as he dragged smoke, satisfying and smooth, deep into his throat, a cop car materialized from thin air. It seemed to be spinning, and shocked by the vehicle crossing his bow, the driver couldn't prevent the white-hot butt falling from his lips. It lodged in his groin. And with the smell of marijuana-seared denim hanging thick in the air, he tried to dislodge the stump. His flailing merely redirected the embers. Desperately focusing on the consequences of flame about his crotch, he let his truck drift into a passing Toyota.

Sideswiped by the F-150, the tiny Toyota careened across the median, and plowed head-on into a Prescott-bound truck. The two young men riding in the back were catapulted from the bed. One hit the road and bounced wildly into oncoming traffic; the other hit the windshield of an Aerostar swerving around to avoid the collision. With a body lodged in his shattered windshield, the Aerostar driver jammed on his brakes, and the rear-ender that followed his unexpected stop silenced the pounding beat of a tailgating low-rider.

At the sight of what looked like a body rolling across the road, a young woman driving a VW Beetle lost all sense of distance and direction. Hitting her brakes, she hung left to avoid the obstacle, and over-compensated. She ran into the low-rider mashed to a stop on the other side of the road. A vintage Porsche following at speed couldn't avoid running up the Beetle's back and flipping onto the verge. And when the driver of a UPS truck pulled to a halt and grabbed his cell phone, he was whip-lashed into silence by a vehicle slamming him from behind.

Cursing everything and everybody, Peterson came to a steaming mangled rest by the Mercedes. He hadn't planned on actually running, but as he pushed open the cruiser's door, he knew the diversion he'd unwittingly created would allow him to duck into the Diamond Valley sub-division and call Rick for help.

Grasping the door jam, Peterson's brain told his legs to swing out. They would not. Then the pain began. Not in his legs, there was no feeling there. In his hips. Up his spine. Into his neck. Rolling waves of excruciating burning wracked him, and dizzying nausea followed. An attempt to throw himself from the vehicle only succeeded in adding to his undulating agony. Then as mind-numbing pulses of electricity radiated throughout his body, he blacked out.

*

When Jim heard tires screeching and the crashing vehicles, he hoped at least one of the collisions involved Peterson. However, at that moment, he was more concerned with seeing how Scott and Holly were. Limping on, he and Ilse rounded the corner, to find two police vehicles parked. One officer was requesting medical assistance, and Jim could clearly hear the dispatcher saying multiple accidents on RTE 69 was complicating efforts to get emergency vehicles into Poets Corner. Expecting the very worst from the confused situation, Jim told Ilse to stay put while he hobbled forward.

Recognizing Jim, the officer left his vehicle. "Jesus, Cromwell, what happened to your leg? Help's on the way but the commotion up top is delaying things."

"I'm okay, what went down here?"

"It's a mess. One officer down, three civilians inside." He anticipated the next question. "Two inside real bad, don't think they'll make it, and by the way dispatch is cranking out EMS, there's a bunch more on the highway."

Limping to the house, Jim saw the first body at the front door. Lifting the blanket draped over, it was a young police officer, dead from a single shot to the head. Stepping into Scott's living room, the scene was no less bloody.

Scott was on his back; head propped slightly with a pillow, a police officer applying pressure to a chest wound. Holly, bloody from head to knees, was seated on the floor, cradling Poppy in her arms. He'd been at enough accident and murder scenes to know from the amount of blood pooled beneath the women that while

Scott's injury might be serious, Holly's ministrations were more urgently needed by his aunt.

Wincing as he squatted, Jim could see that despite Holly's expertly applied pressure, blood pulsed from an impossible wound in Poppy's abdomen. More telling was the unmistakable pallor of his aunt's skin. As he leaned forward and stroked her cheek, she opened her eyes, and attempted a smile. Jim's face, the concerned forgiving face of her favorite nephew, was the last thing Poppy Cromwell saw.

As Jim's color drained, Holly could see it wasn't merely grief affecting him. Squatting had caused the wound he'd tried to ignore, to bleed heavily. Lowering Poppy to the floor, she went to the laundry closet, and pulled out a pile of towels. Then draping a warming towel around Jim's shoulders, she released his tourniquet, and applied a wad of pressure to his leg.

When his shivering began, sweat beaded his brow and lackluster shadowed his eyes, Holly knew shock had set in. "Jim," she gently suggested, "would you mind talking to Scott. He says he's hanging in, but I don't want him drifting off anywhere." She knew if everybody stayed moderately alert, they'd all get out alive.

"What about you?" he whispered. "There's a nasty gash on your temple."

"It's fine. A head wound always makes you bleed like a stuck pig. Now, talk to Scott."

Holly helped him reposition with his leg elevated on sofa pillows, and applied pressure while Jim sat by his friend.

"Hey bud," Jim whispered. "How's it going; can you open your eyes?" Scott's lead-heavy eyelids opened showing Jim the eyes of someone frightened, but nowhere near death.

"This is a hell of a way to get out of doing the dishes." Scott smiled wanly, and re-closed his eyes.

"Hold on, bud; the EMTs are right behind me." Jim was looking directly out the front door, but couldn't see them, and he took up Scott's hand. "Help me out here, Scott; I'm going to keep talking but I want you to squeeze my hand. Come on, Scott. Can you hear me? One for yes, two for no." Scott's chuckle ended in a cough. "I get it, two for no." What he'd said was silly, but as long as he kept talking, Jim knew his friend would survive.

*

Two EMS crews dragging cabooses of equipment rattled into the house. Scott was loaded into the first ambulance, and it was whining into the distance as Jim, Holly and a concerned Ilse packed into the second. And as it slowed to negotiate the traffic backup from the highway accident, Ilse looked from the rear door window.

"You're having a busy day," she said to the EMT. "What happened here?"

"Word is some guy stole a police cruiser, barreled out the fire exit, and plowed into a Mercedes."

"Looks nasty. Anyone badly hurt?"

"Yeah, one fatal, elderly woman driving the Mercedes, and the guy driving the cruiser trashed his legs."

Jim's smile appeared as a grimace, prompting concern from Ilse. "You okay, Jim?"

"Fine. At least Peterson won't be going anywhere anytime soon."

Chapter Thirty-Five

Jim was still smiling as they wheeled him into the emergency room, and as he looked around, the treatment cubicles appeared remarkably empty considering the carnage that had occurred around Poets Corner. However, in a matter of minutes, wailing sirens and the thrashing clatter of helicopter blades accompanied a deluge of injured.

Holly had lain quietly for several minutes before a nurse dropped in to assess the severity of her wound. Pronouncing it minor, she excused herself to take care of the more severely injured. Feeling little more than throbbing around the sight of her gash, Holly slid from the gurney to sit on the cubicle's guest chair. It might have been a lifetime ago, but she vividly remembered being in the thick of such bloody mayhem, and as she listened to surrounding conversations, it seemed nobody in the immediate area was working on Scott. She wasn't unduly concerned, for given the severity of his wound, Holly expected him to be in an operating room. She decided to wait a while before attempting to find out exactly how badly off he was.

When a second nurse came into Holly's cubicle to retrieve a piece of equipment, she inquired after her fiancé; the nurse said he was in surgery. That much, Holly had guessed. A bullet wound to the chest could mean a host of complications, most of them serious, and when she asked to speak with the attending physician about specifics, she was told she'd have a considerable wait.

Long minutes ticked by, and Holly's anxiety built. Casualties were continuing to arrive, and she told herself that staff was busy dealing with the influx, most sounding in considerably worse shape than her. She forced aside selfish notions, and attempted to alley her fears for Scott's welfare. Digging into the recesses of her memory, she ran through a similar situation in her MASH unit and knew a wound such as his required time to assess. However, her concussed mind couldn't help injecting a dozen scenarios similar to the one after Tug's death. Patently aware of the type of organization Scott had stumbled acrcss, she became frantic that information was being deliberately withheld. And her rational thought evaporated, as delirium set in. Determined to find the truth, Holly staggered to the nurse's station, and demanded to speak with one of the surgical team.

"Look, I know you're busy," she whispered. "I was a nurse myself. I know how it goes."

"Then go back to your cubicle and wait."

"You don't understand. My fiancé has been badly shot and someone needs to tell me how he is."

"I told you, whenever there is someone free. It will take a while."

"You're free. Here, now, talking to me, so go find out."

"I'm busy right now."

Holly's voice was now beyond a whisper. "This is intolerable. Somebody needs to tell me something." Her voice became more agitated, and she began pounding the counter as orderlies ran up to help. As she shrugged off one orderly, a nurse came alongside and before she realized what was happening, the unexpected prick of a sedating injection had her drifting into submission.

*

Holly didn't know how long she'd spent in an opiate-induced haze, but when she opened her eyes, an intern was with her.

"You seem to have made quite a statement with the nurses," he said. "We don't usually have to sedate people without giving them treatment."

"I just wanted information about my fiancé," Holly croaked. "I was a nurse, and I saw how serious the wound was. I simply want to know if he made it."

"Ah, so you did the initial work immediately at the scene. Good, you probably saved him from bleeding out."

"He's alive then?"

"And kicking; he was asking how you were until the anesthetic took over." He lowered his voice, "I'll take that as tacit permission to tell you how he is."

"Thank you, doctor."

"It was serious, but you knew that. And the bullet glanced off his sternum and lodged in the pectoralis major. It didn't penetrate the chest cavity, no damage to vital organs, and thanks to your quick action, he lost a remarkably small amount of blood. The bullet came out clean with no fragmentation, and while he'll have to forego golf for a while, he should be just fine."

"Can I see him?"

"I'll see if I can get you five minutes in recovery before he's transferred to a room upstairs. Now, about you—are you going to lie quietly or do we have to zap you again?"

"No, doctor, I have the information I want. I'll behave."

He patted her hand. "Good. I'll send someone in to deal with that laceration."

Holly relaxed, and as she lay on the bed, turning her ring about her finger, she became aware that the intensity of the ER had abated. A nurse came in, removed the temporary dressing, and washed antiseptic over Holly's face. And her tears flowed. But they were not from pain. She was thinking about her dear Poppy, who'd paid the ultimate price for her intervention. Dear Poppy, who'd not only opened up her home and her heart to Holly, but had, on so many occasions, shared her determination. A determination that hadn't died with her. For as Holly had cradled her dearest friend bleeding and broken, she passed on something she said would defeat the man who had killed her. Pulling a gold chain from her pants pocket, Holly rolled the tiny key attached between her fingers.

*

The gash in Jim's thigh required several stitches. However, his pride was wounded considerably more than his person, and he berated himself for thinking a single cop monitoring the gate could keep out a man as resourceful as Bryce Peterson. At the bloody end of another violent confrontation, he couldn't help asking himself, *what the hell was I thinking?* Then it passed. Mayhem was a negative part of his job, an unfortunate adjunct to the man he had become, and no matter how he might wish it otherwise, pain and violence came with the territory. He couldn't stop being a cop, didn't know how to undo his training, and wasn't about to quit doing something he believed in with every fiber of his being. One time, however, he wished someone he cared for didn't have to witness it first hand.

As soon as he was able to put weight on his leg, Jim requested the nurse fetch Ilse. He was loss-of-blood tired, shock-sweated, and with one jeans leg cut apart and the other soaked in blood, probably looked a lot worse than he felt.

Ilse came through the curtain, and stopped.

He held out his arms to her. "Hug me, woman," he demanded. "I won't break."

"I don't want to hurt you."

"You'll hurt me more by staying over there. Come here."

She moved in close and kissed him with a desperation he'd not felt before. "I was so worried about you." She pushed away from him. "I've been out there for hours, and the nurses wouldn't tell me anything."

"That's because they're only allowed to speak to immediate family."

"I sleep with you; I'm closer than immediate family."

"Not to the almighty medical bureaucracy."

Ilse rested her head on his shoulder. "They wouldn't tell me about Holly, either."

"Take it from me, she's doing fine. I heard her yelling at a nurse when we arrived. And rest assured you weren't the only one going nuts. Nobody would talk to her about Scott."

"Is Scott going to be all right?"

"From what I could hear, yes. We'll probably be able to see him later."

"I want to go home."

"That won't happen for a while. I have a mountain of paperwork before I can leave. I can have an officer escort you."

"Don't mean that home. I mean Germany."

A nurse disturbed them. "Excuse me, Officer Cromwell. Your friend Holly is going to see Mr. Morgan, if you'd like to accompany her."

"Well?" Jim looked at Ilse, who nodded.

*

When the nurse brought in a wheelchair, Jim reluctantly sat, and Ilse pushed him to join an orderly who had Holly in another chair. With that, the caravan wound its way along a labyrinth of undistinguishable pastel corridors until they finally arrived at recovery.

Scott was groggy but awake, and his face lit up upon seeing Holly. "Thank God," he croaked. "I thought I'd lost you again."

"You were the one who took a bullet."

"And you would have, too, in the head, if it wasn't for Poppy. She came through for you, darling, she really did."

"I know."

He smiled. It was her stock answer when she was emotionally invested but didn't want to show it.

"You know, Jim," Holly continued. "It was clear Peterson came to the house to either persuade Scott to join his venture or get rid of him, but I'm not sure Poppy knew about the last piece. Also, when I got nasty and challenged her about Phoenix, she genuinely didn't know what had happened."

Jim raised an eyebrow. "You don't need to sugarcoat it, Holly; be honest. I loved my aunt to pieces, but even I find it hard to believe she'd worked with this guy for years and had no idea what he planned for Scott."

"I'm sorry, Jim; she sort of lost direction after your uncle died. I knew she had a funky one-sided thing for this Peterson guy, but I'm at a loss as to what happened to put her under the spell of such a monster. All I can say is, I've been in a similar situation, and love is a powerful drug. Sometimes you can't see the wood for the trees."

"Love is blind, eh?"

"When you say it like that it sounds trite, but you have to think about the type of woman your Aunt Poppy was. She lived life on the edge; pulled everything she could out of every second and never looked back. She lived for the new experience, which resulted in her having a different level of acceptance than most of us, a skewed sense of right and wrong. Getting rid of somebody she didn't know wasn't a thing that would weigh on her conscience. She wasn't a bad person; God knows she's given me so much. I think she simply felt whatever Peterson did was acceptable, as long as he didn't hurt anyone she loved. I have to tell you, she leaped to my defense like a tigress when he aimed that gun at me."

"What about me? That creep almost forced me off a cliff."

"That wasn't anything to do with her. In fact, I'm sure she knew nothing about it until it was over. Look into your heart; you absolutely know she wouldn't condone that. You were the one honest, decent thing she could count on in her life, and she adored you." Holly handed him the chain from around Poppy's neck. "She gave me this key for you. She said it's a safety deposit box at the Bank of America. I didn't know about this one."

He examined the key. "Did she say what was in it?"

"Insurance, in case Peterson turned on her. And the last thing she said was 'tell Jim I'm sorry about the policeman.'"

"What did she mean by that?"

Holly shrugged and turned away. Jim rubbed the key between his fingers and felt his aunt's love. They had been so close, he knew no matter what she had done, he could do nothing but forgive her.

*

It was more than eight hours after the initial incident when an unmarked police vehicle deposited the walking wounded at Scott's house. The police circus was winding down, and as only a small part of the house was compromised, the friends had been allowed to occupy the rear. Entering through the sunroom, Holly was pleased to see nothing had disturbed the tranquility of the indoor garden. However, the presence of yellow police tape around the lounge ensured there was no mistaking what had occurred there.

Within the hour as Holly slept in her room and Jim was in bed, an unearthly calm overtook the house. And Ilse felt a desperate need to be with Jim. She laid down the book she'd tried to get into several times, and crept into their bedroom. She jumped when Jim spoke.

"Hi *fräulein*, what's up?"

Sitting as close as she could, Ilse placed a hand on his chest. "I was alone out there and suddenly got scared. Why aren't you sleeping?"

"Too much on my mind."

"You caught the guy, it's all over now."

"I wish it were. Now we have to prove everything we suspect."

"That can wait until your leg is better."

He laughed. "Not my style."

"You have a serious wound."

"Gashed my leg. It's no big deal."

"Weren't you scared?" she asked.

"About what?"

"Dying."

"From a gash on the leg?"

"Jim, stop it; you know what I mean. That maniac could have killed you."

"But he didn't."

"And that makes it all right. Now you're being deliberately. . ." she jumped from the bed, and began to pace. "*Schizer*, I can't think of the word."

"Come here. I need a hug."

"How can you be so casual about all this?"

"It's how I deal."

"Well, I'm not sure I can."

"Honestly I'm fine; the leg is nothing." He could see she wasn't convinced. "Ilse, listen to me. Cops have to be this way; I have to be this way. I can't fear for my life every time I take on a case. What I do is dangerous, I know that, and I'm cautious and respectful of a higher power, and do everything I can to keep from getting hurt. But shit happens, and I couldn't do my job if I was afraid of every nutcase out there. Sometimes the only way to survive is to be crazier than the crazy."

"That's all very well to say. But how am I supposed to function with you out there doing this macho Rambo bullshit, not knowing whether the next time I see you will be in the morgue?"

"You have to trust me. You have to trust I know what I'm doing, and you have to trust in something none of us has any control over."

"You mean like God?"

"If that's what you need to call it. Not exactly my cup of tea; I've seen too much bad stuff. Between you and me, I feel if I do the right thing, I'm protected."

"Well that's just not good enough for me. I don't want to trust your life, my life, the life of anyone I love, to a belief in doing the right thing."

Jim had heard this before, and didn't like where the conversation was going. "It's all I've got."

"You've got me."

"I'm not sure I do. Sure, I have your body. But what about your mind, your heart, your soul? Are you saying I should change who I am, because it makes you feel better? Are you asking me to give up everything I believe in, because it makes you more comfortable? Or maybe this attitude is simply an excuse because you don't want to be with me anymore."

"I'm not sure what I want."

"Maybe you're the one who needs to get some sleep. This has been a traumatic day for you, though in my defense, I did warn you our being together wouldn't be easy for either of us."

"I'm going home."

"So again, you're running away."

"Why do you say that?" She was angry he understood her so completely.

"Because it seems to be what you do."

She turned to go, and as he jumped from the bed to follow her, a sharp pain coursed through his body. "Jesus H.—"

"Are you insane?" Ilse yelled. "Get back in bed."

"Not unless you're with me. I'm never going to bed again unless you're with me." His eyes had glazed in a show of emotion she hadn't seen before.

"That's the anesthetic talking."

"Didn't have any."

"They stitched up your leg without anesthetic?"

"I'm a tough guy. Now come here and help me before I faint."

Ilse stepped forward to support him, and he dragged her onto the bed beside him.

"Thought you were in pain?"

"Not any more. You really can't leave me, you know that."

"Why?"

"Because I need you."

"You don't need anybody, you have your work; it gives you everything you need."

"Doesn't give me this." He locked his mouth on hers and

despite the searing pain in his thigh, Jim showed her the one thing his job could never give him.

*

Jim watched with mixed feelings as the British Airways jet soared into the blue on the first leg of Ilse's journey home. He winced as he remembered their last heated conversation when she'd accused him of being uncaring because he'd so quickly come to terms with her leaving. It wasn't that. He'd simply been through it several times before. And as the airplane disappeared from view, he recalled the hours they'd spent talking about her feelings, his job, and the pressures of being a policeman's significant other. Confused, and for some time, hurt, he knew in his heart she'd never understand why he immersed himself in a case to the detriment of a relationship. And after that, it was easy for him to suppose it was her own insecurity, which prevented her from coping.

As Jim walked from the terminal, he anticipated seeing Ilse if she testified at Peterson's trial, but even if he did not; he was comfortable with his decision to choose his job over matters of the heart. Resigned and eager to get back to his investigation, he left Sky Harbor and returned to the only woman who gave him unconditional support: Lady Justice.

Chapter Thirty-Six

Jim's temporary office in Prescott Valley's police department had the convenience of white-board walls. Scott's code was illustrated on one, another held the personal statistics of Poets Corner residents, and a third, the names and translations of companies associated with the community. Sitting back on a well-worn leather chair, leg elevated on a desk drawer that wouldn't close, Jim re-read Bryce Peterson's version of the tragic events in Poets Corner. Amused and somewhat troubled by the spin he'd put on the entire episode, the story nevertheless sounded plausible, and anyone reviewing it without benefit of Scott and Holly's statements might well believe everything that was written.

Peterson began by saying Poppy Cromwell had confessed to him about a long-standing affair with Scott Morgan. Upon discovering her best friend, Holly, was to marry Scott, Poppy felt she must intervene. She went to the house to warn Holly about the sort of man with whom she was involved, and he, Peterson, merely accompanied Poppy, his friend and business associate, for moral support. To his surprise, the meeting was not amicable, and Scott Morgan flatly denied any relationship with Poppy. A hostile argument ensued, and the anger escalated considerably until Poppy produced a gun. Peterson handled it, while trying to pry it from her, and during their struggle, both Scott Morgan and Holly Winthrop were shot.

After the shootings, suspecting his friend's derangement would cause her to turn the gun on him; Peterson knocked her to the ground and fled. He was at the front door when Poppy fired another shot, which hit a police officer entering the house. The following bullet flew past Peterson's hip, hitting the fuel tank of their borrowed Cadillac, parked out front. After being momentarily engulfed by the resulting explosion, he was desperate to save himself and jumped in the police cruiser to get help. The last thing he remembered was the collision on Route 69.

As Jim unconsciously rubbed at the ache in his injured leg, Bob Black appeared at his door.

"Hi, boss," he said, holding up a CD. "Finally got the okay to open your aunt's box. I think I'd have gotten into Fort Knox easier."

"Hey, B-ster, come on in; I'm just going over this load of crap Peterson's suits put out."

Bob's derisive snort spoke volumes. "If that leg's bothering you, go home and rest. We can do this later."

"Nah, if I go home, I'll be on the phone every five minutes. What did you find?"

Bob placed the CD before Jim. "Just this."

"Have you run it?"

"Didn't help me much. I released the password so you can get right in; see if it means anything to you."

Jim slipped the CD in his computer. "It looks like somebody has a bit of a God complex."

"According to your aunt, this will completely expose Peterson. Considering his ego, the style is about par for the course, and while some things bounce out at me, I'm not sure a pompous piece of prose is exactly what we're looking for."

"Did you send a transcript to Scott?"

"Yeh, but nothing gelled. Maybe if I put it on a board, we'll have an epiphany?"

"I'm the crippled cop, so I'll read, you write."

From the very beginning, from outside, come, you faithful ones, not for love of one's country but from the heart, with criminal intent. May there be no envy or malice, no offense intended, simply attend to your work, between ourselves, as a favor, not as something owed. And in actual fact within our walls, whether you are willing or not, with full authority, I being the judge, will defend. Standing alone against the world diametrically opposed beholding the sign, I came, I saw, and I conquered, and by that fact, in my own way designed it, and will profit by it . . . 2321512.

When Bob was finished, he stood back. "Very poetic when you see it up on a wall. Do I pass it on to the defense?"

"Not yet; I'd like to get some sort of a handle on it before the lawyers give me ninety million obscure interpretations."

Bob wagged a finger at his colleague. "Withholding evidence? Bad mojo, boss."

"You can bad-mojo my ass. Besides, what's that quaint Americanism about asking first?"

"I'd rather ask for forgiveness than permission?"

"Bingo. Now go get some coffee."

Bob returned with coffee and cookies.

Jim smiled. "Alison in records?"

"She thinks I need feeding. They're pretty good, try one." Bob could almost hear wheels turning as Jim munched on the cookie. "You got something?"

"Well, yeah. The number means zero, which we already know was Peterson's nickname in Vietnam. My aunt said this would bring him down, so we definitely know it's about him. Some of the lines are familiar: 'as a favor, not as something owed,' and 'no offense intended.' Remember what Ilse translated?"

Bob nodded. "Dude, look at the list of companies controlling things in Poets Corner."

"So, we know Peterson's into Latin and is a poetry nut, but the phrasing on this thing reads like a contract."

Bob smiled. "Right-a-mundo, that's what it is. Didn't Carol uncover a bunch of Latin shit from the meeting Peterson hosted in Cabo San Lucas?"

"Yeah, hand me the green file."

Bob held up an olive drab and a lime green aloft.

"Lime green. Okay, give me a second. Here they are. Abextra, from outside; Nolens Volens, whether willing or not; and Judice, I being judge. Jesus, could this epistle give us the names of all Peterson's companies?"

"Flip the screen, I'll check something." Bob's fingers flew across the keyboard. "I've done some phishing on the three you just mentioned, just have to pull up my foreign bases. . . Sicily, Australia, and Russia. If I break this thing down, are we to assume the Cormorant Club is part of a worldwide something?"

"Let's find out," added Jim. "Isolate the phrases we know, put 'em up on the board, and let's see what else floats. Dang, where's Ilse when I need her; who else do we know speaks Latin?"

"Well, I got one here—" Bob pointed at a common Latin phrase.

"No brownie points for that one, kiddo. *Veni, vidi, vici*—I came, I saw, I conquered. Add it to the known entities board."

Chapter Thirty-Seven

After his release from hospital, Scott wallowed in Holly's presence, having almost forgotten how perfect it was to be with just her. It seemed like weeks since they'd been alone, and as she came to him with coffee and cake, as natural as any housewife might be, he pulled her onto his lap.

"Careful," she giggled. "You'll damage something."

"Don't care. Want my women next to me, and that's that."

"Well, be careful, no wriggling about."

"So when?"

"When what?"

"Will I be okay to wriggle about, or do anything else that takes my fancy?"

"Do you ever think of anything else?"

"Not when you're around."

"You could just lie there and let me do the work."

"You're killing me here. Now what are we talking, another day, two?"

"You're impossible. However, I did ask the doctor about that."

"Ah-ha, you hussy. I knew you'd crack first."

"Did not. You made a pass in the hospital."

"Doesn't count, that was the medication talking."

"Like I believe that. Anyway, he said, be careful, and if you feel a twinge, stop and change position."

"Oh, God, that sounds better by the minute . . . so let's go."

"What, now?"

"Yes, now. It's been a century. I'm as horny as all get out." Scott was startled upon hearing the front door. "Foiled again."

"It's only me," shouted Jim.

Holly giggled. "Hi Jim. We're in the sunroom."

"So, Scott," Jim said as he strode into the room. "You ready to start work? We're hitting some glitches with the code. Naturally we have the basics in the system, but any time there's an anomaly, the whole thing grinds to a halt until we get Bob involved. He's got vital computer geek stuff to take care of, so if you could lend a hand on the code end, we'd really appreciate your input."

Holly put a hand on Scott's arm. "You know, Jim, I'm not sure he's well enough to be out and about quite yet. He's not as young as he used to be, and it takes longer for us old types to—"

"Hey," complained Scott, "speak for yourself."

"I am speaking for myself; I've a vested interest in you getting better sooner rather than later." She ran a finger down the side of his face.

"Whoa, mama," said Scott, grabbing at air as she jumped out of reach. "Holly's sort of right, Jim, so how about if I'm on call? I hear you guys have pitched a camp at the clubhouse; I could be available on the phone or by email and if anything bizarre comes up, I can probably manage to stagger down the street."

"Sounds great if Nurse Holly agrees."

Holly nodded. "Typical men—schoolboys, every last one of you. I'm going about my business, so play nice. And Jim, he has sutures, so don't get him too excited."

Scott looked over his shoulder. "After you just—"

"That was a taste of what's to come."

"Do I have to hose you down?" Jim rolled his eyes.

Holly smiled, ruffled Scott's hair and left the men to their business.

"She's something," said Scott, smoothing his hair. "So how deep have you gotten into this mess?"

"We thought we were doing pretty well, but the more we dig, the more convoluted it gets."

"No surprise there."

"Right, so let's start in Poets Corner. Of the twenty-four households here, we've uncovered enough additional evidence to charge four males and one female with murder in regard to fatal traffic accidents. And we're able to re-open the case on Chuck Westlake's murder/suicide."

"I thought my sis and brother-in-law's killer was dead."

"Not exactly . . ."

"What the hell does that mean?"

"We're pretty sure Susan Josephs is the one who forced the Westlake's car off the road."

"Susan Josephs, my neighbor next door? Jeez, she's a total harridan, but her husband Kyle is one of the only people here who was actually decent to me. Besides, didn't Charlotte Messing say it was Sarah somebody-or-other?"

"Maitland; used to live on Browning. She was in the car, but when we dug deeper, we found she wasn't alone. In fact, she wasn't driving; Susan was."

"Holy jeez," said Scott, "how'd that come about?"

"When we ran background checks, we found Susan Josephs is Sarah Maitland's step-daughter, and according to the snippets of information we've been getting from disgruntled spouses, Sarah Maitland was able to stay on here after her husband died because Susan and her husband Kyle, both ex-cops, agreed to work for Bryce Peterson."

"And the Cormorant Club."

"Exactly; I guess Bryce Peterson has a heart after all."

"Believe that and I've got a bridge I can sell you. But you realize the Josephs can't have had anything to do with the current situation. They went on vacation weeks ago."

Jim smiled. "I know; we've been one step behind them from here to Connecticut. Apparently Susan has a gambling problem and left a trail of unpaid debt from Albuquerque to Mount Pocono. We have a strong suspicion she was involved in a fatal hit-and-run in Boonville, right outside the casino, and she and Kyle are also suspected of fleeing the scene of another motor vehicle accident in Connecticut's Wooster Mountain State Park."

"You don't mean they tried the same trick of forcing someone off the road."

"Seems if it ain't broke, they don't need to fix it."

Scott smiled. "Ballsy."

"You better believe it. Fortunately, the Connecticut driver was ballsy, too. He bailed out just before his car went over the edge. And as he rolled into a hollow, he noticed the offending vehicles backend sported . . ."

"A black on gold Cormorant sticker. Jeez, how dumb are these people? Ditch the damn stickers next time."

"Arrogance has its own set of rules," agreed Jim. "Anyway, we've had the word out on the stickers since we began this odyssey, so when we finally caught up with them at the Mohegan Sun in Uncasville, local police had already pulled them in for questioning."

"Who was driving this time?"

"The driver who was hit couldn't say, and for a minute it was up in the air. Naturally, we split 'em up, applied a little pressure and almost immediately Susan said Kyle was driving, and despite her pleading, it was he who made the decision to keep on going after the accident."

"Spousal loyalty obviously not her thing. You buy it?"

Jim shook his head. "Not a chance. The two of them were cops, and they know how the game is played. We couldn't help being skeptical when she broke so quickly. Then when we moved to Kyle and told him what she said, it clearly wasn't the first time she'd dumped him in it. He blew seven sorts of pissed-off, and spilled his guts. Once he got talking, I actually felt sorry for him; Kyle Josephs is not such a bad guy. Turns out he never wanted to be in Poets Corner—his wife was the driving force."

"That much I know. She's the neighbor from hell, a real dragon lady."

"A dragon who knew how to use her claws. According to Kyle, Susan's father Frank Maitland was fully aware she wasn't exactly a true blue cop, so when he got involved in Poets Corner, he told her all about the Cormorant Club. He said he was sharing the information to cover Sarah Maitland's ass after he died, but instead of keeping the secret, Susan persuaded Kyle they should try to get in here. She thought it would be easy money to support her addiction, but when Kyle learned the rules, he wanted none of it. He admitted to being too scared to blow the whistle, and by the time old man Maitland died, Susan had buried them with her gambling. Kyle was also faced with the specter of the widowed mother moving in without a penny to her name. He told Susan to use what she knew, and with enough leverage to get herself an interview with Peterson, she promised the two of them would do anything to be free of responsibility for her mother. The rest is history."

"So when my family was killed, why did Charlotte think it was Susan's mother driving to Jerome?"

"Because Susan planned it that way; she convinced her cancer-riddled mother that this would be her last opportunity to do something to help her only child make a better life."

"So just in case the murder/suicide thing didn't stick, she'd covered her ass by setting up her mom."

"Correct," said Jim.

"Now I know why I never had kids."

Jim smiled. "Some of us turned out all right. Anyway, as I said, we've been using your code very successfully and have managed to isolate a further dozen incidents by joining existing data on the Cormorant Club's meetings, with new stuff. And we've uncovered enough evidence to charge two committee members with accessory before the fact and obstruction of justice."

"Colonel Wright and Allie McCallium?"

"How did you know?"

"Process of elimination, my dear Watson. Most of the original committee members we know. Duke Nyson, Nathan Messing, Joe Beech are dead or out of commission; ergo, who's left? Besides, they were the two that got my goat in the first place and started this whole snowball rolling; something had to stick to them. What about other residents, are they talking?"

"Not a peep. We get the occasional tidbit from a spouse, but generally they're clueless as to what's been going on. I'm amazed how two people can live together for as long as these old timers have, and know virtually nothing about what each other did all day."

"Sorts of makes you understand how Peterson could so easily get this thing off the ground. You know whatever you charge these seniors with won't make a wit of difference to him. The individuals concerned might protect him by banding together, refusing to give statements and stoically resigning themselves to whatever fate awaits them; he'll spend his time devising ways to drop them deeper in the shit, while he comes up smelling like a rose."

"Sort of par for the course; he wasn't the first, and God knows he won't be the last. All we can do is make what we have stick."

"So, as he was dispatching Cormorants right up to his crash, we've established Peterson has steel cojones. What other incidents have there been since then?"

"It's amazing; I don't understand how he can be up to his neck in alligators, look as guilty as sin, and still get people to do his dirty work. We actually received a bunch more information from. . ." Jim consulted his notes, "Cheryl Black—"

"Husband John was military intelligence right?"

"Yeah, but he's in YRMC hospice now with an inoperable brain tumor. She said he doesn't have long and wanted to set the record straight before he goes. Sadly, it's not good. He was attempting to escape a road-rage incident, lost control of his vehicle, and killed three bystanders. While it was recorded as an accident, in the light of the new information we uncovered, it most definitely was deliberate."

"As he's so sick, do you still charge him?"

"In his case, it's about getting justice for the families; we're letting the California boys sort it out."

"Jeez, what a mess."

"That it is. Bob's frantic data-matching also turned up a planned hit in Washington. We got to that one before anything happened."

"Yay, one for the good guys."

"A very small one," said Jim, smiling, "Jake Carmichael, formerly with the FBI, was pulled in and immediately elected to cooperate. He even had his wife turn over a taped conversation. His rationale was 'once a Fed, always a Fed,' and as he didn't actually commit the crime, he felt it was in his best interests to talk to us."

"Any idea who was on the other of his taped message?"

"We hadn't a clue. But as she seems to know most everything about Poets Corner, we ran it by Bubbles Nyson. She identified the voice as that of June Preston. She and another resident, Zack Mitchelman, haven't been seen in the community since the day after the assault on your house, and we have warrants out. Apart from that, we have three individuals new to the community. They've been cleared of any wrongdoing relating to the Cormorant Club, and have been happy to share their joining experiences."

"Were we right about Cabo being recruitment central?"

"Yeah, but while these last three were in Mexico, none met Peterson. They were interviewed by Poppy, and finalized papers with attorney Shapler."

"You've been real busy bees," said Scott, picking up Jim's notes. "But I didn't hear anything about Ben Watkins. Where'd he go after Charlotte's house exploded?"

"Guess."

"Mexico?"

"Bingo. A search of airline manifests found his name on a first-class passenger list to Cabo San Lucas, the day after. However, all attempts to locate him in Mexico have proven fruitless. We were half-lucky with the scuzz-ball attorney Shapler. Miami PD stopped him boarding a flight from Miami to La Paz. He was wanted in Florida for embezzling several million dollars from his legal partnership."

"Who embezzled millions of dollars?" asked Holly, from behind Jim.

"Your favorite attorney," said Scott.

"Marvin-the-sanctimonious-prat-Shapler?"

Scott nodded.

"Hallelujah," she said, punching the air. "Couldn't have happened to a nicer person. I hope you bust his ass from here to Katmandu and take all his money."

"Don't hold back, Holly," said Jim, smiling.

"Oh, you don't know the half of it. This is a major cause for celebration. I've opened some wine, so come on, dinner is served."

"Now you cook dinner?" said a surprised Scott.

"I've learned to do a lot of things while you've been in the hospital."

Scott smiled. "Anything I might enjoy after dinner?"

"Good grief," interrupted Jim. "Do the Penthouse people know about you two?"

"Not yet," smiled Holly.

Chapter Thirty-Eight

The police spent countless hours with Poets Corner residents over the next several weeks. Those spouses identified as being unconnected with the Cormorant Club pressed to be allowed to leave, but were told association made their continued residence mandatory. Only Bubbles Nyson and Sandy Beech, who'd rendered considerable help to Jim's team, were permitted to go to approved relatives until they were needed. However, when Bubbles attempted to take the nest egg her husband left her, she was told it came from an illegally funded account in the Cayman Islands and had been confiscated. She was not happy.

The residents of Poets Corner directly associated with the Cormorant Club remained resolute in their loyalty to Bryce Peterson. It was as if they expected his reach to extend beyond his hospital bed and eradicate all evidence of their wrongdoing. And during extensive interviewing, while protecting their benefactor, several of the elderly felons, inadvertently exposed the leading part that Allie McCallium and Colonel Carl Wright played in the organization. Bob's diligent cross-referencing of both community and Cormorant Club minutes quickly established both were at every meeting, and each subsequently admitted to having met Bryce Peterson on many occasions. Nevertheless, they doggedly upheld their belief that he—and they—were members of a philanthropic organization dedicated to giving retired government workers a better standard of living in their golden years. Moreover, when questioned about the activities of the Cormorant Club, neither wavered from their assertion that it was a legitimate ornithological fellowship, which on occasion provided members with field trips to exercise their passion. Both were held in custody as flight risks, pending further investigation.

Chapter Thirty-Nine

When Bob finally broke through the multiple encryptions of Poppy's CD, he could barely wait to present his findings to the team.

"As Jim anticipated," he began, "the linguist took Peterson's epistle apart pretty easily. She pointed out it wasn't written by someone who actually studied Latin, and it read like a bunch of random phrases cobbled together, but that isn't significant. I told her we weren't looking to decipher the scriptures, as long as she pulled some names from it, she'd earn her fee. Anyway, your aunt was sort of right, Jim. What we need is all here. I already ran the names; they're all foreign companies, and while I've got preliminary data for you to look at, I need more time to dig the deeply embedded info out. The ones I give you here," Bob handed out lists, "we already know a good deal about."

Jim smiled. "Looks like there are twenty-four companies, same as the number of houses in Poets Corner." Jim looked at Carol and back to Bob. "Coincidence or meaning?"

"Still working on that, only mentioned it because I know how the coincidence thing bugs you and Scott. So, let's review the companies with data. First, I made information requests through normal channels, but when I encountered reluctance to share info, and in a couple of cases got responses which didn't remotely jive with what I expected, I used the expertise of 'proctologist Bob' and slipped in the rear."

"Do I want to know about that?"

"Best not." Bob couldn't miss the expression on Jim's face. "Don't worry, by the time the defense asks me, I'll be a hundred and ten percent kosher." Jim smiled and Bob continued. "On the surface, all the companies appear legitimate, but they have such severely sophisticated protection, it got me wondering. I mean, dude, it's a mess."

"Maybe that's all Peterson wanted," said Carol. "Discourage the looky-loos and buy some time from the experts."

"Doesn't matter to me, I can get into anything, given enough time. In fact, when I uncovered programs encrypted within programs, potholes, and pitfalls, the old noggin near exploded; I knew something huge was hidden. Anyway, Guillermo Rialto heads Abextra, and amongst other things runs a local newspaper in Sicily called *Il Corvus*."

"He's an international businessman," said Carol. "I'd expect diversity."

"Hold that thought a minute, next, Patterson Booth behind Nolens Volens; he has similar publishing aspirations in Australia, with a news-sheet called *Pica*. And finally Fiers Antipov of Judice; he's really testing me, didn't get squat on him—yet. Anyway, the publications connected with the other two are radical underground periodicals popular with young people, and anti-government wannabes."

"So?" said Carol. "We have a bunch of those rags here."

"I know, *Enemy Mine* and *People Power* to name but two. However, Corvus, loosely translated, means raven, and Pica is magpie. When I scanned some of the other companies, I found periodicals that translate to Albatross, Sandpiper and Hawk. Didn't get much info so far, but the word is they're a means of recruiting mercenaries."

"You mean like *Universal Soldier*?"

"That's what it looks like. I'll continue spoofing, but I'll need a bit longer."

Jim tapped the papers against his leg. "I wonder if these rags are just blowing smoke, or really do recruit killers."

"But Jim," said Carol, "the people we interviewed from the Cormorant Club indicated they were recruited by word of mouth."

"I know; but there's more than one way to skin a cat. Maybe the free weekend in Cabo is simply Peterson's way of doing things.

Get onto our European friends; see if they have records of anything like the Cormorant Club, pictures of accidents where the cars have stickers, anything which might establish that Peterson and his merry men are a small cog in a much bigger wheel."

"You got it." Carol hurried off.

"Bob, are these rags available openly on the web? Can we get copies?"

"Already on it," said Bob, "I couldn't get at them without using valuable time, so I have friends pulling examples, and they'll be transmitted by this evening."

"Excellent; whatever it takes, keep going. I'll release the CD to the defense, tell 'em I just found it in a bunch of my aunt's papers. I'll also take the opportunity to arrange a chat with Peterson."

Chapter Forty

When Jim returned to his office, a smiling Bob was waiting.

"Well at least you're happy," said Jim. "What gives?"

"As requested, I ran all the companies through the wringer, and found some doozies. Also received this newsletter." He held up a periodical. "Found the usual ads for security guards, bodyguards, and such like, but spotted these." Handing Carol and Jim photocopies, Bob had highlighted several one-line ads.

"Security specialists wanted, no age limit, housing, generous benefits," said Carol. "So that sounds Poets Corner-ish, but how is it going to lock Peterson in? We already have our killer community, but no one directly involved will stand against him."

"I'm getting to that; I contacted all the periodicals numbers and they're all out of service."

"Kicking us back to Square One," said Jim.

"Not exactly, because I blew a bunch of heavy-duty favors on the newsletters and when I got squat, it made me mad. So mad, I went back to the CD."

"But you scoured the thing and while the epistle helped, it didn't expose Peterson," said Carol.

"Hold your horses. You don't wanna see a computer nerd with his back against the wall. Not pretty, and we bite—get it?—bite, for byte, computers and all."

Jim looked at Carol and couldn't help grinning. Bob was clearly on a roll, so they let him have his fifteen minutes.

"Anyhoo," Bob continued, "I sat there for a couple of hours letting it flow over me. I knew Jim's aunt wouldn't have said the disc would bring Peterson down if the information wasn't all there."

"We established that hours ago," chipped in an impatient Carol.

Bob ignored her and went on. “Suddenly, I realized I'd been concentrating so hard on the epistle and its companies, I'd overlooked 2321512.”

“Zero; so how does Peterson's nickname help?” asked Carol.

“Embedded files, my impatient friend—deep, deep chasms, stuff from the under wall. I tried every combination of numbers, zero words, words that mean zero, sound like zero, are zero, until kapow—I had this thought. The dude is obsessed with birds, poetry, Latin, the whole spiel, and this file was primarily a contract between him and all the other groups. What word would a guy like Peterson deem symbolic?”

They looked at him blankly.

“Thought so, but me being the B-ster and all, I entered the word ‘chavish’. And kapow, the freakin' file popped open.”

“What the hell is chavish?” Jim asked.

“The sound of a bunch of birds chirping and singing all at once,” Bob smugly replied. “Anyhoo, the file was mostly pictures.” Bob threw a pile of black and whites on the desk.

Jim's eyes lit up. “Well I'll be a—will you look at these.” He handed some to Carol.

“One of the file names was caboexec,” said Bob.

“Of course,” said Jim, “the meeting Duke Nyson noted, and holy shit, thank you Aunt Poppy. I recognize Peterson, Poppy, Rick Nyland, and judging by the demeanor of this trio,” Jim showed the picture he had to Carol, “we probably have Rialto, Booth, and Antipov. I'm guessing the others are bird fanciers in Peterson's other companies. Poppy was right, once we identify everybody, we'll have direct and irrefutable connections every which way we want.”

Bob blew on his knuckles, and rubbed them down his shirt, and Carol smiled big enough to light up the room.

Jim gave him a fist bump. “Not bad, B-ster, not bad at all. Man, this is wild, now there's no holding back. Carol, get back on to Scotland Yard, Interpol, the Sûreté, YAMAM, MVS, the

Masons, any damn agency you can think of; I want passport pictures, driving permits, photo IDs, names, addresses, inside leg measurements if we have to, and let's get 'em quick."

Carol fanned the four pictures she had in her hand. "Okay, but before you get all macho doo-daddy on me, we might find some joy a little closer to home. See these?"

Bob leaned across. "Oh mama, she's something. Wife of, maybe?"

"Not a chance. Remember in Cabo, when the receptionist was talking to us, she said even when wives were there, Peterson brought women in."

"So she's a hooker?" Jim took the pictures from Carol.

"Not just any hooker; I know this one. High class, agency darling, busted her about a year ago."

"You remember every hooker you bust?" said Bob.

Carol smiled. "It was a sting, and before she knew who I was, she offered me a job. Said she had exclusive clientele, a thousand bucks a trick, traveled the world, private jet, first class all the way."

Jim could hardly believe their luck. "This is too sweet, know where to find her?"

"Scootch over, Bob, need a quick look at the files." Within seconds, Carol found what she needed. "Eleanora Karen MacQuaid, professionally known as Karen Q; Las Fuentes, 1486 East Chaparral, Scottsdale, Arizona. Guess you two get to reach out to the world, while I head south."

Chapter Forty-One

After the guard strapped down the bulky electric wheelchair, the prison ambulance set off for the courthouse, and during the ride, Peterson contemplated the simplicity of his companies' wrap-up. They and Poets Corner had been dumped for cash, thanks to an arrangement he'd long since set in place, and the new owners had already transferred funds to a series of anonymous offshore accounts. They had cost a small fortune to set up, but even with Jim Cromwell's extensive resources, they would take so long to identify, he'd have siphoned the bulk elsewhere. It was at such deliciously triumphant times Peterson missed Rick; the only person with whom he could let down his guard. But no matter, Cromwell's case was flawed, his lawyers couldn't hold a candle to the Peterson team, and he'd soon be a free man. Then with tens of millions at his disposal, he could buy an army of Ricks to have a beer with and keep him amused.

As the ambulance pulled up at the courthouse, the radio crackled. "Take Peterson straight into the judge's chambers," it said. "There's been an incident at the safe house." Peterson knew exactly what had happened. The house was compromised, and though police officers had fired shots, which generated some residual heat, someone had efficiently executed his favorite hooker and the female cop living with her. A self-satisfied smile crossed Peterson's lips while a momentary pang of guilt flashed, *Pity about the female cop,* he thought. *She was a fighter, single-handedly putting her kids through school. Still, it's never personal. Absit invidia.*

Resigning himself to the final minutes of his captivity, Peterson mentally applauded the new circumstances he'd created, knowing they made the rescheduling of his trial inevitable. His plan was simple and perfect; he'd wheel inside, the judge would order a postponement, and as he trundled back to the ambulance, his friends would liberate him from the area.

*

Electric blue sky radiating bone-warming sunshine makes Prescott a haven for seniors, and many make the clean mountain air of the desert state their retirement goal. Some of the lucky ones had gathered on the Courthouse Plaza. However, those gathered weren't just any seniors; they were residents of the exclusive Poets Corner, in town to support their benefactor Bryce Peterson. Illness and death had made them fewer than when Peterson was arrested several months earlier, nevertheless the elderly veterans, some sporting squadron caps and campaign ribbons, felt a show of solidarity was the least they owed their brother-in-arms.

Next to the men, a quartet of stone-faced woman stood haughty, ice-cold, and dressed to the nines. With the pinched, vindictive look of widows not yet comfortable with their reduced status, the feelings they harbored for Bryce Peterson were a lot less gracious. And on the periphery of the mature crowd, groups of tourists gawked, wondering what had caused a fellowship of seniors to gather at the courthouse that day.

Not everybody present noticed the elderly group, let alone cared why they had assembled. They were in Arizona to soak up the cowboy history ruggedly etched in every mesa, butte, and cactus of Maricopa, Yavapai and Coconino counties. These closet cowboys, trail-bosses, and gunslingers from around the world, had wound an irresistible trail from Phoenix, to Old Tucson. They had toured back to Apache Junction and the Superstition Mountains' Lost Dutchman mine, then headed north to see Arizona's old territorial capital of Prescott, visit mines in Jerome, the red rocks of Sedona, and hang over the abyss on the Grand Canyon's Skywalk. Mario

Marzetti and his friends were such people.

From a small village in Sicily, they'd spent hours in a one-reel cinema watching anything western; from ancient Tom Mix shoot-em-ups, to Steve McQueen's *Junior Bonner*, they now stood where their celluloid heroes had walked. But it wasn't simply hero worship that brought this group to America. After visiting New York, Chicago, Miami, and Las Vegas, at least one was on the last leg of a mission to prove himself a modern day outlaw.

As vivid images of the old west transported him elsewhere, Mario Marzetti turned his camera on the courthouse. Snapping above the crowd, he imagined a rustler being brought to trial, or the gathering of suspicious town-folk upon discovering a sleeping stranger, like the cowboy, immortalized in bronze, at the end of the plaza. And he could almost taste the salt sweat of a ten-gallon hatted marshal, six-guns strapped to his thighs, running the bad guy out of town.

Mario was angling for a different view of the cowboy statue when the ambulance obscured his view. He let the camera drop to his chest, annoyed that the square metal box in his viewer wasn't the stagecoach his gunslinger psyche had in mind. Nevertheless, when a six-foot something trooper emerged, wearing a cowboy hat, with a gun strapped at his hip, Mario knew he was on the right track. Motorcycle cops, a disappointing sign of the times, pulled up behind the ambulance, but his boss, Signor Guillermo Rialto, owner of his town's local newspaper, had said to take the best shots he could, because anything relating to modern cowboy America would amuse the folks back home. Assessing the area, Mario saw a position on the other side of the crowd offering a superior vantage point, so he slung his tripod over his shoulder and separated from his friends.

When the doors of the ambulance opened revealing Bryce Peterson strapped in an electric wheelchair, his feet, for reasons only obvious to law-enforcement, were shackled. It took some time to unthread the supplementary chains clamping the conveyance to the floor, and reposition the chair for offload. And Peterson badgered, eager to get going with the final phase of his liberation.

Moving the hulking chair gingerly onto the ambulance lift, Peterson breathed deep of the only fresh air he'd felt since his transfer from the Yavapai Regional Medical Center to a prison hospital ward. And as he looked into the crowd, he recognized Poets Corner residents and other supporters. Nodding acknowledgement as the lift lowered his chair to the sidewalk; a veteran from the crowd grabbed his hand, and told him to, 'kick ass for the little guy'. Peterson smiled benevolently as the elderly man was swept away by police officers. Then rolling forward, his legal team closing about him, he again acknowledged the crowd as if in a procession of the magi.

As the crowd parted to let the cavalcade through, Peterson looked beyond the seniors to a group of young foreign faces. He knew somewhere out there was the group who would help him flee the scene. He turned and smiled; freedom within his grasp. And breathing deeply amid euphoria borne of certain knowledge, he lifted his arms to wave.

Mario had his tripod steady and focused to take his shot. And as the hands of the courthouse clock jerked spastically to nine fifty, and the morning sun beat down on anyone foolish enough to be in the square without a hat, he squeezed the trigger.

Mid-wave and smiling confidently, all Peterson heard was a sharp zipping hum, like that of a nectar-crazed hummingbird or a hornet. And as he instinctively clutched at his forehead, the pinpoint hole in front blossomed to a vermilion chrysanthemum at the back of his skull.

With blood pulsing from the gaping wound, and shredded tissue plastering the headrest of the electrified chair, a legal assistant, in pale beige, screamed hysterically as she attempted to wipe Peterson's bloody gray-green essence from her suit. And with total surprise frozen on his face, a thin line of crimson seeping from his nose, Peterson slumped slowly to the side.

Mario smiled as he watched the dead weight of the elegantly dressed cripple shift, his hand death-frozen atop the controls. And as the chair set in a dizzying circle, it hit the curb and toppled, spinning Peterson like a top.

Conditioned to gunfire, many dumbfounded veterans had hit the ground, and anticipating more shots, police officers drew their guns, took up firing stances, and aimed skyward. They were trying to establish from where the shot came, but they would never know. Mario was already back in the plaza, tripod case shouldered, photographing the bloody scene. And he'd made exactly the shot he came for.

Chapter Forty-Two

When Jim and other officers spilled from the courthouse, the square was in chaos. People were running from the scene, while several seniors were on the ground waiting for assistance to get back on their feet. Peterson's ambulance medic was performing CPR on a man who'd had a heart attack, and another was dealing with the legal assistant and several of the crowd in varying stages of shock. And while officers from the adjacent police station had cordoned off the area to dissuade people from leaving, nobody noticed the departure of two limousines and a VW bus.

Jim knew exactly what happened; the pattern of confusion was all too familiar. And he could see Peterson's wheelchair, on the ground, twenty yards ahead. He jogged to the spinning chair, its footrest gouging deep into the courthouse lawn. Avoiding the chair's perfect circle of blood, he deactivated the controls. He could do little but stand and shake his head. Then, as he squatted, lifting his sunglasses to view Peterson's wound, a piercing flash of a camera exploded in front of him. He flipped down his glasses, and before a second flash blinded him, he made out the face of a young Asian woman. The hairs on the back of his neck bristled as she disappeared into the crowd.

Jim ran forward but knew he wouldn't find her, for whoever orchestrated this event had pulled off the perfect coup. He couldn't help admiring the expertise that resulted in the assassin getting away after so publicly reducing the back of Peterson's skull to pulp. His only regret was that he'd never exact judicial payment from a man who'd hurt so many.

He was almost back to the courthouse when Scott joined him. "Dead this time?"

"Yeah."

Scott pulled Jim to a halt. "Could you have proved who and what he was without his favorite hooker?"

"Doesn't matter now. The case has gone in a completely different direction."

"It's closed, right?"

Jim smiled. "For me, maybe. I did my part."

"So you'll be looking for another assignment."

"That's what I do."

"I have something vitally important to the heath and well-being of some people if you're interested."

"Sounds promising."

Scott put an arm around his friend's shoulder. "Will you be the best man at my wedding?"

About the Author

Born and raised in Warwickshire, England, Anji immigrated to the United States in 1986, and now resides in Northern Arizona. She has written five novels, *Desperate Obsession, Everything Comes If. . .*, *Lonely Hearts Cry*, *The Cormorant Club*, and *How Many Freakin' Frogs Do You Have To Kiss?* She is a member of the Mystery Writers of America, the Romance Writers of America, the RWA-Women's Fiction, NARWA, the Kiss of Death mystery suspense group and the Chick-lit Writers of the World.

You can e-mail Anji at *anjinolangrasso@cableone.net*

In the mood for more Crimson Romance? Check out *Unbound* by Nikkie Locke at *CrimsonRomance.com.*

www.ingramcontent.com/pod-product-compliance
Lightning Source LLC
Chambersburg PA
CBHW010857130726
47900CB00017B/2809

* 9 7 8 1 4 4 0 5 5 2 3 2 8 *